THE HYDRO GENE

Chase Peter Josef

Titles in *A Compendium of Magiks*
(in reading order):

The Hydro Gene

A Cider Web
(Avail 2019)

Battle-Axis of Evil
(forthcoming)

THE HYDRO GENE

Book One
A Compendium of Magiks

by
Chase Peter Josef

FRAGMENTED SPACE BOOKS

First published in the USA in 2018
Fragmented Space Books (An Imprint of Fragments Production House Ltd)
19 9955 140th St, Surrey, BC, V3T 4M4

The Fragmented Eye and Ocular Maze Logos are trademarks of Fragments Production House, Ltd. This book is typeset in Anurati, Noteworthy, and Georgia.

First Edition

Paperback	ISBN: 1-9994081-0-1
	ISBN-13: 978-1-9994081-0-7
EPUB	ISBN: 1-9994081-1-X
	ISBN-13: 978-1-9994081-1-4
Kindle	ISBN: 1-9994081-2-8
	ISBN-13: 978-1-9994081-2-1
Hardcover	ISBN: 1-9994081-3-6
	ISBN-13: 978-1-9994081-3-8

Table of Contents

Acknowledgements

Edited By:

Kyla Yeates

Series Editors:
Kelly Gosselin
Tawnya Gosselin

Special Thanks to:
Scott Button
Carmen Flannery
Dan Mizuguchi
Laura Palermo

Prologue

Admiral Idras footsteps echoed. He raced down the hall. Underneath the thin veneer of calm, was layers of freaking the fuck out. Managing to keep his composure, he thought, *don't sweat. You'll be fine if you don't sweat.*

Admiral Idras had conquered quivering tendrils. He no longer blushed. He had no personal quirks to set her off, but she had a way of making you sweat.

He stopped. The Captain of the Guard himself checked his paperwork. Admiral Idras reminded himself this meant nothing. He handed over the papers, and skimming the documents, the Captain signalled for him to follow.

They strolled into the foyer of the imperial chambers. The admiral would have liked to admire the spectacle. Besides catching a hutch littered with pewter serving ware, there was no time. His full name and rank announced him. He entered the imperial court and knelt before his Empress.

"Your Imperial Majesty," he stared down.

"Speak," she commanded.

"We have a security breach, Your Imperial Majesty," Admiral Idras said.

"Yes, I am aware," she said. "What happened?"

The Admiral insufflated a moment.

"We should not call it a breach because no one broke in and stole anything," hoping to ease some of the pressure. "They..." Admiral Idras steeled himself, he ripped the bandage. "They pinged us with a subspace frequency allowed them to create a full-scale 3D map of our systems. All the territories we control."

The last few words ran together, and the Empress leaned forward. "Eyes at me," she commanded, and he stared into her deep cobalt eyes. "Where is the map?" Her expression is serious.

"The mapping is omniversal and universal. The Strangers did not appreciate it either." He tried to stay confident.

"Odd." Her tone cutting like a dagger.

"They have removed the Terran technology," Admiral Idras continued. The Empress remained laser-focused on him.

"And the map?" Her tone made it clear she no longer wanted to wait.

"They eliminated the threat by taking it for themselves," Admiral Idras held his breath.

The Empress leaned back, her eyes on fire. A bead of sweat dripped off Admiral Idras' cheek.

"Unfortunate, Admiral," the Empress turned to the Captain of the Guard. He hovered near the Admiral; the Captain pulled out a sword and drove it through Admiral Idras' chest. The expression drained from his face. He sputtered up thick blue blood that ran down his chin.

"I liked you," the Empress said.

The Captain removed the sword. The first guard swooped in and caught Admiral Idras' lifeless body with one arm. The Captain stood at ease.

The second guard grabbed a pewter pitcher from the hutch. She strolled over. She held the pitcher under the waterfall of blood gushing from the hole in Admiral Idras' chest. The pitcher overflowed, and the first guard let go. The corpse slid to the floor.

"Contact the Order and inform them Terra made contact," the Empress ordered.

The Captain snapped to attention. A splash of blood splattering across his forehead. He bowed before turning and marching out of the room. The second guard poured Admiral Idras' blood from the pitcher into a crystal glass. The first marched back to his post. The Empress's long-fingered hand grasped the glass.

"You aren't going to drink that, are you?" A man stood in the middle of the room, staring at the Empress. She waved her hand at the second guard, who left and closed the doors.

The man strolled over to the glass, clasping the pitcher in his fingertips. He sniffed the blood; its silver blue swirls and sweet scent did little for his gag reflex. He could drink it.

"Want a taste?" The Empress picked up her glass and shook it at the Man. He put the pitcher on the sidebar.

"Is this how it's going to be from now on?" The man paced the room like it was his. "Is this your way of breaking up with me?" He betrayed a hint of a smile.

The Empress put down the glass. "Don't be cute." She leaned back and let the moment between them hang there. "You forget your place."

"And you," the man reached for the handle of his sword, "forget where you came from."

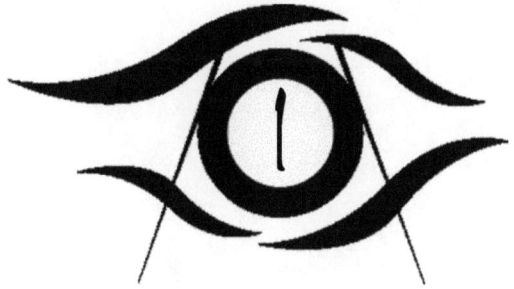

Trials by Ire

Chapter 1
Enter Sad Man

Friday, April 13, 1995
9:32 p.m., TST (Terran Standard Time)
Quibble Creek
British Columbia, Canada

David stared at the small device. It sat there on the rough worktable. He picked it up and turned it over in his hand. He admired the possibility contained within the little metal frame. He put the device down and examined the laptop on the desk.

"Eighty-three percent complete." David arched his back. He sighed and reached up to massage his sore neck. He eyed the dark, dusty workspace, which had once been this house's garage.

A pair of halogen tubes buzzed from opposite walls. A third light, a bare incandescent bulb, hung from the ceiling above the table—his working light. The walls of the room lined on all sides by a combination of toolboxes and racks. The racks holding plastic bins, tarps, larger tools, and machine parts.

David stared at the small device he made. The metal framework and repurposed LCD, with the bundles of wires he alone understood. All connected to a circuit board resembling something alien; a design of his own chaos. David responded when his laptop whistled. He ejected the device and disconnected the cable.

There was a hard quality to his eyes. He glanced at the device while his finger hovered over the start button. He held his breath; he made himself shake it off.

David exhaled.

He was ready, and, holding the device up, he held down the button for a few seconds. The screen flashed on and his personalized boot sequence chimed.

"Gl/xyPhone," his graffiti logo art read, "Subspace Communicator Beta V0.1." It was a simple name, and David liked it; he was going for function over form.

"Loading {modules}" popped onto the bottom of the screen. It was between "unpacking {dishes}" and "taking {app naps}."

David forced his breath out in a long, thin stream. He watched the boot sequence. The command prompt materializes at the top of the black screen. *Now, this is it,* he thought, and he clicked near the prompt, watching. A digital keyboard slid on-screen. Going to ping the universe, and it's over, no big deal.

He typed "run {gl/xyZMaps [0.4.3]}" on the keyboard and hit Enter.

A flood of code scrolled past. The program booted and executed.

"Welcome to Galaxy Maps Beta." The program opened, with "enter command" on-screen. Below that, a cursor blinked. David watched it flash for a minute, staring at it before he clicked. The keyboard slid up. He entered "\ping" and executed the command.

This time, the program spat out the code fast, it was impossible to see. A blur of lines showing the progress of the program. It pinged across the universe. He hoped to create a 3D digital schematic of the universe itself—a set of master blueprints.

The program completed, and David stared at the on-screen runtime: "7.06s." Jesus fucking Christ. It was too easy, and it compiled. He put down the communicator and turned. He jumped up to cheer.

"Yes!"

A horrible, gut-wrenching pang came over him. He caught movement on the communicator's screen. He turned and sat back down, staring at the communicator. A virus ate it alive, a fucking good one. It was striking with sniper-like precision, code unseen. It destroyed the operating systems, any software, and all the data.

The device was hot. David dropped it. It fell to the ground with a crunch. The screen cracked into a thousand tiny shards. David stared at his hand. The symbol burned into it.

He surveyed his computer, to back up the software at least, but they had gotten to it too. With a loud electrical noise and several sparks, the laptop went black.

David overloaded. It wasn't a virus; it was a program engineered to seek out and destroy his technology.

Someone had sent it because of the data he had collected. David had made first contact.

He dressed in sweatpants and a wife-beater. David paraded into a dinner with their queen. He grabbed a bottle of champagne, and on his way-out bitch-slapped the prince.

His head swam. He stood, his left arm went numb, and he lost consciousness. The pressure on him grew. He fell to his knees, clutching his chest with his right arm.

His right arm was numb. It fell to his side. David's eyes widened before his body collapsed onto the floor.

Gabriel strolled in.

Entering from the shadows the room got smaller, shrunk by his presence more than his actual size.

His angular facial features set in a half smirk beneath thick blackout sunglasses. His arms, crossed in front of him, hidden by the sleeves of his cloak.

Gabriel's expression equalized. He glanced at David's body. He surveyed the scene before him. He channelled his mana, the first form of magik, *Wizardcraft*. Gabriel's eyes filled with purplish-white smoke, in a process called spectering.

He unfurled his right hand and reached out. A wisp of smoke floated in the air for a moment before dozens of tendrils burst forth. It created a ball suspended over his palm.

Gabriel knelt beside David's corpse. He dipped his index finger into the ball of thick, viscous liquid magik like finger paint.

His finger traced a rune on David's forehead. Gabriel stood and clenched his fist around the ball, leaving a few fleeting wisps of smoke.

Gabriel took a step back from David's corpse.

The symbol on David's forehead glowed a bright blinding white.

Meanwhile, Gabriel raised both arms, and, bending them at the elbows, placed his hands one on top of the other. Light spilled out from between them. He lifted his top hand, revealing a small model of David made from particles of light. Channelling his spirit, the second form of magik or *Enchantment*.

David and his light echo rose. He lifted until David was a few feet off the ground. The light echoes dissipated. Gabriel closed his hands.

Gabriel raised his left hand. Mana tendrils twisted around his fingers, pouring forth. Gabriel twirled his hand through the air. A sizeable swirling vortex of moving liquid smoke opened in front of David's corpse.

Gabriel grabbed David's shirt collar with one hand and his jeans with the other. He straightened up, swung back, and threw David forward, letting go. David hit the vortex face first with a horizontal splash of purplish white. David's corpse sank into the vortex.

Gabriel turned and jumped up. He pushed off the corner of the work table with his right foot and reached his left arm out. The communicator rattled on the floor. Mana snaked out of his sleeve until, with a final shake, the device flew into his hand.

He slipped it into his cloak and spread his arms. His body entered the vortex, folding into the liquid. When the last of Gabriel had gone back into the portal, the vortex imploded.

Friday, April 13, 1995
9:41 p.m., TST
The Edge
The Whitespace

The portal swirled out in concentric circles amid unending whitespace, indistinguishable from a field or the entire expanse of a universe.

Gabriel exited the vortex first. Even when transmuting from one dimension to another. For every action, there is an equal and opposite reaction.

Gabriel's feet hit the ground running. He turned around and stepped back toward the portal with gentle grace. Gabriel stretched his arms out; David's corpse fell into them. The entrance closed.

Gabriel stood there for a moment, taking in the body in his arms, and let out a long, exhausted sigh. He turned around and paced. A small group of dark, shadowy figures and objects surfaced in the distance of the Whitespace. Growing closer and more defined with every single step he took.

The structure and people he strolled toward solidified. A mirage forming one hundred meters ahead of him. He went on toward the large, white marble structure. Several steps led up to a large platform holding sixteen stone slabs in pairs. Each piece had a corpse on it, save one.

Gabriel creaked up the steps and glanced around at his family. The cloaked figures attending to the corpses on the slabs. The Primum Immortales—or Prims, also called the First Immortals. They were the guardians of the elements, the forces of nature, the keepers of the Four Magiks.

Lucy, Prim of Light and Life, had long light-gray hair and gave off a sinister vibe. She could make the calmest person's nerves break with a view. Lucy was standing on the far side where Gabriel, Prim of Death and Time, had entered. Her discernable crow's-feet the only hint of age.

The Terrans on the slabs, called acolytes, are individuals whom the Prims had chosen. Gabriel had collected them over the years. He lifted them from the timeline, in stasis.

Lucy tended to the body of Asher, their Doctor. She reviewed his shiny black linen turban, dress shirt, and khaki pants. Lucy held her hand over the three wounds in Asher's chest and healed them.

Opposite Lucy stood her daughter, Zed, Prim of Love and War, her coppery-red hair pulled up into a slutty ballerina. The goddess of love wasn't like her mother; her personality was warmer, brighter.

Zed finished with Bennett, who was still in his World War II flight suit. Zed took the mask off his face, and the goggles, removing the helmet to reveal a mass of thick, curly hair and dark skin. Zed held her hands over the chunk missing from his side.

It repaired itself, his skin sparkling in the light from inside the hole in his suit.

Zed held her hand over his body, her eyes spectering red. The suit moulded itself over Bennett, turning into a gold crew-neck T-shirt and slacks. Zed wrapped Bennett in his shroud. Gabriel crossed into the centre of the circle and veered toward the right slabs.

On the remaining side, his daughter Rafi and niece Mica worked across from each other at a pair of slabs. Mica, the round-faced goddess of water, giggled like a kid. Her face lit up at something Rafi said. A wry smile crossed her striking face.

Gabriel approached the empty slab, seeing his son. Ariel, Prim of Fire and Truth, was leaning on the next tile over, tending to Kay, their Templar. Having updated the button-up shirtwaist dress to a slate gray, he was going over each of Kay's injuries one by one.

His five-foot-ten-inch frame made him like a god among mortals when he was with the girls. Ariel straightened up in Gabriel's presence.

Ariel sauntered over to match his father's position across the slab. Gabriel laid David, their Necromancer, on the cold, gray stone. Ariel helped him adjust David, moving his body into position. They finished placing him.

Ariel surveyed his father. "You look like shit," he said. Gabriel smiled.

"I do, don't I?"

"Should we wake Zeke, then?" Ariel spoke of the pink elephant in the room: Zeke, Prim of Thunder. "I ask because you gave me the key."

"I guess," Gabriel lifted his arms, placing his palms forward, and took a deep breath.

A burst of purplish-white smoke unfurled in the centre of the circle. Gabriel let go, lowering his arms. The mana dispersed. In its place was a gilded metal cell suspended in midair. It crashed to the floor, waking Zeke with a literal bang.

"Jesus fucking Christ!" Zeke roared out of bed and charged into the cell wall. The whole cube slid toward Gabriel, who did not even change breathing patterns. Zeke's six-foot-three-inch frame left him face to face with Gabriel.

Zeke struck at Gabriel, who countered and blocked the fist with his forearm. Zeke reached through the next space, going for Gabriel's free arm.

Gabriel, in one movement, pulled his son's arms forward until Zeke wrapped around the pair of bars. Gabriel leaned down. He brought his mouth close to Zeke's exposed ear. "You forget I made you," Gabriel let go and stepped back.

Zeke stumbled a few paces before running into the cot. He nursed his wrists; "I suppose I don't have much choice then, eh?"

"It's like you thought you ever did," Gabriel said.

Zeke huffed and stood. Ariel trudged toward the cage and pulled a key out of his cloak. He inserted it into the lock and let go. The key rotated in place.

Zeke stood and stepped up to the doors, the locks clicking and whirring. The bars stretched forth until the entire façade of the cage was a pair of hinged metal doors. The key stopped turning, and the doors swung forth.

Ariel, Rafi, Zed, Gabriel, and Lucy moved to stand in front of the cage doors. Zeke stood unmoved, staring at Gabriel who was uncomfortable.

Gabriel had missed it. A slight limp distinguished Gad, Prim of Wisdom, from his twin Zeke. Gad was no longer in charge of their shared body.

Ariel realized their mistake and pivoted in place. Gad threw out his hands, his eyes turning yellow. He spectered.

"Turbo," he incanted, and the air around his hands swirled. He cocked his head to the side, smiling, and pushed forward.

Zed, Rafi, and Ariel all spectered and transmuted themselves out of harm's way. Lucy and Gabriel withstood the winds, while Gad fled the cage.

Mica reacted to Gad's incantation, dropping her clipboard she turned toward the sound. Mica's eyes turned a deep Caribbean blue. She ran toward the fray.

With a slight jump, Gad kicked back, his spell hitting the back of the cage with gale-force winds. The cage launched at the advancing Mica. Gad flipped up and backward in an open pike. The remaining prims had recovered and moved in on Gad.

Gabriel saw Gad was performing a mid-air boomerang, heading back toward the cage. Gad reached out during his flip to send a gust of wind at Mica and push the cage toward her. She extended her small arm and hand, catching the enormous cage aloft like a pair of keys.

"Arma," Ariel incanted, with one arm aside, one arm aloft. A trident expanded in his hands in a puff of red smoke. He was rusty, and Gad had been waiting. Gad hit Ariel in the chest with his leg, stopping and reversing Ariel's forward momentum.

Gad kept going. Walking up Ariel's body, he folded his left leg into Ariel's chest. He dropped his right leg and swept Ariel's kneecaps, flipping him.

With a final, firm kick, Gad stepped down and forward. Ariel skidded along the stage behind him and charged away from the cage.

Lucy, Zed, and Rafi had stopped moving in a stunned moment.

Lucy and Gabriel exchanged the briefest of looks. They talked without words. They could speak for minutes by exchanging a glance.

He's toying with them, Gabriel thought, but Lucy had a way when it came to Gad.

Mica had stopped the inertia of the cage. She had slid backward for the few seconds Gad's takedown of Ariel had taken. Mica pulled back her arm and launched the huge cage. Mica was the smallest of the Prims. She threw the pen with no sign of strain, and it flew forward at an incredible speed.

Meanwhile, Zed and Rafi had advanced on Gad, who met them in the middle. Gad crouched down, sweeping backward with one leg, and catching Rafi. Zed faltered, a chance Gad exploited. He finished his leg sweep, he stood and turned to face Zed.

The cage initiated its return trajectory. Gad put his forearms together. His palms pointed toward Zed's chest. Time slowed. The air became electrified.

Gad spectered, his hands filled with a ball of mana suspended between him and Zed. She had enough time to protect herself. Her eyes consumed with bright orange.

"Praemium," Gad spoke, letting go of the spell. The ball of magik exploded, launching them in opposing directions.

Gad used the momentum, trying to cross the stage on impulse alone, but Mica still had control of the cage. Like the moon itself, she changed the tide of the cage, causing it to roll back toward Gad.

He saw it coming, shifting to the side in time to grab the cage. He whipped around and barreled past the edge of the theatre. He let go before the cage collided with the marble floor into a heap of twisted metal.

Lucy vectored off now that Mica had changed the tide of the cage. She raced forward alongside the cage. Gad concentrated on the giant flying metal box. Gad let go, he arched to the side, and Lucy pounced. Jumping into the air, she collided with Gad.

They became entangled in a mess of limbs, hair, and fabric. They fought for control. Careening downward, Lucy gained control and held both of Gad's arms behind his back. She brought her hand around and scooped up his ankles, holding them together. Her knees were in the small of his back. They hit the marble with a loud crunch.

Gad cried out. Lucy let go of him and tucked in, rolling to the side. She popped up on her feet a few meters from Gad's body. He flailed for a minute, his limbs contorting. He tried to force air into his lungs, tried to breathe in or out. His anxiety activated; he lost control.

The walls closed in on Gad. All he could hear was the deafening tap of Lucy's heels. He rolled onto his back, and she knelt beside him. With one swift motion, she slammed her elbow into his sternum with measured force.

He gasped and fell back onto the floor.

"What is wrong with you?" Lucy said, with a slight hint of aggravation.

Gad struggled to breathe; his chest rattled.

"I don't know," he said with more than a hint of venom. "The cold marble floor in place of my lungs?"

Lucy raised an eyebrow.

"Very funny, but did you think you could get away?" Lucy traipsed over to him. She grabbed him by the arm and counted "One, two—" before heaving him up onto his feet.

He wobbled, steadied himself against Lucy, before pushing away from her. He took a few stumbling steps, jerked back by his left foot. He glimpsed his ankle, now clasped in a manacle, and Lucy's outstretched right hand.

"Son of a bitch," Gad swore, his frustration building. Lucy pulled back on the chains, and he lurched forward, landing on his face, arms out.

She let go of the chains and stepped back toward the theatre. Gad sat up in a huff, legs spread, arms crossed, like a petulant child. He got up and followed Lucy.

❧

By the time they reached the dais, the remaining Prims had assembled, except Samael. They were going to have to break him out of a different prison.

Gabriel stood over the pair of corpses, lost in thought; Zed, Rafi, and Mica worked their way toward him.

In slow, measured movements, the three of them moved in on Gabriel. He stopped, not expecting them. They closed in with precision and speed.

Rafi grabbed his left arm; Mica his right. Zed had moved in front of him, a katana materializing in a puff of orange smoke. Mica and Rafi kicked Gabriel's knees in, forcing him to kneel. Zed raised the katana above her head.

"Reversio," Zed incanted. She swung the sword. Time slowed. Gabriel fought back. Gabriel took a deep breath, focusing on letting go. Time ground to a near halt. Mica, Rafi, and Zed spectered. Mica and Rafi fought back, counting together.

"One, two, three," they said in unison, and with one quick, synchronized movement, they each bore down. There was a set of loud, wet snaps.

Gabriel cried out. The pain stopped his spell, allowing Zed to follow through. Mica and Rafi fell over, half of Gabriel dropping on each of them.

Ichor, the blood of the gods, sprayed Zed. Gabriel came apart. Mica got up, wringing ichor from her sleeves. She stepped over to Rafi, who to be struggling, and pulled her up.

Mana had already escaped from Gabriel's two halves. Pooling in the middle like a clogged storm drain.

It swirled upward until it reached critical mass and the magik dissipated. Left in its wake was Samael, the last Prim they needed to complete the ritual, lord of sorcery and gravity.

He put his hands up and pulled a dark hat out of thin air. Placing it on his head, he stepped out of the centre of Gabriel's body parts. The space between the two sides swirled with white mana. Each side sprang back to life, and both halves pulled together. The magik stitching him back together.

Gabriel came to, coughing and sputtering. He took a deep breath. He tried to sit up but rolled over with a groan.

Samael had the spring of a twentysomething, while Gabriel was the opposite. Creaking when he moved, his body was like an old oak: harsh, inflexible, and slow moving.

The eight of them stood around for a minute, no one sure what to do in the awkward silence.

"You're breaking the accords, Gabriel, aren't you?" Gad shattered the silence like glass.

"They are already broken, son," Gabriel breath rolled out like fog.

Gad, intrigued, popped an eyebrow, and straightened up.

"May I ask what happened, dear Father, or is your heart too cold for even that?"

Gabriel smiled. He had made this monster; he could deal with the fallout.

"Why don't you see for yourself?" He removed the communicator from his cloak and tossed it across the stage.

Gad fumbled it for a minute before he turned it over in his hand.

"What is this piece of junk?" he said. Gabriel opened his mouth, but Gad saw it glaring up at him. The symbol he had missed the first time.

"Talk about burying the lead," Gad said, still awestruck.

Gabriel reached up, and the communicator floated out of Gad's hands. It flew into Gabriel's open, outstretched hand. He put it back in his cloak.

"Is this why I am here?" Samael said. "Glad to know I am good for something."

"Would it bother you if I dealt with this first?" Gabriel asked.

"Please, don't stop on my account," Samael leaned back against the nearest slab. He examined at the shrouded woman lying lifeless on the marble.

Zavannah, their Oracle, was in her mid-twenties, five feet seven inches tall. From the looks of her citrine-yellow clothes, she was from the late 1800s. Samael turned back to the conversation.

"You're saying Jericho too?" Gad asked. The look on his face was one Samael had never seen him have before.

"If you agree to see this through, Nephew, I'll give you carte blanche," Gabriel said.

Gad and Samael sensed something was not right.

"What could they have done for you to let this waste of magiks out in the first place." Samael watched Gabriel remove the communicator from his cloak again.

"Here; take a closer look," said Gabriel, and he watched Samael examine the device.

"Shit," Samael said, his heart sinking. "This has a dimensional gravity signature." His head swam for a moment.

"Yeah, what else is new?" Mica said. Making a final check of Bennett, she finished by marking off her last item on the clipboard. It faded away.

Gad laughed.

"This is not your release of me," Gad managed to sputter. He stepped toward Gabriel. "This is you doing your job." He turned to Lucy, sticking out his ankle.

"Mother, you can undo this because we both know there is no point in running," he said, turning back to Gabriel. His expression changed. His face became sad and sullen, "that's suicide."

Lucy gave her son a once over; the manacle solidified on her wrist in a puff of smoke. She unclasped the restraint and let it open; it fell off her wrist. The shackle disintegrated. The chain crumbled with it, destroying the last of the connection.

Gad shook his ankle a few times, flexing his foot to make sure he was free. He eyed his family; this freak show was his best hope of surviving this thing.

"I assume we're taking the acolyte route?" Gad was drunk with freedom. "Otherwise, this is super weird."

Samael stopped examining the communicator and scrutinized Gad. Samael marched toward him, handing the device to Gabriel as he passed. Samael stepped across the centre stage and reached the other side.

"Should we get this show on the road?" Samael said in a low tone.

The remaining Prims all regarded him for a moment, and Lucy spoke:

"I don't have anything better to do."

Sunday, April 15, 1995
3:42 p.m., TST
The Megatorium
Parathas, Lyra Inferior

Starlight fell upon the top of the large rock, which on Terra would have constituted a small mountain. The formation was half of the crescent shape Megatorium emerging from the mount.

An enormous, pitch-black cave opened into the middle of the arena.

The vast amphitheatre's ruddy-brown and silver structure became a matte terra cotta. The starlight poured over it like paint.

When the starlight reached thirty meters from the centre of the arena, a shimmer generated. The line moved toward the arena's centre. It's starlight shimmering across the bodies of the acolytes now visible on the ground.

Light reached the centre of the arena, revealing a much smaller volcanic formation. About two meters in diameter, the top was big enough for Gadreel to sit upon.

The shimmer continued to the centre of the arena and got thinner. The other half of the acolytes became visible. The shimmer shrank to a single spark and dissipated, the starlight continued.

Gad sat up and scrutinized the right half of the Megatorium.

The stands were overflowing with gods, deities, and spirit-gods. The Egyptians to the Inuit, along with the archangels, the lesser angels, and saints.

The raven god of Kamchatka and Chukotka sat perched on the upper edge of the Megatorium. Below was Lucy, sitting on an obsidian throne. Standing twelve feet tall, it took the form of a gargoyle Lucy had once fought alongside.

Lucy had created the chair to honour him but also to remind them all grace is a way of life. The remaining Graces sat below her; Ariel, Samael, and Zeke.

Lucy stood and walked up to the few steps at her feet. She stopped at the edge of her platform. She glanced down at Gadreel, and her eyes turned black.

Gad inspected the left side of the Megatorium, observing the sea of Hindu gods and goddesses. Gabriel stood from his throne.

Less ornate than Lucy's, Gabriel's throne was solid white marble, the capstone of the Lost White Pyramid. Inverted, it stood base up. In front of and below his throne sat his fellow fates—Rafi, Zed, and Mica.

Gabriel stood; his expansive white robes flowed behind him. He held his left hand out, and a large staff popped up. He gathered up his robes and took a step down. The tapping of wood against white marble boomed through the Megatorium.

It continued—step, tap, step, tap, step, tap—until Gabriel reached the edge of his platform. He looked back down at Gad. His eyes filled with white. He looked over at Lucy, who now held a Sai dagger in each hand. She nodded.

Gabriel held out his hand, palm up, focused on manipulating the time stream.

The Megatorium went silent. Gabriel closed his eyes and lifted his staff.

He struck the floor hard. The wave rippled through time and space, taking a celestial shard from each spirit. The third form of magik or *Witchery* passed through the crowd.

Tiny dots of pure light floated out of every being the spell hit. A constellation map of some foreign star system.

Gabriel let go of the spell and put his arm down.

The celestial shards flowed up from the stands. Swirling together like bees, they loomed before Gabriel at twice his height.

Lucy pulled her right arm up and threw the Sai dagger into the air, catching it by the point. She nodded at Gabriel, who could see her past the edge of the celestial shards.

Gad put his hands down and pushed off, standing upon the rock. Gabriel and Lucy counted down together without words.

The mass of celestial shards vectored toward the centre of the arena. Lucy let the Sai dagger go. Whistling through the air, it headed straight toward the middle of the platform and Gad's head.

The spell's magik was audible. The pure celestial essence grew out of his sleeve, reaching upward past Gad's fingers.

The branches spread outward and extended down. The tendrils stopped. The black-and-white branches each sprouted a coloured bauble which generated an orb.

The dagger ran into the barrier, which shimmered to life in a rippling wave. A billion points of light slammed into the spot on the ripple, flowing through the ripple towards Gad. Weaving around his arm, its tendrils went for the swirling baubles.

The Sai dagger bounced off the barrier, toward Gabriel's face. The shards finished flowing into the orbs of mana, they hit the force of the wall. The spheres dislodged from the branches and shot off in every direction, like pool cues.

The orbs ricocheted around the space. Gad held his hands in front of his chest, a light echo in his palms. Gad focused his spirit. The balls slowed and stopped.

The dots of light were stationary. They sprang to life, and the orbs followed suit, zipping around. They left a trail of coloured light in their wake. The circles hit the acolytes in the chest.

Bennett, their Monk, gasped. He examined his hands. Asher awoke, and rolled onto his side, coming back to life.

Pierre stuttered. He woke, surprised by the back touching his. Jonah, their Mage, sprang to life with a few coughs. The two of them turned right, left, right, trying to see each other like the Three Stooges.

They separated, surveying each other, Jonah taking in Pierre's forest-green logger ensemble. Pierre assessed Jonah's pastel malachite suit with a cashmere turtleneck and flared bottom pants.

Ronnie arched her back and sat up in her tangerine work jumper. A cloth tied at the front to hold the broad mass of copper curls.

Hayden, their Enchantress, opened her eyes. With a persimmon jumper dress, a striped T-shirt finished, and a large-brimmed hat, it was like she was about to go for tea. Hayden sat up and glanced around.

Kushia's chest rose. He sprang to life and sat up at the same time Maya did. They looked at each other. Maya's violet V-frame jacket and floor-length skirt glinted at Kushia, the

Valkyrie, who held up an arm of his sparkling amethyst three-piece suit. They moved away from each other, aware they were not alone.

Kay opened her eyes and sat up. David inhaled and sat up, continuing to try to solve his virus problem.

Avery, their Warlock, rose like Beetlejuice and coughed. Her canary yellow cowboy boots, boot-cut jeans, and button-up shirt shimmered gold in the light. Zavannah rolled over on her side, her eyes wide with amazement. Zavannah wiped off her pastel citrine pants and blouse. She saw Avery and shuffled backward.

Zavannah was about to apologize when Avery beat her to the punch.

"I'm sorry, miss; I didn't mean to scare you," Avery got up and walked toward Zavannah. She held her hand out to Zavannah, who hesitated.

"C'mon now, you're going to ruin your dress," Avery continued, signalling to Zavannah to take it. Zavannah glanced at the hand and took it. Avery pulled back, and she was on her feet.

"Avery," the woman said, shaking Zavannah's hand.

"Zavannah."

Hudson coughed. He pushed his body up and got onto his knees. Pushing his cerulean pants-and-vest combo and long-sleeve button-up shirt into the dirt. Slate, their Barbarian, gasped, her eyes opening wide before she sat up to survey the scene. The midnight-blue khakis, cuffs, and Poison T-shirt made the juxtaposition much odder.

Wearing crimson argyle knee socks, loafers, knickers, suspenders, and a button-up. A Naugahyde jacket curled up in the fetal position under an oversized flat cap, Aiko. With a cat stretch, Aiko awoke and, putting her hand on her hat, rolled over. She yawned, and tears streamed down her face.

Harry, their Mechanic, coughed. He jolted awake. His rust-coloured Canadian tuxedo and t-shirt blended into the background. He gasped. He fought backward, protecting his face. Harry had one arm up and reached with the other. He found the sand, grabbed a handful, and threw it at a ghost in front of him. He put his arm down and looked around.

At the last second, Gabriel moved, catching the still-flying dagger in his hand. He flipped it. Holding the point, he threw it at Lucy—return to sender. It barreled toward her head, and she moved at the last millisecond to catch the dagger in her hand.

Siblings.

Chapter 2
Love is a Sharpshooter

Sunday, April 15, 1995
4:22 p.m., TST
The Arena, the Megatorium
Parathas, Lyra Inferior

"You two," Gad said, his voice booming through the arena. Hudson and Slate jumped out of their skin. Gad cleared his throat and spoke again.

"Sorry. Hudson, Slate, for your safety." His eyes filling with yellow. His expression grew serious, "I would suggest you move!" Hudson, their Priest, sprang to attention and toward Zavannah and Avery.

"What the hell are you talking—"

Hudson reached Slate, interrupting her. A cloud of canary smoke rolled in. Hook swords fell from the sky. Slate shrieked. The rest of their weapons crashed to the ground. The smoke evaporated in the clangour of metal and wood. Slate stumbled backward into Avery.

"Careful, hon," Avery grunted. She heaved Slate up.

Slate rolled with it and took a step forward, turned and stepped back toward Avery. Slate held up her hand. "Thanks, my name is Slate."

"Avery," she said, "but you can call me Boots. Everybody does." Avery pointed to the cowboy boots on her feet. They both turned at the sound of Gad's voice.

"David, Kay, Aiko, Harry," Gad motioned to them to join the others on the right side. "Join us over here by Hudson. Put up your hand, Hudson."

Hudson held up his hand and waved at the four of them. They looked at Hudson's hand waving in the air and at each other. David shuffled toward him.

"Why not?" David said. He turned around in stride and shrugged, before continuing toward Hudson. Aiko, their Huntress, fell in behind him, while Kay and Harry exchanged glances. Harry turned and put his elbow out for Kay, and the two of them walked together. Gad turned to the other half of the acolytes.

"If you would, ladies and gentlemen, move over here and we can have a bit of a chat." He gestured toward the other side of the weapon pile, smiled again, and gestured to the spot. "I promise I don't bite."

They moved. Asher still viewing Gad, bumped into Pierre.

"Je m'excuse," Pierre said. "You OK?" Asher dusted himself off.

"Yeah, sorry," he held out his hand. "Name's Asher."

"Pierre."

Asher strolled toward the spot Gad had shown them, Pierre fell in line behind him. The two of them walked over to an endless set of pleasantries. Gad cleared his throat.

"You're all wondering what is going on, but there are more questions than we have time for. Trust me, all your questions will get answered."

David wanted to ask a question, but when he went to, Gad shot him a look. Something about the way Gad talked—you knew you needed to listen.

"My name is Gadreel, but you can call me Gad. Gadreel is formal," a bit nonchalant.

"Like zee anjel?" Pierre, their Druid, said before he could stop himself. Gad smiled.

"We should not get hung up on semantics. We have over five and a half minutes before Schrodinger's cat dies." He said, no one laughed. "Let me rephrase. If you have not left this dome in, five minutes, you never will."

"It's a dream," Kay had been repeating to herself the whole time. "It can't hurt you; it's a dream." When, Gad, was it? When he said they had a few minutes to leave or they would be stuck here, Kay lost her ability to concentrate on the mantra. Her heart raced, and her head spun. She became paralyzed with fear. She was watching Gad and listening to him, but he was a million miles away.

"I can tell you the secret of how to get out of here. The barrier is simple to conquer if you know how," Fourteen hearts beat faster.

Aiko did not care, stuck in the same place she had been all those years ago.

"And what do you want in return?" David asked. "You don't give away such precious information free of charge." Laying it on a bit thick.

"Astute observation, yes, I can't tell you my secrets." Gad's body became enveloped in canary-yellow smoke. "There is a way for you to earn information." Gad continued talking. His face grew and floated upward.

"Earn it?" David asked. "What do we have to do?"

The smoke finished growing and dissipated. The body of an eighteen-foot-tall lion formed in its place. It still had Gad's head. He lied down and put his paw on the rock in the centre of the dome. They were the same size. He held his other leg up.

"All you have to do is solve three little riddles," Gad said with a wry smile.

"Of course; you're the Sphinx," David said. "Because this couldn't get weirder."

"Careful, words have power. OK," he leaned closer to the acolytes. "Are we ready?" Without waiting for an answer, Gad continued:

> I welcome the day with a show of light,
> Quiet, I came here in the night.
> I bathe the earthy stuff at dawn,
> But by the noon, alas! I'm gone.

Avery looked down, kicking the ground with her boots. "Dew," she spoke quieter than she had intended.

Gad lifted his head and put a paw to his ear.

"I'm sorry, dear; you will have to speak up. I'm thirty-five hundred years old."

Avery stared at him, in case she was wrong.

"Dew," Asher shouted. "She said the answer was morning dew." He was speaking to Gad but looking at her, impressed. "Which is the right answer."

"It is," Gad continued.

To you, rude I would never be,
though I flag my tongue for all to see.

He rested his head on his paws, thinking they might need a second.

"A dog," Zavannah responded off hand.

"Correct," Gad raised an eyebrow in surprise.

One of us bears no ill will but does not forgive,
One of us misses nothing but cannot relive,
I give birth to her, she gives birth to me,
but she hides away, and I allow you to see.

Pierre rubbed his temple. His brain hurt from the multitude of things in his head.

David pondered, *what is the point of this? Why is he toying with us?* In the end, he wanted to get out of this prison; he could go from there.

"Day and night," David said. Gad sighed, lifting his arm to rest his head on his paw.

"Correct," he said, deflated. The mana engulfed him, returning him to Terran form. "And with over three minutes to spare." Gad stood next to the boulder.

"I'm assuming you will want the secret to getting out of the dome?" Gad asked, and most of them stared at him. Tough crowd.

"All right, look," he paced backward. "You have to think of it like this." He continued to step backward, focused on the acolytes. "It's a matter of faith. This space is an elevator." He closed the gap between him and the shimmer. "You have reached your floor." He kept stepping backward, one step from the barrier. "The doors are open." He took the last step back. "You step out." He proved this by turning and stepping out of the dome. He stepped through the barrier like nothing was there.

He turned around and bowed to the acolytes before snapping his fingers and dissolving in a puff of smoke. He popped up next to Lucy, standing on the ledge. There was no seating for the Furies.

The acolytes looked around at one another, each one more confused and unsure than the next. Aiko was the only one who was not spiralling. She did not understand what was happening and figured the grown-ups would tell her what to do.

Then she saw the cave in the side of the mountain, a great expanse of blackness carved out of the side of the rock. She spied a three-headed dragon at the mouth of the cave and froze. *Did none of them see it?*

Tuesday, February 19, 1935
1:41 p.m., TST
Madame Ling's Parlor and Salon
Vancouver, British Columbia, Canada

"Protect your brother," her mother told her, "and know I'll always love you." When the disease had taken her—typhoid, they called it—and Aiko and Kenji had been alone. She had gotten a job as a paperboy by dressing like one.

It had not fooled the owner of the paper distribution company. He told her he liked her moxie. He offered her a job on a trial basis and the condition the boys didn't know she was a girl. She wasn't sure what "moxie" meant, but she took the job anyway.

A week later, she was the best boy in the city. She could work any corner, in any part of town. Everyone tipped her, and she never forgot any customers or their paper preference. What moods meant she should or should not offer them a paper.

She worked hard enough to afford a small bedroom rental in the house of a woman. A widow whose children lived nearby. She rented them a room with breakfast at first, for thirty-five dollars. The woman was old and needed help around the house.

When Ester suggested Kenji do some handiwork in his spare time. She would also pack them a lunch and make dinner for them to share. Aiko held her tears, remembering what her father said when she had fallen off her bike, crying in the street.

"Tanakas do not cry!"

Kenji did some housework and went to school, and she helped him finish his homework at night. He was going to get an education, and she was going to make sure of it. She picked up some extra shifts with the evening editions and even got Ester to co-sign on a bank account.

Aiko paid for the milk delivery. Ester tried to stop her, but the pleas of a twelve-year-old orphan are hard to ignore. In the end, the milkman conceded and signed up Miss Aiko Tanaka.

Having managed to carve out her own slice of life, she came home one day. She ran back from the dispatch, up her street, and into Ester's yard.

When she flew through the door, though, Kenji had a sullen look on his face. Something was wrong. She found Ester sitting on the couch, a handkerchief to her mouth. Ester held up her other hand. Don't come any closer. She put her hand down. Aiko saw the blood. Typhoid.

Her head was spinning, Kenji was like a ghost. They held each other for a moment, and she racked her brain on what to do. She pushed off him and grabbed him by the shoulders. Intending to tell him it was going to be all right. Kenji coughed. He was unable to cover his mouth, and the bright-red spatter hit Aiko square in the face.

She stumbled backward into the kitchen table.

Thursday, December 19, 1935
10:14 a.m., TST
Saint Paul's Hospital
Vancouver, British Columbia, Canada

In the ward, Mrs. Smith and Kenji continued to get worse, but Aiko never seemed to develop symptoms. The doctors guessed who the carrier was. The disease, like the newspaper, Aiko got from her mother; she brought it to Ester and Kenji when she made them cookies.

Unlike her customers, she never read a single edition of the paper. Unlike her brother, her mother, and Ester, she would never be sick.

All she had wanted was to fulfill her mother's dying wish, and she had been the one to hurt her brother the most. She slipped out when the guard was taking his nap.

Aiko went into her and Kenji's room and found her emergency money. She had eight dollars and thirty cents, and she knew what she was going to do with it.

She would do what her mother had done when they took her father to the internment camps. All they had gotten back was a letter confirming his death in some labour accident. Her mother sauntered into the nearest opium den and never again stumbled out.

She was already a walking zombie, the weight of everything dragging her down. She shuffled down a set of stairs where she had seen junkies coming in and out before. She entered the den, and the woman running the place eyed her. Her one arm on her hip, the other holding the cigarette she smoked on a foot-long filter.

"Are you lost, little boy," the woman said.

Aiko pulled out her money and put it on the table. "Not a day in my life." Looking up, she locked eyes with the woman, showing the depth of her pain.

The woman considered Aiko, and the amount on the table.

"Are you celebrating or something?"

"You could say that," Aiko said. "Tomorrow is my birthday."

"Dare I ask how old you will be?"

"Older than I am now."

The woman laughed. "How much do you want?" She took a drag on her cigarette.

"Everything," Aiko's tone serious.

"I have never seen you here."

Aiko gave her a cold look again. "What is it to you?"

The woman blinked for a second, and she glanced down at the money.

"Are you sure you want to do this?"

Aiko thought about how Mrs. Smith's children reassured her they did not blame her. But there was no place to go, and she had the plague. She would do the right thing. Besides, this way they would not waste a bed in the wards on someone who wasn't sick.

"Yes, I am," she said.

Sunday, April 15, 1995
7:26 p.m., TST
The Arena, the Megatorium
Parathas, Lyra Inferior

She had given up once, and she would not let it happen again. She wasn't sure who these people were or why she was here. But, she knew her purpose was to defend them. These people were her wards. Her brother had been, and she would not let them down.

David noticed Aiko was staring at something, and he looked over in the direction of her gaze. *Shit* was what came to mind when he saw the hundred-foot-tall monster. It stood in the mouth of the cave.

"Of course, it's the fucking Hydra, not a problem. Go ahead, defeat mythical beasts."

He looked back at Aiko, but she wasn't standing there anymore. She reached the pile of weapons and stopped. She closed her eyes and held out her hand, concentrating. The composite bow shook in the middle of the collection and made its way out, with its quiver right behind.

David was still focused on the beast, calculating how to keep track of the heads. I guess *I'll name them,* he thought, inspecting each one from left to right. *Lefty and Righty are self-explanatory. What to call the centre head...hmmm.*

David remembered Aiko, wanting to tell her to stop before he realized he did not know her name. He had heard it before; he was sure Gad had said it. He had no idea what to call her. The bow, unstrung, reached her outstretched hand, and she grabbed it. She put out her other arm to grab the strap of the quiver and threw it over her shoulder, though it held no arrows.

Gabriel glimpsed David and pitied him for a minute. Aiko turned away from the group and vectored toward the Hydra.

The boy can run. Shit, David thought, and Gabriel snapped his fingers. Lucy shot him a dirty look across the Megatorium.

"Aiko," David called out to her, the words leaving his mouth before he could even process the situation. "Wait!" He knew who she was. *Guess the girl can run,* David thought.

She kept running but glanced back, a determined look in her eyes. She winked at David.

She approached the shimmer, a few feet from the line, and kicked off. The first of the acolytes to discover the power of the force of will. Aiko determined she would jump through the barrier and advance on the serpent. She willed it, her kickoff launched her ten feet into the air, through the wall with a tickling ripple.

David looked around and caught Slate's eye. She popped an eyebrow, and he shook his head in the direction of the Hydra. She glanced over and ran. *Shit,* David thought.

"You need a weapon!" He shouted at her. She continued toward the beast.

She reached back with her hand, the pile rattled. An enormous double-sided axe flew out. Ronnie, their Paladin, leaned back with her outer shoulder. She saw her reflection in the chrome of the blades. They whipped by her face.

They were all aware of their surroundings. The remaining thirteen people turned toward the mouth of the cave, watching. Aiko approached the midpoint of them and the Hydra.

"And the rest of us stand here," David said aloud, not sure what to do.

Kushia, Ronnie, and Bennett all responded to what David said like a set of orders from their commander. Bennett dashed forward. This time Lucy snapped her fingers while Gabriel got to look daggers her way.

"Bennett," David said, "weapon!"

Bennett did not stop but held up a hand. "Already got two of them," he pushed off, flipping through the shimmer.

Ronnie and Kushia stuck their arms out toward the pile of weapons, and four javelins flew out. Two landing in each of Ronnie's hands. She turned and ran for the Hydra. Two morning-stars launched out of the pile. Kushia grabbed them on Ronnie's heels.

Aiko slowed down. Each of the three dragon heads moved, staring at the little girl. She turned sideways, sliding along the sand. She leaned down and reached into her quiver.

A dozen crimson arrows materialized in a puff of mana. Aiko grabbed one. A string of golden light strung the bow in her hand. She cocked the bow and, closing one eye, fired and took another arrow out of the quiver. The Huntress of Love fired five shots in the span of a few seconds before sliding to a stop.

The three heads of the Hydra each screamed. They reared back. Slate, Bennett, Ronnie, and Kushia all stopped in their tracks. The snouts dropped, each one hitting the ground with a thud, the middle one landing at Aiko's feet. A crimson arrow in each of its catlike eyes. It came to David. *Bob*, he thought. *Would have been a good name for the middle head.*

❦

"*eighty-one, eighty, seventy-nine—*"

Gadreel was counting down inside David's head.

Why me? David thought, pleading with Gad.

"*Because the game is follow the leader. Seventy-six, seventy-five.*" Gad's voice boomed in his head, and David jumped, not expecting a response.

Which makes it worse, he thought, but Gad kept counting. He sighed.

"All right, we have over a minute before we have to be out of here, I guess—"

"Ande who made you ze bause?" Pierre asked.

David got angry, tired of this, and he looked at Pierre. His body electrified like he could do anything. His eyes were pure white, and his face expressionless.

"Do you want to run this thing?" David's words were like venom, "make the lives of fifteen other people your responsibility."

Pierre didn't want to be in charge anyway. "What do we do?" he said to David, a begrudging look on his face.

David calmed down; everyone staring at him. He took a deep breath.

"OK, all we have to do is walk out, I'm assuming." David paced when thinking. Kay sauntered over to the boulder and sat with her back against it. David took in the pile of remaining weapons. "I assume we should arm ourselves?" he still paced.

Kay's eyes closed. She muttered to herself, repeating over and over.

"It's a dream."

David would deal with it later. "*Sixty-three, sixty-two,*" Gad kept counting down.

"Yes," David said, this time with confidence. "We grab our weapons and leave. It's simple." He stopped pacing and examined the group of acolytes before him. They looked at one another, no one willing to ask: Why?

David lost his temper. "Fifty-five seconds and you're trapped in here for the rest of your life. Is that what you girls want?" He looked at them.

"Look, I have no idea what I'm doing," he confessed. He took a deep breath. "Hell, I'm not even sure this is real. If it is, I don't want to be the guy who stood here and got entombed while a thirteen-year-old girl fought my battles for me."

The whoosh of a slight wind audible. Nine heads turned at once. Hayden said it first.

"She's a girl?"

"Yes," David continued. "A thirteen-year-old girl who did not hesitate but headed toward the danger in our defence."

Some of them were moving before David spoke. By the end, they all headed toward the weapons on their way out of the dome. David stopped Zavannah.

"We've got forty-three seconds before we're trapped. Can you get the rest of them out while I deal with Kay?" He pointed to Kay. She rocked back and forth next to the boulder.

"Yeah," Zavannah said. "You make sure you get out of here, though, OK?"

"Deal," David smirked. The ground around them rumbled. The thirty-nine-second mark. "Go."

Zavannah headed toward the others.

Three white lines of smoke—mana—travelled up the dome, equidistant from each other. Stopping halfway to the top, the horizontal white lines expanded. Like a gated community, locking them in.

Harry reached the weapons, and he put out his hand. Hudson and Maya, their Sorceress, stepped up beside him. The weapons pile rattled. A gladius shot over to Harry, who caught the flying sword. He turned and headed toward Kushia, staying away from the gates.

Pierre reached the weapons. A trident flew into Hudson's hand. A fistful of shuriken flew at Maya. Pierre hesitated. Asher arrived, and Maya caught the first few shuriken.

Pierre reached up. Maya caught the remaining projectiles. His longbow flew toward him faster than he expected. It hit him in the chest, and he fumbled it but managed to hold on. *Snap out of it;* he thought. Asher turned, holding two bolas in each hand. The two of them headed toward Maya and Hudson, picking up speed. The gates closed in.

David had already held up his hand, his two hook swords flew forward. He passed them both to his off side and held up his palm once more. Kay's bastard sword erupted from the remaining few weapons and flew into David's waiting fingers.

"*Thirty-three, thirty-two—*"

David lifted his hand and put the bastard sword on the boulder, bending down to put his hook swords on the ground. He looked at Kay, who had tears streaming down her face. He knelt beside her.

"*Twenty-eight, twenty-seven—*"

Zavannah reached Jonah, Hayden, and Avery. They stood at the remaining weapons, arms out. A quarterstaff flew into Jonah's hand. Zavannah stopped beside Avery. Jonah headed for the opening. Two Korean fighting fans flew into Hayden's one palm, and Avery inspected Zavannah's dress.

"You won't be able to sprint in that," Avery said. Zavannah looked down. She put up her arm. "Go," Avery said to Hayden, who had been waiting for them. She was off, and Avery transferred the first sickle to her off hand.

Zavannah looked back up. "Do you have an idea?" Avery caught her other sickle. The metal loop holding sixteen chakrams jingled like a tambourine. It flew up, the last of the weapons claimed.

"Do you trust me?" Avery stared at Zavannah, who hesitated and moved her proximal leg forward. The ring of chakrams flew into her hand. Avery spun the sickle in her hand and tossed it into the air, catching it. The blade pointed forward.

"Kay, it's not a dream," David said, pulling her hands off her face. "Kay, you have to tell me what the problem is, I can help you. Kay?" He had been trying to calm her down since putting down the swords. *Shit, twenty-one seconds,* he thought. He gazed at her.

"I need more t-t-time..." She stammered. "I need t-to th-think." She looked at him.

He couldn't think either.

⟡

Avery dug the point of the blade into Zavannah's skirt at midthigh and split the dress. She sliced through the hem. "Should work," she smiled. "Let's go."

She turned and headed toward the now-closing gap. Zavannah on her heels, her long, muscular legs glistening. She flew past Avery. She went for the gating and got to the midpoint. The two sides met at the bottom, zipping upward in the middle.

Zavannah turned toward Avery. Bending down and interlocking her fingers and laying them on her knee, she looked up.

"Avery," Zavannah called out, "jump!" Avery was a few steps away and put her head down. She jumped up, Zavannah caught her left boot and heaved, and Avery launched through the air. She landed on the wall a little to the left.

⟡

David was unable to think of a solution. He always had the answer. *Twelve seconds,* he thought. *Twelve seconds to go.*

Straddling the wall, Avery reached down and grabbed Zavannah by the arms. Avery fell backward off the wall, her momentum pulled Zavannah over the wall with her.

David watched. Avery and Zavannah faded away.

"*Ten—*"

The walls rose around them. "*Nine, eight—*"

They were becoming entombed. David was shaking Kay now, screaming at her she needed to snap out of it, eyes full of white.

"*Six, five—*"

David couldn't take it anymore. Kay was giving up. David did not know what overcame him. "*Four—*"

He wound up with his arm and swung forward, aiming to backhand the refusal out of Kay. "*Three—*"

At the last moment, her eyes filled with gray.

"Stop!" She yelled.

"*Two—*"

She launched David up and away with the force of the spell. "*One.*" The interval finished, and time froze. The mana stopped, feet from encasing the whole barrier, and David hung in midair. Kay stood and walked over to David, poking him.

His body moved like it was in the vacuum of space. Weightless, it floated away.

The walls forming around the barrier were closing, but Bennett wasn't looking at the dome. He was viewing the Hydra. Its body was still standing, even though Aiko had taken out the heads, and Bennet had an instinct. He saw something—some things—moving inside the body of the beast. *Of course,* Bennett thought. *You can't kill the heads.* He rushed toward Aiko. Aiko was staring the other way.

Bennett poured on more speed. Each of the three necks moved, the new heads snaking through the old ones. It was like a snake about to regurgitate three small mice. Bennett was too far away, a few yards back and unable to close the gap.

Three new heads burst through Lefty, Righty, and Bob. Let us call these ones Lobby, Bobby, and Robby.

Aiko turned. Bobby reared up and bore down on her. Aiko couldn't move. Ronnie's javelin slammed into its snout and pierced through it.

The javelin stopped when it hit the sand, pinning Bobby's mouth closed and its snout to the ground. Its screams muffled by its closed mouth. Aiko was launched backward by a huff of air through its nose, flying past Bennett. His fingertips brushed her arm to catch her.

Bennett slid to a halt and ran the other way. Lobby came up and around, splitting the dead flesh of Bob apart and heading for Aiko. Bennett jumped up. Lobby whipped past, and he landed on its neck. Bennett grabbed its horns in each hand and squeezed the neck with his thighs. Bennett, calm eyes filled with silver, twisted Lobby's head to one side. He broke its neck, the head dropped like a stone. He lifted himself up by the horns, standing on Lobby's head until it hit earth. Bennett rolled forward off it, popped up to his feet, and kept running.

Robby headed for Aiko. Bennett reached Bobby, still fighting the javelin in its snout. Bennett jumped up and ran over the scales of Bobby until he vaulted off its nostrils. He vectored through the air toward Aiko, who was struggling to cock an arrow.

"No," Slate yelled. "No more heads."

Aiko froze, unsure what to do. Robby was behind Bennett, coming in from outside, but it was moving too fast. Bennett wasn't going to make it, he realized. He reached the mid-point of his arc, and Robby closed in.

Bennett was five feet from Aiko and the serpent's head about four when time froze, suspending him in midair.

Gabriel looked at Lucy and smiled. She sighed in relief.

"This does not change anything," she said, strolling back to her throne.

Gabriel sported a wry smile. He shuffled back to his throne, his step, tap, step, tap, step, tap, not echoing this time. The sound caught in Kay's spell. When he turned to sit down, Lucy was already leaning on her throne.

Gabriel and Lucy were back in their seats, they heard a clamour. The two hook swords flew up out of the hole in the top of the white dome. Arching over the wall and falling to the ground with a clatter. Kay's bastard sword flew out next, whipping around until it landed, blade first, in the sand.

David, body frozen in midmotion, floated up out of the gap by about three feet before slowing to a lazy drift. Kay's hands grabbed the edge of the white mana wall, and she hung on to it by her fingers. Kay grunted and heaved herself up to straddle the fence. Kay was about to turn around for David when she saw it—the whole scene. Aiko retreating from Robby's advancing head. Bennett ran toward her. The second javelin caught midair. Ronnie froze, arm forward, one leg up, mid-release. Pierre, longbow in hand, stuck with his arm pulled back. A hunter-green arrow between his fingers, cocked and ready to go. She saw the rest of them in various states of disarray. They tried to regroup.

Kay had an epiphany: She had not stopped the walls from closing in; she had stopped time altogether. The silence was deafening. She examined the Megatorium, unmoving. Kay glanced at Aiko, discovering she was in serious trouble. Bennett would not make it to her before the Hydra did. Pierre had not been fast enough either; his arrow might strike right, but Aiko would be in the Hydra's mouth.

Kay was still holding on to the spell; she was still in control of it. She wasn't sure how it worked or, should she let go, if she could recast it in time. Kay sensed something in the magiks—resistance. She met the strength of each being in the Megatorium. Like hairs on the back of her neck. Even the small opposition from her fellow acolytes.

There were millions upon millions of larger bodies of resistance. The imprint of the gods in the stands. She realized the footprint a god created was comparable to a planet. Like Mars or Terra, looming behind her in the millions. There were even seven gas giants. The power emanating from the three fates and the three graces on either side of the arena, and the lone fury.

She noticed three large footprints were behind her, but they were not resisting. They were not even frozen, and one was far away.

Kay should have known she couldn't freeze a star on her first try, but why were they were sitting there, staring at her? It was like gazing at the Sol on one side and a black hole on the other. A neutron star unseen but there in the distant background.

She focused on the mountain-sized footprint in front of her. The faint signal of resistance was hard to isolate in the cacophony of magikal echoes. She blinked, her eyes turning gray again. She made a game plan. She adjusted her stance and braced herself, holding her hands out, palms forward.

She focused on the spell, concentrating on the echo of Robby, and setting it in her mind. She let go of the magik, and the scene sprang back to life like someone had hit Play. The booming taps of Gabriel's staff caught up in quick succession. She focused on Robby, trying to keep it frozen. It moved forward.

Bennett looked sideways at the beast, a confused expression on his face. He passed the head. He faced forward and hit the ground running. Kay was sliding backward. The Hydra fought against her enchantment, her feet grinding in the sand. She lost ground.

Bennett was three steps ahead of Robby and two steps away from Aiko. His foot hit the sand. The beast broke the spell. Kay flew forward. The head lurched forward. Bennett closed the gap and crouched down with this last step. He scooped Aiko up. She panda-hugged him around the middle. Her chin resting on his shoulder. She watched his back.

Bennett took another step. Robby closed, about to overtake the two. The second javelin slammed into the dirt. The beast's skull kept moving. Its spine pinned to the ground, Robby's head lurched forward. It turned to the side, Pierre's arrow connected, hitting it square between the horns.

Bennett kept running, turning toward the others.

"Thanks, mister," Aiko said, leaning back to look Bennett in the face, using one hand to hold on to her cap.

"No problem," Bennett glanced back over his shoulder. Bobby reared up with the javelin in its snout.

"Do me a favour," he looked forward again and poured on more speed. "Try not to kill any more heads."

"Yeah," Aiko more mesmerized than shocked, glanced back. "That's a safe bet."

They had made it three-quarters of the way back to Kushia and Hayden, the farthest out of the group. The others were rushing toward Kushia. He and Hayden were talking fast.

"OK, we had to take out two more heads," Bennett heard Hayden saying. He slowed down on approach. "Now there will be thirteen heads instead of nine. That's not the issue. Without knowing how to kill it or stop it, it doesn't matter."

"I get your point, but there's a difference between insignificant shift and abandon," Kushia said. Jonah jogged up last, and Bennett put Aiko down.

"What part of it was abandon?" Bennett asked, and Kushia turned, confused.

"Girls," Kay said, but everyone focused on Bennett and Kushia.

"Sorry?" Kushia became defensive.

"You said 'abandon.' What part of it was abandon?"

"Girls." Kay got louder, staring at the Hydra.

"My point is," Kushia continued, his tone becoming irritated, "we can't chop off heads until we know what we're doing."

"GIRLS!" Kay yelled.

Everyone stopped and looked at her. She was still staring at the Hydra.

"What does it mean if there are ten heads?" Kay finished, and they all followed her gaze. The Hydra was moving. Three more heads burst out of the folded-over neck of Robby. Nothing came out of Lobby.

Bobby-Joe, Bobby-Sue, and Bobby-Lyn shook off the flesh of their predecessor. Bobby-Lyn pulled the first javelin from Bobby's snout. Bobby-Sue grabbed Robby's head, pulled it off the javelin. She tossed it to the side. Bobby-Joe grabbed the second javelin. Bobby-Joe and Bobby-Lyn pulled back. They threw each of their javelins back at the acolytes.

"Girls," Kay reiterated.

"Stop saying 'girls,'" Maya glanced at Kay and back at the Hydra.

Lobby, the one whose neck Bennett had broken, lay on the ground.

Bobby was staring at its fallen sister, before noticing Maya. He screeched at her.

"It's not impressed," Maya took a step back and ran into Hudson. She stepped forward and said, "Sorry."

Zavannah dropped to her knees. Her head tilted forward, and her body went limp. They all turned to her, Asher taking a step toward her before she floated upward. Her feet dragging on the ground. Zavannah lifted her head, her eyes filled with canary yellow. Her arms raised up by her sides. She opened her mouth wide and left it open.

"The Leonean Hydra," something echoed out of Zavannah's still mouth. "The three-headed dragon. A self-regenerative, multiheaded serpent originating from Lake Leona. The offspring of the Echidna and Typhus, the Hydra is not mortal."

Everyone breathed out.

"Do you mean immortal?" Hayden asked, and they all held their breath again.

"The Leonean Hydra is immortal while it has a living head; otherwise, it's unable to regenerate," the voice said. Aiko was about to protest she had killed all three of the heads at once, but Zavannah's head turned toward her. "You managed to take out all three cerebellums. If the medulla oblongata can send back a signal and keep the lungs going, that is all it needs." Her head turned back. "This happened when Heracles could cut off each head below the lizard brain. He had Iolaus cover each neck in pitch and set it on fire, sealing the bronchial tubes. This leads to death by asphyxiation."

The Oracle turned to Bennett. "Another method of elimination is the severing of the spinal column at the C3–C4 joint. This leads to a loss of motor control over breathing functions and death."

Bennett was horrified.

"It's not..." He couldn't bring himself to ask the question.

"Dead?" The voice again. Bennett glanced over at the beast and saw its eye moving.

"No, it's paralyzed."

Friday, May 21, 1971

8:43 p.m., TST
Allan Gardens
160 Gerrard St E, Toronto, Ontario, Canada

Harry was having the time of his life. He had been confident enough to tell his date his full name was Harold. She had laughed and mocked him, and he had enjoyed every minute of it.

It was intoxicating. His head was drunk, but his heart was wide awake.

The two of them strolled the pathway to the entrance of Allan Gardens. They reached the fountain out front and, on a whim, Harry marched to the nearest side. He hopped on the sidewall.

Harry started walking along the side, and he stuck his arms out. He put his hand on his hat and took a step back. Harry's foot missed the side and he slipped backwards. He tried to recover and managed to turn and stumble forwards. His arms flailed. Harry took a few steps and headbutt the fountain's central basin.

Unconscious, Harry fell into the water.

Chapter 3
Put on a Cave Front

Saturday, March 19, 1998
7:43 p.m., TST
An Alley off Oxford Street West
Moose Jaw, Saskatchewan, Canada, Terra

Tara Macintosh, or Tarmac, turned the corner into the small alley. She walked over to a graffiti-covered wall. She put down her pack and pulled supplies out of it. She spread the drop cloth out and pulled out a paint tray. There was a rustling noise. Tarmac examined the alley before turning back and putting the tray down.

She stepped down the alley up to a garbage bin next to the gate at the end. Grabbing a corner of the container, she moved it forward and bent down to grab the supplies.

Tarmac stood and turned around, she sensed eyes watching her. She stood there for a moment, frozen in place. Was she crazy?

Tarmac walked back to the drop cloth and dropped the paint cans. She opened the first can, poured the pale gray paint into the tray, and adjusted her fabric; she was ready.

She reached into the bag again and pulled out something like a nightstick. Tarmac stood and flicked the baton, which became a pole, eight feet in length. She screwed it onto the paint roller, dipping it into the tray to cover it in the thick paint.

She turned to paint. Samael stepped out of the shadow behind her without a sound, holding up his hand. His eyes became consumed with thick, viscous purple mana. Her last memory was a flash of light. She made her third stripe along the wall.

Tarmac stopped, Samael incanting behind her. The arcane symbol for sorcery drew itself in glowing purple on her forehead. Samael faded in a swirl of purple smoke, and Tarmac went back to work, eyes hollow. Her body moved on autopilot.

❧

Tarmac came to, folding the drop cloth into her pack; she walked out of a haze. Tarmac stood up in confusion. She glanced down to see her pack full. The hair on the back of her neck stood on end. She stared at the wall. She could recognize her writing anywhere.

Thursday, July 15, 1999

11:26 a.m., TST
The Arena, the Megatorium
Parathas, Lyra Inferior

Ronnie's internal alarms blared. Her head spun. Something was happening inside her skull. *The javelins,* she thought, and she ran. She weaved between Pierre and Jonah, Ronnie looked up at the two projectiles. She had time to stop one.

The first headed for Harry. Ronnie saw the second, which drew for Zavannah, and she skirted past Maya on her way to intercept it.

The first javelin should have sliced through the meat of Harry's thigh and smashed into bone. The Mechanics' instincts were better than that. His body moved for him. Harry sidestepped the projectile with a half turn. His arm reached out and grabbed the javelin.

Zavannah's eyes drained of the canary magik. Her body went limp, and Bennett rushed forward. Bennett caught her torso. He slid down to his knees with Zavannah. Ronnie whipped past her. Her head fell forward.

Ronnie's outstretched arm grabbed the tip of the javelin. She slid to a stop. She managed to stop the javelin before her arm pulled back. The point stuck out of her fist, half an inch from Zavannah's forehead.

Zavannah came around and raised her head, opening her eyes. When she saw the point sticking out at her, she screamed. She scrambled backward. Ronnie flipped the javelin around and stood it up.

"Zavannah, you're OK now," Bennett said, peering into her eyes. She stared back, her face softening. She calmed down. "Do you know where you are?" Bennett asked her.

"The Arena, the Megatorium, Parathas, Lyra Inferior." Zavannah rattled off the info.

Bennett stared at her.

"Your brain could be a blessing or a curse. Let's forget what you said for the moment. You OK to walk?"

"Yes," Zavannah said, straightening up and stepping forward. "I am well now." She stepped forward. She was shaken, and Bennett took a step back.

Ronnie strode over to Harry, who turned to face her.

"You OK?" She asked him, seeing the awestruck look in his eyes.

Harry shook his head, coming back to reality.

"Yeah," he said. "I'm fucking badass." Harry was smiling, but his eyes belied a mind racing with possibilities. He tossed Ronnie the first javelin, which she caught in midair.

"Thanks," Ronnie said, turning back to the centre. "Anyone figured out how we are going to kill it yet?"

Silence, they had no clue how they were going to fix this.

"Heracles," Slate offered.

"Who?" Kushia was confused.

"In mythology," Slate said, "Heracles defeated the Hydra. He cut off the heads and had his nephew Iolaus hand him a firebrand to cauterize the wounds."

Bennett had been staring down since Zavannah had sauntered away, not wanting to do what he knew he would have to. He knew how to defeat the beast, or at least the best way to try. He did not want to handle any more lives.

Hayden was looking at her hand, a voice telling her to snap her fingers. The hair on her entire body standing on end; she glanced up. The Hydra was more than three-quarters of the way to them, and the heads were getting too close for her liking.

"Girls," Hayden said, "we did it again. It's on top of us."

"I know of anozer way we can cripple ze monstère," Pierre said. Fourteen heads looked over at once, and he blanched. Pierre saw the Hydra coming toward them, its heads taking turns seeing how far away they were.

They backed away from it, exchanging glances. The advancing beast was closing, and Pierre stopped, power coursing through his veins like he had licked the third rail on the metro.

His eyes filled with hunter green, and he put his hand out. The ground shook underneath the advancing Hydra. The dirt broke open under it, and thick vines emerged from the cracks to wrap around each of the Hydra's four legs.

The beast lurched to a grinding halt and fell forward, crashing to the ground. Its heads screamed. They became a tangled mess and fell. They untangled themselves and tried to get up, tried to break through the vines, to no avail. The closest of them was several feet from its targets.

Pierre, back to his old self, was staring at the vines attached to the Hydra.

"You were going to say something before," Hayden said. "Please, continue."

Still staring at the vines, Pierre said;

"I was going to say; ze problem is zat we don't have any sing to make rope."

They stared at him.

"I don't think it is a problem anymore," said Jonah.

Hayden looked down at her hand again. The voice to call once more, telling her to snap her fingers. She did it, figuring, what is the worst outcome? When Hayden did snap her fingers, a spark flew out from between them. She gasped and tried again. Snap...spark.

She was too timid, and she snapped again, harder. Her fingertip exploded with fire hotter than oxyacetylene. She held her hand up.

"Could this be of use?" She said, pointing to her finger torch.

Bennett made a fist.

"I have a plan. "Pierre, can you do the vines again?"

"Yes," Pierre said.

"Kay," Bennett continued, "that sword of yours is the one long enough to go through the entire neck. Can you wield it?" Kay at him, slight panic in her eyes. Bennett looked at her. "If we bring the heads to you, and all you have to do is chop them off, can you do that?" He asked again.

Kay turned confident.

"Yes, that I can do."

"OK then," Bennett said, "here is what I'm thinking."

Wednesday, December 11, 1941

10:17 p.m., TST
Consolidated B-24 Liberator
Airspace over Hong Kong, Terra

Bennett flicked a switch on his console, releasing his first set of bombs over the flotilla of cruisers below him. The Japanese forces had surprised them, launching an attack without warning. Bennett stared down at the yellow decked carrier leading the group.

The cruiser he aimed for exploded. He turned wide, exiting the battlefield to reach radio range. Understaffed and undersupplied, Bennett and 1st Battalion, The Winnipeg Grenadiers, CASF, left for Hong Kong from Jamaica on October 27th.

It was him *and* The Winnipeg Grenadiers. Bennett was a man without a company. He had no assignment when they decided a Bomber with a transmitter and receiver would be an appropriate solution for the limited supply of wires.

"Liberator, come in, over…for God's sake. Ben, pick up." His Commanding Officer's voice breaking with an unusual vibrato. "I can see you."

Bennett grabbed the handset. He held it to his mouth. He pushed the button.

"Liberator to Command, over." Bennett let go of the button.

"Liberator, what the hell are you doing? You're supposed to be watching the air base, over." Bennett bit his lip. He pushed the button.

"Yung Street is gone, they overran it. I managed to make it out in Darla here. Over." He let go of the handset.

There was a vast expanse of dead air.

"Is she all we have left?" There was a long pause, and then the CO added "over" like an afterthought. Bennett held the mic to his mouth, much closer to his lips than before. Bennett, soft-spoken, often seen walking with the help of a big stick, wavered.

"Yes Sir," he let go of the button but did not drop his hand. He saw the Japanese Air Force heading for his position. He grabbed the steering column with both hands and turned back at a sharp angle. He levelled out. He pushed the button.

"I left the receiver and the transmitter connected., Sir. They triangulated the signal. It was my fault, over." Bennett pulled away from the handset and looked over his shoulder. The Japanese forces closed in, faster than the bomber and more agile.

He could make it back to the carrier.

Bennett keyed the handset one last time.

"I'm sorry, Sir. I got in the air, I didn't have another option. Over." Bennett dropped the mic.

"Liberator, you get your sorry ass back—" Bennett switched off the radio.

The fighters on his tail opened fire well before there effective range. The bullets close enough to hear. He approached his target. The fighters closed in. Bennett flicked the last two switches.

His left engine exploded.

Saturday, September 14, 2002
3:41 p.m., TST
The Arena, the Megatorium
Parathas, Lyra Inferior

Maya, Asher, Slate, Kay, Hayden, and David were Team Omega. Pierre, Ronnie, Jonah, Avery, and Harry were Team Gamma, and the rest were Team Omega.

Team Omega was to take out the right set of heads, Righty's descendants: A-Righty, B-Righty, and C-Righty. They'd work together to take out all three heads using Bennett's technique. The goal was to have three or four runners to distract and attract the heads. One of the team supplied cover fire and the other disabled heads, one by one.

Team Gamma was to do the same with Lefty's offspring—A-Lefty, B-Lefty, and C-Lefty. They used Pierre's vines to immobilize them. Team Omega was to tackle the Bobbies and would be able to cut off their heads and cauterize the wounds, all in one fell swoop.

But it all sounded a little too crazy. Maya had believed in the supernatural all her life, yet when faced with this, she did not know if she could handle it. The defensive formation of the heads, even and equal sitting in three rows, creeped her out.

"Ready?" Bennett yelled at the other two groups.

"Ready!" Pierre said, nodding to Bennett.

"Ready!" David said.

Maya wasn't sure, but they were going anyway. While the vines trapped the Hydra, its necks could move fine. Pierre was having trouble catching one.

"Go!" Bennett yelled.

The sixteen of them responded together. Maya headed forward, toward the middle, and pulled out her shuriken. She needed to make sure she got the attention of all four heads. She threw shuriken at Bobby-Joe and Bobby-Lyn. They each took one to the face and roared. They sought Maya, with Bobby and Bobby-Sue in tow.

Maya slid to a halt. Kay and Hayden reached her. She waved to them she was ready. Hayden snapped her fingers, lighting her torch and heating up Kay's sword.

Team Omega had gotten C-Righty already, Bennett and Jonah out in front. A-Righty shot toward them. Jonah shot ahead and veered to the side, taking the head's attention with him.

Bennett took the opening and jumped up onto its neck. He turned and ran along the spine to the head. Jonah was outrunning the Hydra. Bennett grabbed it by the horns. Bennett sat behind its head, squeezing with his thighs, and twisted to the right. Until he heard the pop and A-Righty dropped out of the sky.

Two down, one to go, Bennett thought.

Team Gamma was dealing with the last of the three Lefties. C-Lefty wasn't moving, hanging back in the air, and trying to figure out a way around them. The team waited, and Ronnie ran toward its right flank, and it shot after her.

Pierre, his eyes hunter green, held up his hand, and a crack formed in the earth. Ronnie jumped it and turned around. C-Lefty stopped trying to turn around. A vine shot up from the fissure and wrapped around its neck. C-Lefty struggled against the vine, Pierre closed his hand into a fist. The vines tightened around the Hydra. It couldn't breathe, and its eyes popped out of its head until, with a crack, its hyoid snapped, and C-Lefty fell to the floor.

David stopped running. He had reached his mark, and he looked back at Bobby, the last head. It barreled toward him. David kept calm and waited for the right moment. Bobby got close enough it couldn't miss him, and he jumped sideways and hit the deck. Bobby blew past him, slowing down and turning toward him when it passed.

The red-hot tip of Kay's sword sliced through the flesh of the Hydra. The half with the head dropped, while the body kept going. David sensed the heat by his leg and saw the tip of the blade was a few inches from his thigh. *A little farther,* he thought. He got up and looked around.

All the heads were gone.

The crowd exploded, cheering for their respective champions.

Lucy and Gabriel exchanged a glance and stood. Gad got up from Lucy's ledge. The three Prims phase-shifted to the ground in front of the black sphere. Lucy standing in the middle, with Gad and Gabriel on either side. The crowd died down, and the three gods waited.

The acolytes saw each other panting, dishevelled, and tired. David glanced up at the sky, glanced back down, and stepped forward. The remaining acolytes followed suit. They stood across from the Prims and waited, unsure if they should go first.

"Well done," Lucy said. "You work well together." She glanced at Asher, at Bennett. "You have completed two of your trials. Now you have two more to go."

"What do you—"

"Please," Lucy said, "no questions until the end." She turned back to the group. "To make it to your next trial, you need to enter the cave in the mountain behind you."

They all turned and inspected the darkness. The Hydra's body was gone. They looked toward the gods again, but they were gone.

"Shitfuck," David almost collapsed.

Friday, June 10, 2005
4:27 p.m., TST
The Arena, the Megatorium
Parathas, Lyra Inferior

The acolytes approached the blackness. Not much had changed since the Prims had left, and they were now standing at the mouth of the cave.

Everyone looked to David for guidance, and he sighed, conflicted.

"Should we go?" He asked the group.

They were all hesitant to answer. Harry piped up.

"What if it's not our fort?" Harry turned to David.

"I would assume we would, like, take it over?" David said, and Harry reacted like he was speaking Greek. "I'm sorry, what are we talking about?" David asked.

"You know, what if it's not something we are good at? Not our fort; f-o-r-t-e."

Pierre had been confused, but by the time Harry got to e, he burst out laughing. Unable to contain himself at the confused but comedic comment. His hearty laughter echoed in the now-empty Megatorium. Ronnie joined him, giggling to herself. David glared at the two of them; they died down. He looked back at Harry.

"Forgive them; their French is showing," David said. "It's pronounced for-tay." Harry was mortified, but David managed a reassuring smile. "You bring up a good point, Harry," David continued, taking them in. "We don't know what is going on, what we are doing, or why we are here. We have nothing on us but the clothes on our backs and the weapons in hand. We are going to an unknown territory, for an unknown purpose. To fight another battle, against a different class of monster. Am I missing anything?"

"That's a bit blunt, but yes," Hayden said.

"There is an excellent chance this won't be our fort." David looked up at the blackness ahead of them. He turned to face the group—*No, my team*, he thought. *Guess this is where I make some inspiring speech.*

They were dishevelled, dirty, disheartened. The one who stayed the same was Aiko, but she was rough around the edges. He wasn't in the mood to pander.

"Look," David said, "I have no idea what is going on here. Do any of you, besides Zavannah?" He thought of the last bit when he opened his mouth, in case the Oracle triggered.

"We have two options. One, we stay here, since I don't see anything resembling a door. We'd stay here for three to five days, the amount of time it would take us to die of dehydration. Or, we go into this cave and take our chances. At least this way we have a chance. Anyone disagree?"

They looked at one another, seeing if anyone dared, but David was right.

"Great," David said. "Let's get the fuck out of here. I'm sick of this place." He turned and stepped into the blackness of the cave.

Sunday, December 24, 2006
9:06 a.m., TST
ABC Ultimo Centre
New South Wales, Australia, Terra

Bradley Jamison walked out of the hall and into the newsroom. She stepped up the few steps with the copy she had received moments ago and moved into the anchor chair. The executive producer didn't give her enough of a count in to use words. She held up two fingers, one finger, and pointing at a more composed Bradley, showing they were now live.

"Breaking news. Sixteen people have reported the same experience while remaining thousands of miles away from one another. I'm Bradley Jamieson, and we apologize for interrupting your regularly scheduled programming. Sixteen graffiti artists are at the centre of a global mystery. Plus, panic in several nations. Jess Bergen with the scoop. Jess?"

"Hello, Bradley," Jess said.

"Tell me, Jess, what is going on?"

"I'm standing here next to a mural I'm going to show our viewers in a moment. But before I do that, let me tell you more about the situation. In a twenty-four-hour period, sixteen people worldwide performed beautification tagging, and claim they blacked out. No memory of anything after setting up, and they ended up painting the same thing." She paused for dramatic effect. "While none of them planned to paint anything like it. In fact, none of them knows how to replicate it."

"Wow. What did they end up painting?"

"Bradley," Jess said, "it's an image of the sky, realistic enough to be the sky at night. The problem is not what's painted, though. It's what wasn't."

"How's that, Jess?"

"The murals have writing made from the negative space, where the base coat emerges but not the mural." A shorter pause. "Each of them wrote the same message"—brief pause—"but none of them wrote it in the same language."

"Wow, Jess. How can something like this happen?" Bradley asked, intrigued and a bit concerned.

Jess continued, "the first possibility is it could be a hoax, and the second is it's a rare form of shared delusion. After those options, many national security agencies are considering enemies. Some are investigating the countries which took part. Most other organizations which do things like this are too violent. Others would have taken credit by now."

"OK," said Brad. "What, if anything, does all this mean?"

"It could be a warning something, or someone, is coming, and they are telling us not to be afraid," Jess continued. "Others question the motives of such a message.

"Meanwhile, there are riots in the streets of Islamic and Judeo-Christian countries. The creation of new religions based on these paintings in Russia, Africa, and New Zealand. The United States has seen a mixture of both reactions. In France, they have already created an attraction based around it. In Canada...nothing has changed."

"Got to love the Canadians. Always commendable," Bradley added.

"Ha, yes. Canada takes ineffable to a new level," Jess said.

"OK, what is the message?"

"Why don't I show you instead of telling you, Brad," Jess said, sweeping her hand to the side. Her camera operator panned over. There, on a brick wall, was an image of the night sky, but it was like the building was missing a large chunk. A hole punched out of the middle. In the lime-green base coat, was a message in Maori:

"While angels are coming, and demons are here, the gods arrive first. Greet them without fear."

"Wow, a new one," Bradley said.

"Yes," Jess agreed, "but the government is stressing the message is positive. Thus no one should worry. Otherwise, we should go ahead like normal. I'm Jess Bergen, live here in Christchurch, and this is ABC News. Back to you, Brad."

"Thanks, Jess," finished Brad. "I'm Bradley Jamieson for ABC News. We now return you to Doctor Who, here on the Australian Broadcasting Corporation."

Monday, April 16, 2008
11:32 p.m., TST
Mount Olindias
Olindias Territories, Lyra Superior

David stepped forward and became enveloped in complete darkness. He stopped, unsure what to do, and Asher bumped into him. David took a couple of steps forward and apologized, but "sor" was all Asher heard before David was gone.

"David?" Asher called out, trying to figure out what had happened. But there was no response from David.

"Hey, you girls OK?" Avery asked from nearby, invisible.

"I am," Asher said, speaking toward where he hoped Avery was. "I bumped into David, and he walked forward and vanished."

"Huh," Avery's voice more visible than she was, "do we need to keep walking?"

"Do we want to stay here?" Hayden said from farther away. "What is the problem?"

"Don't be hasty. We don't even know where we are. For 'all we know, David could be dead on the other side," Jonah's accent thicker than the darkness.

"OK," Avery said. "Why don't we put it to a vote? Say aye if we should keep going, and nay if you want to stay here and figure out where we are." She waited for any objections, but none came. "OK, if you want to continue on, say aye."

"Aye!" Eleven voices spoke at once, and Avery smiled, hoping no one could see her.

"Those opposed," she finished.

"Nay!" Three semi-enthusiastic voices replied.

"The ayes have it," Avery said, "let's forge ahead." She took a step forward. She was striding through water, and her hand dissolved. She followed it, falling through to the other side.

Tuesday, December 21, 1965
11:37 a.m., TST
Northwest of Ulyankulu
Tanzania

Asher's movements were slow and deliberate. He held the elephant gun with a firm grip. The tall grass obscuring the bottom third of his body.

He had managed to make this trip after all.

Asher's lifelong dream was to return to Africa and hunt some of its wild and dangerous game. The years in the war left him with a greater sense of being the hunted rather than the hunter. The enemy stuck with speed and precision, leaving nothing in its wake.

When the tide had turned the rush after liberation was second to none.

It was no surprise that his closest confident through the years had remained after deployment. The two captains had been together since they were thrown into the deep end of the North African Front. They spent the war patching and repairing the men in between telling the nurses they were too far gone and eating, while sleeping and other forms of life hovered just out of reach.

Captain Millhouse started going on safaris right after the war, using the trophy money to fund his life. With the decline of the trophy market his purses had dried up, having never been the smartest he had invested in several failed expeditions.

Asher had funded half of the current Safari cost to help his friend. He didn't care about the money. He was after the thrill of the hunt.

His partner was after the life insurance policy he took out on Asher after he generated a vested interest in his life by having him become a sponsor of this trip.

Asher faced away from him. Captain Millhouse pointed his elephant gun at Asher's torso, and fired.

Monday, October II, 2010

11:33 p.m., TST
Beneath Mount Olindias
Olindias Territories, Lyra Superior

"Sorry," David said. He fell through the darkness, submerged. He tumbled out and fell onto the floor. He stood. "You OK?" David turned; he froze. Around him were the walls of a midsized cave, four torches lit the space, and no door in sight.

David paced the room in a circle, talking to himself. It was going on for several minutes since he had come out of. David wasn't sure where he had come out, but it had vanished once he was through.

Muttering to himself, he tried to figure out how to get them a message, some way to tell them to keep going. His pacing changed to a back-and-forth pattern, faster and faster, and he heard a thud. Looking toward the sound, he saw Avery getting up from the ground. The rest of the team came tumbling after.

Once they were all back on their feet again, the rest of the group noticed it too.

"There is no exit," Hudson confirmed he could talk and speak English. The rest of the acolytes searched, but no one could find a way out.

"It's a trick of the light?" Hudson grabbed a torch and pulled it out of its holder.

Slate was near another torch. She grabbed it out of its holder, and the two of them searched the walls. Kushia took a torch and examined the nearest wall. When Kay pulled the last torch out the entire room filled with wind, blowing out each of their flames.

The wind died out, and they were in darkness again for a moment. The ground lit up in a circle of white light and writing formed on the floor.

Sacrifice by pure love gained.
Courage of the one who waned.
Unity through a defeated wraith.
Trust to take a leap of faith.
Walk forward to escape from dark.
Touched by the angels' mark.
Reach new levels with cooperation.
Mortal sacrifice gives elevation.
Fight together through the haze.
Leading to your own dark maze.

David repeated the words inscribed before them, trying to memorize them. Everyone except Zavannah stared at the ground. She looked around the cave, and she spotted it.

The little bit of light coming from the symbol was a fraction compared to the glowing circle on the floor. Easy to miss, Zavannah strode over to the place on the wall where it shone.

"Hey, girls," she said, "I know what our next move is."

Every head turned, but Hudson still looked at the ground. "Does it have anything to do with this list of instructions?" he spoke and Zavannah turned.

"The point," Zavannah said. "We've done the first five things on the list. Now it's time to do the next five." She acted like this was common knowledge, a reasonable assumption.

Zavannah crouched down. Her finger tracing the lines of the symbols, causing them to glow brighter.

"Should she be touching that?" Maya asked, but she realized it did not matter. She glanced down at the ground. A spiral staircase twisted around them several times. It headed upwards and stopped. The two halves of the floor reunited.

"I'm guessing we head up the stairs," David said.

"No shit, Sherlock," Ronnie's dry wit showing. She sized up the stairs and stepped forward. She stepped onto the bottom step and looked down, testing it. "See, safe enough," she said. She went to take a step up. When her foot reached the level, it went through empty space. Ronnie fell forward, and Jonah lunged in time to catch her.

"Might want to wait a moment."

Wednesday, October 23, 2012
9:46 a.m., TST
The Capital Isles
Thoth, Atlantis Prime

The shuttle initiated its descent into the Capital airspace. An officer of the Interspatial Transportation Agency, or ITA, popped up. Lieutenant Taros saluted, and the Corporal returned the gesture.

"Entering Capital airspace; please identify." The Corporal's voice chirped in the Lieutenant's earpiece.

"This is VPTAM Gi Tis Apangelías," Lieutenant Taros referred to the ship with its designation. "Informing Island Control of the arrival of Her Imperial Majesty I Ayona Empress. Imperial Code iota lambda zeta psi rho omicron one six tau fife mu niner."

It was a formality or course. Even if the sweat dripping down the Corporal's shoulder wasn't a dead giveaway. He knew Capital Island would be in full panic mode. The moment a maintenance worker accessed the Empress's private shipyard and every little mouse in the city had squeaked. When the mice talked, people listened.

Every citizen of the Seven Siblings would always want to know the Empress's every move. It could save their life. The ship had pulled away from the palace. Mathematicians and physicists around the city were working out trajectories. She had once gone in the wrong direction on her way to the financial district.

She turned away from the children's hospital. Seventeen physicists and mathematicians had committed suicide. Another eight had dropped dead of coronaries or strokes. One poor woman killed her co-worker in a fit of rage. He suggested she stop calculating until the ship finished correcting course. The Empress had made it clear from that day forward. They were to triple-check before leaving.

By the time they had landed on the western edge of the island, the capital had rolled out the blue carpet. All eyes were on the doors. They opened.

The Empress stepped out, standing at least a head taller than any Atlantean on record. She was a full foot taller than most hybrids. The closest of the relatives to the Terrans, the Humannecs, in the crowd reached her ears at best.

The Empress sat on the massive throne, it became normalized. The members of Parliament, or MPs, settled in. The Speaker of the House called this session to order. The Empress waited for due diligence. Even she had to play by the rules. The calmer she was, the funnier the scene before her was.

"On to new business," said the Speaker. "I now open the floor." The MP from Amphitrite, the smallest of the Seven Sisters, stood. "The House," the Speaker said. "Recognizes the Honorable Epimel of Andrea, district of Pathos, Amphitrite."

"Thank you, Mr. Speaker," Epimel said. "I propose that we reopen Resolution 67B to imperial review."

"The House recognizes the motion," said the Speaker. "Do we have a second?"

This time, a member of the official opposition, a Humannec, stood. An MP from Ouranos, the Terran planet in the system.

"The House recognizes the Honorable Kattavallo of Antix. The representative for the district of Elpida, Ouranos," said the Speaker.

"I second the motion," the representative said.

"The Representative of Antix seconds the motion," the Speaker said. "Let us put it to vote. All in favour, say aye." After a moment, every MP chimed aye, in perfect unison.

"All opposed say nay," the Speaker said. The prime minister, the chancellor, and the president all stood.

"Nay." They were firm but did not oppose the motion. The Rules of Parliament state that all resolutions must pass with one vote in opposition. Imperial ballots required three nay votes. They sat back down.

"That is one thousand four hundred seventy-two for, and three against." The Speaker banged a gavel. "The motion passes. Resolution 67B is with this reopened for parliamentary debate. I open the floor to Her Imperial Majesty I Ayona Empress."

The room went silent; you would have thought that someone had unplugged the speakers.

"Thank you, Mr. Speaker," the Empress said. Three thousand MPs, officials, and aides unclenched. She let time hang there until her smile dissipated.

"From the efficient way you run the House," the Empress said. "I would assume that an imperial motion would be in and out of these walls three times in mere months." The room became suffocating for those in it like the air had gone out.

"My first question is simple," she said. The average heart rate in the room spiked.

"Can anyone tell me why, then, it has been seventeen cycles? My motion to increase our military forces still has not left this room once."

She looked forward, seeing if anyone blinked. The Empress was no fool. They were in a troublesome situation.

"The House recognizes the chancellor of the exchequer," the Speaker stood to say.

"My sincerest of apologies, I admit our failing, Your Imperial Majesty." He paused, taking a deep breath. "But if I may be direct," he said to her.

"You may," the Empress said. She had not liked the Chancellor of the Exchequer when appointed, as he had been picked by the PM and the President of the Seven Sisters, or POTSS, but the Chancellor's bravery had grown on her.

"You are a wise Empress who already knows of the predicament we are in....unless I am mistaken?" The Empress did not move. He continued. "We are trying to find a way to justify increases in the Armed Forces without a disclosable reason."

"How about because I said so?" The Empress remained calm. The chancellor laughed.

"How about because I am going to sit here and wait until you do. Since there is no time limit on an imperial inquisition. I can sit here forever."

POTSS motioned to his head aide, who rushed over.

"Contact the vice president's office. Tell him that he must call an emergency session of the Senate. Tell him it's for me."

Friday, February 12, 2016
7:29 a.m., TST
Beneath the Aegean Plateau, Mount Olindias
Olindias Territories, Lyra Superior

After several minutes of trial and error, they had solved the puzzle of the stairs. Wide enough to accommodate two acolytes, each step would solidify for someone. Thus, they had to work together to make progress. One of them would find his or her footing, which Ronnie discovered by accident. If he or she stayed on that step, it remained stable, and others could walk on it too. This allowed them to find the next person's place. They would stand on their steps while acolyte after acolyte tested steps to see which ones held weight.

Bennett stepped down, and solid stone met his foot. Bingo. He saw lights at the top of the stairs. He moved to the side, and Hayden stepped up from the bottom to test the next step. No dice.

They repeated this, having to skip steps. The pattern became more random and harder to manage. By the time they were five steps from the top, three of the spaces were two steps wide. Some of them had trouble bridging the gaps. Aiko navigated the areas without a problem.

Aiko stepped on the fifth step and hit pay dirt, climbing to the side.

"Ze platform is not zolid," Pierre said, reaching over the wall, and meeting empty space.

"Ever heard of one problem at a time, mister?" Aiko glared up at the French giant. Pierre looked down at her, taken back.

Ronnie put her foot on the last step, and connected. The platform lit up and solidified. One by one the acolytes stepped up and out, onto the platform. Ronnie stepped off the stairs, and with a rumble, they descended.

They stood on a round platform about twenty-five feet across. On one side was a ledge leading to a second platform, twice the size. The lighting of the floor was bright at the ridge and dim farther away.

"Anyone see what I see?" David asked.

"The lights seem to be telling us that we should go that way?" Avery said, looking around at the others. They were past the point of pleasantries and extraneous commentary.

David went first over the ledge. He needed to stay out in front for safety but didn't know why. Once he was across, he signalled that it was safe and turned to look at the new illuminated platform. He stood in a smaller circle, several feet across. It connected to a small bridge on each side, leading to another platform.

This continued until the bridges met on the opposite side, in one final circle. David counted sixteen spots.

"Alternate sides," David said, turning to Maya, who nodded. "One person per circle. Stop when there are no more empty spots in front of you. Pass it on." Maya turned around and gave the message to Jonah behind her; David went to the left.

By the time everyone had settled on their circles, they had ended up staring at one another. The rest might not know what to do next, but David did.

David thought about the writing on the floor. None of them understood that this was where some people had to sacrifice their lives for the good of the others.

"Any idea what happens next?" Kushia asked, hoping someone had an idea.

David looked at Zavannah, who realized what he was about to do.

"A mortal sacrifice gives elevation," David looked up at the sky. Visible hundreds of feet above them, the top of the chamber. He leaned back and closed his eyes and fell backward off his platform; at peace.

"No!" Zavannah yelled, but it was too late. Maya and Jonah both headed for him, but the sixteen platforms moved. Rising, the bridges crumbled away, and they were stuck one to a pillar, the earth moving beneath them.

Sunday, February 11, 2018

2:51 p.m., TST
Near the Base of Mount Olindias
Olindias Territories, Lyra Superior

David's eyes closed, he fell backward; his body limp. He took some solace in the fact that this might make up for what he had done. While he continued to fall, he thought about how he had never focused on the consequences. His sisters often had accused him of being uncaring and inconsiderate. David never meant to be unkind; he lived in his head.

David heard the rumbles of the crumbling platforms and opened his eyes. He saw the bridges falling and closed his eyes again.

His inability to separate the reality of his mind from the existence of the world around him, was a product of not understanding how to. David had never suspected that his selfish actions would lead to this. An assumption he made after sizing up the other acolytes and realizing he was the oldest one. Or the most recent?

David knew he was in 1995 when he died. Some of them were from the sixties, the thirties, and Zavannah was from the turn of the century. Avery and Jonah might be from a later year, but they each gave him an eighties vibe.

A piece of the bridges clipped his arm, spinning him around. David continued rotating until he fell backward again, not wanting to look down.

It isn't a coincidence that I had used the communicator and then I'm here. How stupid did Gabriel think—

David hit the stalagmite-covered floor. His head slammed into the point of one, which protruded from his orbital socket. Another seven of the razor-sharp formations were sticking out of his body, in his arms, a leg, and his torso. His remaining leg hung limp, in an absurd position.

❧

They had reached the top of the chamber, some of them by clinging to their platforms. The platforms rose. Slate focused on the ceiling. Sections pushed forth from the edges. There were sixteen slivers set in a circle above, they matched the platform locations.

Slate watched. The holes closed near the centre and rounded off around the edge. Perfect little circles to hold perfect pillars. They were closing on the ceiling fast.

"Everyone let go of the edges," Kay announced. "Keep your body near the centre of your platform."

Everyone except Pierre looked up and understood. They settled into the centres of their platforms, some more eager than others. Caught by his fear of heights, Pierre had been on his knees, clutching opposing edges of his platform. His knuckles were pure white. They were now at fifty feet and closing.

Slate looked at Pierre on the next platform over and judged the distance. She knew what the problem was, and the few seconds they had wasn't enough time to fix it. Slate heaved her axe and embedded its tip into her platform. She hopped, turned, and ran the two steps she could before jumping the gap between them.

Pierre was saying something. His thick accent and the fact that it was in French led to Slate understanding none of it. She had made the jump and was finding her balance. Slate grabbed Pierre by the arms and pulled his hands off the edges before wrapping him around her. She hugged him, pulling their bodies close together. The hole above them was now two feet wide, and neither of them would be what you consider small.

They stopped the platforms beneath the smaller holes. Each of them stepped off, their platforms descended, and the openings closed. Slate and Pierre realized they were still holding each other; they disengaged.

"Thank you, Madame," Pierre said to her, and Slate could swear a blush flashed across his face. She looked at the six-foot-two man standing before her. Pierre was significant. Anyone could tell from a distance. Slate couldn't shake the memory of his ab muscles against her. She also couldn't shake that she had moved her hand down from the top to the bottom of the small of his back. Slate hoped that he would not bring it up, but he was a Frenchman. It was a bit of a gamble.

"Anytime." Her response came out at a higher pitch than she intended, and she coughed before finishing. "We are a team, us."

They both remembered and looked around.

"Sorry...I..." Slate was saying something when Aiko walked past her.

Aiko reached the edge of the platform and saw that they were above the clouds. She did not know whether to be happy or sad that David had gotten them to the haze. She was glad he had gotten to do something useful with his death.

She turned back to the others, all a bit shell-shocked.

"Over here, girls," Aiko said. They looked up at her with hollow eyes. She did not get it. David was already dead, and he wanted them to make it. What was the point of giving up now? "I know what we have to do next."

"How can you be thinking about that...you're...David is gone!" Hudson burst out.

"Because," Aiko said, "he's gone, and he gave his life to finish this, the way to respect his memory is to keep going. Otherwise, he died for nothing. Trust me." Aiko fought back the tears, regretting her last moments. "That is the worst death."

2

Let Me Drink on It

Chapter 4
Run and Games

David's platform hit the bottom of the chamber; the other pillars reached the top. Gabriel stood on the platform, in his cloak again, waiting.

David's talent kicked in. He came back with a jolted, jerking motion. David could see again, stared up at the wall at a funny angle. His head ached, and he went to sit up.

David moved and froze. He came to the realization that he had struck half a dozen or more stalactites. Or was it stalagmites? His instinct was to get up.

There was a large calcium deposit where his skull should be, and David tried to take a deep breath. The result was a visceral reaction of his whole body to the sensation.

David managed to pull his head off the spike. Air coming in the hole in the back of his head as it finished closing. He lifted himself, one peak at a time until his legs remained.

David saw Gabriel and jumped. He was still stuck at the legs. "You could help me up," he said, giving Gabriel a dirty look.

"I can't," Gabriel held a measured voice. "It's not allowed."

David continued to pull the stalagmites out of his one leg.

"What do you want?" he said. "If you can't tell, I'm a bit busy."

"Trust me, Davie, if I oversaw the testing, it would not be easy."

David froze in place. No one had ever called him Davie except for his mother, and she died when he was five. After that, his father would not tolerate the nickname.

"Now, we don't have much time." Gabriel's smile faded. He held his hand out to help David onto the platform.

"I thought you couldn't interfere," David grabbed Gabriel's Hand.

"I can't help any of you in any way," Gabriel said. The platform rose. "This is true, but there are no rules against me telling you a story." David glanced at him and nodded his understanding.

"Good," Gabriel said. "Listen; we don't have much time."

Wednesday, March 8, 2023
2:59 p.m., TST
China Central TV HQ
Beijing, People's Republic of China, Terra

The producer was counting Destiny Xa in. She adjusted her paperwork. *"Wu, si, san, er,"* the producer counts with his fingers after getting to 'san,' pointing to Destiny instead of counting 'yi.' She breathed in and commenced her broadcast.

"Continuing coverage tonight. The Canton Province sees another bout of the international phenomenon. I'm Destiny Xa, and this is CCTV National News at eleven.

"New developments as scientists have discovered evidence supporting the Canada theory. Since every round has hit Canada or, on two occasions, Canadian embassies. This leads many to guess on its involvement.

"Researchers have flocked to Canadian cities, along with millions of immigrants from all over the world. Now they have discovered a series of previous tags. They're hidden by the demolished buildings and structures, dating back to 1999.

"The Canadian and US governments pledged over seven trillion Canadian dollars to upgrade. Receiving funding for upgrades to everything from infrastructure to urban developments. News of the US investment caused a massive sell-off in foreign markets.

"The TSX surged in response to major investments into companies that acquired contracts. In other news, an explosion in Tehran kills thirty-seven and leaves hundreds wounded in a building collapse—"

Saturday, June 11, 1977
1:03 a.m., TST
The Arms Public House, South Park St
Halifax, Nova Scotia, Canada

The doors to the public house burst open, and Jonah stumbled out at the hands of a bouncer. He adjusted his coat, flipping up his collar. He flipped off the bouncer with effortless grace and two fingers.

He adjusted his hat, and leaning forwards, paced towards Spring Garden Road. His smug expression and quick step gave him an exuberant bounce. Jonah's trench flapped wide as if it had a life of its own.

Jonah reached the intersection of South Park St and Spring Garden Road. He kept walking.

He turned to see the headlights as the driver tried to slam on the brakes.

Thursday, February 22, 2024
3:17 a.m., TST
Aegean Plateau, Mount Olindias
Olindias Territories, Lyra Superior

Everyone was looking for a way down, peering over the edge, pacing. Maya threw rocks down without hearing a response. They let the confusion over what to do next push the reality of what had happened out of their heads. Kay stared at them, sword in hand, the tip in the dirt, caught in a surreal moment.

What the fuck is wrong with everyone? Kay thought, unable to understand how they could be moving on. Not three feet behind her was a hole in the ground where David should be. Leave no man behind; it was what her father would have said.

"Are you all for real?" Kay exclaimed, yelling at them louder than she intended. A rumble became audible beneath her. They all stared at her. Kay continued to chew them out. "What is wrong with you? David's...he's down there without us, without anyone." The rumbling got loud enough to cause reverb on the ground. Kay did not notice. Her voice cracked. "Gods, he sacrificed himself for the good of the group."

The remaining acolytes froze, caught between the odd and sudden juxtaposition of David's head popping out of the hole behind her, and Kay's admonishments.

"And all you girls can do is look for ways out of here?" Kay kept yelling at them. Her gesticulations getting wilder. David reached elbow height. His arms crossed, an eyebrow raised. He watched Kay.

"Kay," said Hayden.

But Kay did not stop.

"I mean, yes, I don't have any clue what to do, what we even could do."

"Kay," Jonah said, David still observing. His knees cleared the ground.

"But I can't imagine why we would all be together like this—"

"KAY!" Hudson bellowed.

"WHAT!" Kay screamed at him.

David's platform stopped, and he stepped forward. Kay was breathing heavy in the resulting silence. David smiled.

"It's good to know you care."

Kay dropped her sword, her eyes widening. She turned around. She slapped David across the face, hard. She had never hit anyone before, but he seemed to take it, nursing his jaw. Kay grabbed him and hugged him. The disparity between his six-foot frame and her five-foot-three-inch body was evident.

"Woah," David said. "Did not mean to scare you." His tone was cheeky but sincere. Kay let go and stepped back, punching David in the chest. "Ow," he laughed.

"It's not funny," Kay said. "We could have lost you."

David's face went grim, and the others gawked at him.

"You can't," he said, holding up his arm. He sliced through the fleshy part of his forearm, forming a massive split. There was no blood. The layers of the dermis, the structure, but nothing worked. Ivory mana formed at the end of the divide and stitched his flesh back together.

"What the—" Maya said.

"Can't kill what is already dead," said David.

The rest of them were getting that shell-shocked look again. Aiko went to slice her hand to see if she was dead. Fifteen people moved toward her in unison.

"Sorry, my fault," David said. "I have always had a flair for the dramatic. It's me, but if you want to check that you're alive," he strolled over to Aiko and bent down, holding out his hand for hers. She gave him her hand, which he pulled forward. He put her two fingers on her other wrist.

"You have to see if you have a pulse. Is your heart beating?" David asked Aiko, and she nodded. "You're alive, little one." He finished by rubbing her head. She grabbed either side of her hat and stuck out her bottom lip.

Kushia had put his fingers on his own wrist.

"Curious," Kushia looked at David, "we're alive, but you're not? I thought we all got resurrected or something?" David stared back for a moment, not sure why he was special.

Hudson saw Mica on the horizon, standing on a cloud in the distance. She held up her hand and snapped her fingers, vanishing. At the same time, Hudson turned to Kushia and spoke.

"We're incarnations, manifestations of the Elemental Forces in former Terran hosts." Hudson looked over at David, "the incarnation of death is dead."

An awkward silence hung over the group.

"OK, now that we have that sorted," Zavannah stated, trying to find the next step.

"Anyone look up?" David said.

For a moment everyone stood there, they never glanced up, and they did. Above the group, about forty feet in the air was a cable, anchored on one side to the mountain behind them. The other end dissolved into the haze.

Pierre looked like he was going to faint, and Slate and David exchanged looks. There was no way he was going up there. Pierre, caught up in protest, didn't notice David motion to Slate. David gave her a suggestion for a solution.

Slate tried it. Walking up to Pierre from behind, she lifted her axe and, with one quick motion, hit him square in the back of the neck. She knew what she was doing because he went down hard.

"B. A. Baracus style," David said; Avery laughed.

⤜⤛⤚⤙

When Zavannah had said there was a staircase leading up to the anchor, this wasn't what Asher had in mind. If you could consider some of them steps. The widths varied from a few inches to several feet across. They had a slant, and Asher thought they couldn't look worse for wear.

Asher stepped on a rock, and it came loose and tumbled down the side of the mountain, hitting Bennett in the head. Bennett lost his balance, his arms jutting out. He wind-milled them. Bennett arched back. He tried to catch himself. Hayden grabbed him by the shirt collar, twisted, and pulled him back on the ledge.

Bennett slumped down, his back to the rock. He breathed hard. "Fuck, thanks, babe."

Hayden stepped over Bennett. She continued up the steps. "Don't call me babe."

Bennett's heart skipped a beat. Harry grabbed him by the arm and heaved him up.

"Careful, tiger," Harry said, helping Bennett balance out. He stared back at Harry. "I've seen that look before," he continued. He turned Bennett around and directed him up the steps. "Trust me, that one's more trouble than she's worth."

Bennett pushed him off and pushed forward.

"I'm sure I don't know what you're talking about," he said, inhaling, and exhaling in a systematic manner.

Harry leaned forward, murmuring in Bennett's ear.

"Word of advice. I would keep my pants on. All I'm going to say on the subject."

Bennett glanced back at Harry, who had straightened up. Bennett raised an eyebrow before turning back and continuing up the steps.

David and Slate were last up to the steps. The two of them carried Pierre up the mountain. Slate went in front, holding Pierre's knees. David had his arms under Pierre's armpits at first, and held on to Pierre by his fingertips in the end as Pierre's torso kept trying to escape.

They reached the plateau, and, after a few steps, Slate stopped. David ran into her. They put Pierre down for the moment.

Everyone was confused, and, once David saw what he had thought was the anchor, he knew why. What they had seen from a distance wasn't an anchor. It was a grip attached to the middle cable of three steel cables above them. The grip was part of an arm that extended from the base of the platform beneath them. David now realized that it was a tremendous platform for the cable car. It attached to the ropes that faded into the mountain above.

"What is this?" Kushia's stress showing. "Some sick joke? How do we get out of here!" He was going stir crazy the closer they were to the end.

"It's an aerial tramway," Zavannah said in that creepy voice.

Kushia was confused. David went to jump in.

"Cable car," Avery said. "It's a solid-rock cable car."

Recognition sprang to everyone except Aiko, who still looked confused.

"Ropeway?" ventured the voice inside Zavannah.

Aiko tilted her head. "Like they use outside the mines?" She asked.

"Yes," David said. "Like they use outside the mines." He examined the platform, trying to find a lever, a button, a symbol, something.

Most of them had given up and were sitting on the platform or against the mountain itself. Asher was tending to Pierre, whom they had propped up next to the base of the tramway arm. He and Jonah were fussing over Pierre's body.

"How long has he been under?" Asher asked. Jonah pulled out a pocket watch and glanced at it.

"Twenty-seven minutes, thirty-two seconds," Jonah put the watch back in his pocket. He leaned forward and checked Pierre's temperature. "Temperature's normal."

"This is super bad for him," Asher said to David.

"Indeed," Jonah said.

"What do you want me to do about it?" David asked. "I'm a corpse. I'm sure my power's not healing based."

Asher glanced at David. His mind raced. Then, looking down at Pierre's head, he heard a voice calling to him in the distance. Asher's head darted to the side. He tried to find the source of the sound.

"You OK, eh?" Jonah asked.

Asher turned back, but his eyes stared through Jonah. He heard the voice again. Clear this time; it stuttered somewhere in front of him. "*Heal...him*," the voice said. Asher sensed it was mocking him, and frustration was building inside him. "*Heal him*," the voice called to him again.

"What do you think I'm trying to DO!" Asher yelled at...nothing. In reality, no one else was hearing what he was. His voice rang out and echoed into the twilight. Jonah put a hand on his shoulder, but when Asher turned his head, his eyes filled with black. Jonah stumbled backward. Asher turned back and held his hand out, his palm above Pierre's forehead.

Asher's magik built, like the charging of a flashbulb. Black magik shot forth from his palm. He blasted Pierre for a moment before a final burst of magik launched Asher backward. He hit David straight on, and they both landed in a heap on the ground.

Zavannah had been watching the horizon. The sun was setting for the day. It had finished its journey. She glanced over at Pierre, the shadows growing. The sun got smaller on the horizon. Zavannah stared at Pierre. The sun set, and dusk was upon them.

She looked away, her shoulders dropping. Pierre opened his eyes and sat up.

David saw him from his position on his elbows.

"I'll be," he said. The platform beneath them shook and rumbled.

Pierre glanced around and realized that he was on a mountain. The colour drained from his face, he scrambled backward, heading toward the side of the hill.

The platform detached from the wall. A crack formed at the place where the platform and mountain met and the whole chunk of rock tilted forward. Pierre turned around. The remaining part of the tramway detached. The platform lurched forward. By the time Pierre reached the edge, it was too late.

Everyone was scrambling to get hold of something, or someone. The floor dropped out from underneath them. The platform swayed forward to balance out its lateral forces. After a few sways, they were descending along the cable at a measured pace, level and steady.

David got that sensation in the pit of his stomach. *Do corpses have feelings?* He asked himself. He glanced up at the cable and saw it. It was like something out of a future *Popular Mechanics*. About ten meters from where they were, was a midspan junction suspended in midair. No tower or structure to support it. There was a conversion junction showing that the top and bottom cable were the same.

But the surprising part was the fact that it was about to turn their aerial tramway into a straight-up zip line. David glanced at the grip holding the middle cable and saw how it would flip around at the junction.

They were a few meters away from the converter.

"Fasten your seatbelts," David warned them, pulling Asher toward the arm with him. "We're about to experience some turbulence."

The platform stopped with a jerk, swaying. The cogs and gears of the junction did their work. The grip's two halves worked their way around the intersection. With a loud click, the grips cleared the converter. The entire structure went into freefall.

Jonah saw the colour drain out of Pierre's face and knew what that look meant. Without being able to help it, Pierre was going to be sick, nauseated by the sensation. Jonah was quick on his feet.

Alcoholics tended to vomit at a higher-than-average rate. The look that people got varied, but their eyes did not. He could get his mother to the nearest toilet bowl, seat up, hair back, and be rubbing her back within twenty seconds.

That had been covering fifteen or twenty meters. He closed the less than a meter between them. Jonah reached Pierre. He planted, grabbed Pierre by the waist and spun him until he was facing the way they were coming from.

Pierre released everything he had in him. The force projected them backwards. Pierre wondered if it would ever stop. The pain clouded his judgment. He struggled to breathe. His ab muscles constricting even though he had nothing left. Jonah grabbed him. Pierre fell to his knees and Jonah rubbed his back.

They entered a thick fog. The platform was still dropping, but it was not the same, the rig had balanced out. David stepped into the middle of the platform, trying to understand the mechanics of what was going on.

The fog rolled in, pouring around them like a white blackout curtain. No one could see in front of themselves for a few seconds. David whipped sideways, and he was somewhere else, but where, he did not know.

The haze cleared. There were eight copies of David standing around the edge of the platform in a circle. They moved in perfect sync.

"What the fuck happened?" Eight Davids said in unison, looking around at one another in bewilderment. *They must be able to read my thoughts,* David thought before realizing he had to clear his mind.

"These other ones aren't me, girls," eight voices said together again. "Shit." It hit him. They had picked the wrong one to copy. Was it because he stood in the middle? In any case, he was dead. He knew when other things were dead, and these creatures were alive.

"I know how we can solve this. I'm dead," eight voices said. Eight pairs of eyebrows raised. "And they aren't," one David said.

The furies screeched. They morphed back into their natural form. Slate, axe in hand, sliced a creature in half in mid-transformation, and it burned up into ash.

Jonah used his staff to sweep the legs of a second creature. Asher pulled out a bola and threw it at a third, entangling its legs. It went down hard. Harry had already stuck his gladius into the chest of the second creature, who burst into flames. Hudson skewered a fourth, who crumbled into dust. He struck his trident into the back of the third creature, which disintegrated.

The other side of the tramway dealt with the three remaining furies. Kay tried to cleave a creature, but it moved too fast for her. It wasn't too fast for Avery, though. She put her sickles on opposite sides of its waist and pulled inward. She sliced it around the middle, causing it to burn up.

The second remaining creature had crossed over to Avery, approaching her from behind. Before it could reach her, Kay thrust her sword forward, impaling the beast on the blade and it turned to dust. A shriek pierced the sudden quiet. The last of the monsters flew away.

Hayden pulled out a fan and turned toward the fleeing creature. She flicked her wrist, and the fan opened. Five daggers flew forward, launching out of the fan's folds. They connected with their target, hitting the creature in the back. It fell out of the sky it became embers that floated in a nonexistent wind.

"Shit," Ronnie said.

The haze lifted, and the group could now see where they were headed.

Below them was an interweaving series of pathways and corridors. The paths, formed by trimmed hedges, wove and expanding in every direction.

They came out of the haze close to the terminus. The line anchored to the far side of a large circle in the centre of the labyrinth. A few acolytes braced themselves before the bottom of the platform touched. The grips hit the stone, stopping the tramway but not the acolytes. Sixteen bodies tumbled through the air to land on a cushion of Terran bones. The entire group ended up splattered over a hill of skeletal remains twenty feet high. They crashed into the pile of bones and sounded like a Jamaican steel-drum band warming up.

The sixteen acolytes struggled to right themselves among the ever-shifting bones. Ronnie's head popped up. "I may have spoken too soon."

Sunday, April 13, 1947
12:02 p.m. TST
Lakehead Psychiatric Hospital
Thunder Bay, Ontario, Canada, Terra

Maya pushed the cart of pill cups along a long white hall. She stopped at one of the doors and abandoned her cart.

Inside, a man lay in bed.

Maya crept over beside the bed. She floated down onto the soft surface and extended her arm until she could reach the pillow. She removed it from behind the man's head in one quick motion.

The man's eyes opened wide and fast.

Maya grabbed the other side of the pillow and pushed down. The man's scream muffled from the start.

He clutched at Maya's arms and flailed. He kneed Maya in the head. She lost her concentration and eased her grip. He pushed her off, hard.

Maya flew into the wall.

She tried to get up but couldn't get her footing and slid down the wall.

The man threw the pillow away and got out of bed. He closed the gap between Maya and himself before she could recover.

He wrapped his hands around her throat.

Wednesday, November 17, 2032
12:37 p.m., TST
Chamber, Minasyan Labyrinth, Far Reaches
Olindias Territories, Lyra Superior

Maya flailed; she was suffocating. She swam through the sea of bones. Her skin was crawling like a toddler. This was her visceral reaction to the dusty bones that she was unable to escape. Maya had sunk too far into the pile and couldn't find the exit. She hoped that whatever direction she was digging in was the right one. Her movements got wilder and more panicked. She wasn't making much progress.

A hand connected with her ankle and, grasping her leg, pulled her out of the pile. Her leg hit the air, followed by an intense sense of relief. Another hand on her arm and the bones fell away. She flew, landing on Kushia. They both collapsed onto the floor.

Maya scrambled up and grabbed Kushia's arm and helped him up.

"I got her!" Kushia yelled.

"Kushia has her," Maya could hear Hayden yell off to the side.

"Thank you," Maya said, smiling at Kushia. She brushed herself off, a cloud of dust forming around her.

Kushia checked to see if the others were coming. Maya examined the room, seeing it for the first time with open eyes.

They were in an enormous rectangular atrium. The walls must have been fifteen meters or taller. The room had no real light source except the circular hole in the ceiling.

Maya could even swear she heard a small clicking sound. She wondered if they had triggered something. A time-delay device counting out by spring and cog: click, click, click.

The rest of the group joined them, everyone looking a little gray due to the thick layer of persistent dust.

"Where are we?" Maya asked.

The Oracle returned. "Antechamber of the Minasyan Labyrinth. Far Reaches, Olindias Territories, Lyra Superior." The yellow drained from Zavannah's eyes, and she came back.

"Great. Of course, we end up in a labyrinth," Avery scanned the room until she saw David's face. It was more like a corpse than before, if that was even possible.

"No," David said. Maya noticed the clicking sound was getting louder. "Not *a* labyrinth, *the* Labyrinth," his voice warbling in an unusual display of concern.

"What's the difference?" Hayden wondered.

Maya realized that the ground was shaking in time with the deepening clicking noise.

Jonah was staring up at the ceiling right above the top of the bone pile. There, suspended above the collection, was a skeletal chandelier. Woven together, the bones made up five segments resembling flower petals. They attached in the middle by a socket with a giant Tesla bulb hanging at a funny angle. *It's not screwed in right*, Jonah thought. *Is it supposed to be that way?*

"The way out of the Labyrinth is to use a magik ball of string called Ariadne's thread," David said. "I forgot to pack mine and unless you have one I'm not even sure we can get out of here."

"Does not mean you can't make one," Maya heard someone say from somewhere off to her left. Her head darted back.

"Also, there is the minor problem of the—" David's eyes went wide, and the ground shook.

"Minotaur," Maya yelled, looking back at him.

Everyone except Jonah stared at the far wall. Bones fell off the pile and slid down. The chandelier moved, and Jonah snapped to attention. He glanced at the others and in the direction of the ground quakes.

"I'm sorry; did you say Minotaur?" Jonah asked. Clouds moved above the ceiling, blocking out the twilight and driving them into total darkness.

"*Fix the lights,*" Jonah heard a voice say to him.

How can I do that? He thought, hoping it would be that straightforward.

"*Concentrate on the bulb and return things to their natural order,*" the voice replied.

Cryptic—perfect, Jonah thought, forgetting that the voice could hear him.

The voice sighed. The shaking stopped, and the pitch-black room went quiet. Jonah's blood ran cold.

"*Think 'Bulb, turn,*'" the voice said.

Jonah was incredulous and thought *Bulb! Turn!* Mocking the situation;

"*Don't say I didn't try,*" he heard before something took him over.

In the darkness, he faced toward where he knew the bulb was, the malachite of his eyes glowing in the dark.

"Turn," said the voice from his mouth. The bulb aligned itself and twisted upward into the socket. It kicked on, filling the chamber with blinding white light. The petals curled downward and closed around the brightness to form their own bulb. The room was no longer blinding.

There, standing in front of an archway that had not been there before, was the Minotaur, in all its glory. Its breath a dense fog that sprayed down from its nostrils, a ring hanging from its nose.

Jonah came back and saw it. He screamed, and the other acolytes stared back at him in surprise. A man's body on bull legs, with a half-and-half face. The Minotaur's large curved horns and sheer size caught Jonah off guard.

The Minotaur smiled and ran for them, the ground shaking under its feet. Ronnie threw a javelin at it, and Pierre cocked his bow and fired. The beast deflected them both with his arms. The projectiles bounced off the manacles that still bound his hands.

The others scattered. The beast headed toward the group, but Aiko stood her ground. "*Let your hair down,*" a voice said behind her, but she knew it wasn't there.

What? Aiko thought while the Minotaur picked up speed.

They had all moved, but Bennett saw Aiko standing there. He scrambled toward her. Aiko held up her hand, telling him to stop. It made Bennett pause before heading toward her again.

Kay stopped him.

"This is her fight."

At the same time, Avery's eyes went citrine, and the clouds above them darkened.

Harry was spectering too. His eyes filled with rust. The bones behind them rattled, pieces falling off the top. The skeletons reformed and stood up before marching toward the oncoming beast.

"Or theirs," Kay said. "I guess, in any case, you have to trust her. She trusts us."

Bennett stepped back and out of the way of the three dozen skeleton soldiers walking toward the Minotaur.

The beast slid to a halt and looked at the skeletons, trying to figure out what to do.

Avery took her moment, and the sky cracked. Lightning struck the beast at the horns, followed by the reverb of the thunder. Avery came back to, the clouds rolling away. She took a step back and looked at her hands.

The Minotaur leaned his top half forward, bending at the hip, and kicked twice with his hoof. The beast charged into the oncoming skeletons. It knocked most of them over. Bones and parts flew in all directions. The Minotaur kept charging through the skeletons. It slid out of the other side, a soldier skewered in its horns. It stood and shook it off, sending the bones flying against the wall.

Harry's eyes drained of rust. He let go of his control over the skeleton army. The bones fell apart behind him.

The Minotaur turned to face Aiko.

"Let your hair down," the voice said again, and Aiko reached for her cap but hesitated, wondering if she should do it. The Minotaur was running toward her, twenty meters and closing, full steam ahead. "Believe," the voice said, this time insistent. Aiko took a deep breath, steeling herself, before she pulled off her hat, shaking her head. Long, black hair poured out of her cap, flowing down until it stopped at her ankles.

The Minotaur was fourteen meters out when Aiko turned and looked into its eyes. Hers filled to the brim with crimson. The beast's eyes became glassy. It stopped running and dropped seven meters out. It slid on its knees until it was a foot from Aiko.

He stared into her eyes. Aiko lifted her right arm and extended it to hold the beast's face in her hand. The Minotaur, drawn to her, leaned its head down, allowing Aiko to put her other hand on its head. The Minotaur's breathing slowed. He placed his forehead against Aiko's, closing his eyes. She leaned her forehead forward, taking a moment. Everyone else stared, mouths agape, unable to reconcile the image before them.

Aiko rubbed his head and twisted in place. Her feet remained planted, while her body turned until her back was to the Minotaur. She reached back and grabbed the beast's horns.

In one quick, fluid motion, Aiko turned around, breaking the Minotaur's neck with an audible crack. She now stood in the same place, holding him by his now upside-down horns. She let go and stepped back. The Minotaur's body slumped forward, hitting the ground with a loud thud. The earth shook.

"Jesus," Bennett said. "You may be right, Kay. I'm sure she can take care of herself."

He and the others were still gawking. Aiko turned toward them, the crimson gone from her eyes. She saw the way they were looking at her, and, blushing, she twisted her hair around itself.

"Thanks?" David said, unsure.

"No problem," Aiko said. She got to the end of her hair and coiled the twisted locks into the cap. She reached her head, and she pulled the hat down, sealing the hair in.

"Huh," Slate said. "It was the beauty that killed the beast." Hayden elbowed her. "Ow," she said and saw Hayden's admonishing expression. "Sorry."

Aiko gazed at her, without pretense.

"Should I not have?"

Slate understood the expression *from the mouths of babes* for the first time. She stared at the others. The remaining acolytes looked back at her, everyone unsure what to say.

Slate cleared her throat.

"No, Aiko," Slate said. "I guess you did what you needed to." She hoped that covered it. They needed to move on. "How do we get out of here?"

Monday, February 22, 2038
9:00 p.m., TST
SABC Studios, Uitsaaisentrum
Johannesburg, South Africa, Terra

"Good evening. Thank you for joining us here on the South African Broadcasting Corporation. I'm Saia Govender, and this is SABC *News at Nine*. Our top story tonight is the release of a global immigration trends study that shows that the ever-increasing trend of migration to Canada is not stopping. The country has broken the record for the highest immigration by any nation for twenty years. But those numbers are bolstered by developing countries, like BRIC, MINT, and Next Eleven nations.

"The population of Canadian citizens approaches 150 million. A new examination of immigration before and after July 27 of last year shows a change in trends. Emigration from developing countries remained stable but developed nation immigration rates have doubled.

"Speculation into the growth rate of Canada estimates—"

Saia stopped talking, his eyes going hollow. The production team became a flurry of questions and answers. The executive producer stared through the window, everyone around her searching for guidance.

"Keep 'em rolling," she said, and the order went down the chain of command.

Saia stared straight ahead, his eyes still hollow. His mouth opened, and released a voice:

Angels and demons fight,
Gods' hearts take flight,
In peace, we come,
Balancing the zero-sum.

Monday, November 15, 2039

4:13 a.m., TST
Chamber, Minasyan Labyrinth, Far Reaches
Olindias Territories, Lyra Superior

"You must lead the way," the voice said. "Look for the thread of truth inside you." Maya examined her hand, staring at its back. Purple lines formed a circle on her skin. Then, spreading inward, the lines drew an inverted five-point star, a pentagram.

How many books had she read on the occult? It was real, and it was terrific. But watching it happen, reading about it—that was child's play. Now she was in it. There was no turning back and nothing to turn to. Maya had always been lost and alone in her life, and she was to lead them out of the Labyrinth?

She was having an out-of-body experience. She was looking at herself from above. She tried yelling at herself, but the Maya beneath her did not care, did not to notice. She froze in place. Above herself, Maya swam downward, toward her body, but she hit an invisible wall, like plate glass. She yelled. She pounded on the invisible wall, getting more desperate to return to her body. It stood there like a statue. Maya hit the wall harder, using her two hands together to pound against the barrier. She got frustrated, she wound up and punched the wall straight on.

The barrier broke, and Maya flowed right back into her body. Her arm shot out. She held out her hand. She looked at David.

"What did you say we needed?" Maya said, and he forgot the name of the—

David's brain stalling out. She was in his head; he could her exploring it.

"Ariadne's thread," David spit out, the answer pulled out of him.

Maya turned and gazed at her hand, fingers extended, and incanted;

"Ariadne filum." The words boomed out of her, and a small cyclone of tyrian mana swirled out from her hand. The magik swirled in place before a giant ball of golden thread came out of the top. The cyclone dissipated, and the thread fell to the floor.

Ariadne's thread was on autopilot, springing into action. It hit the ground with a bounce. The ball unravelled. Individual strands anchored to the ground. Ariadne's thread continued rolling along the floor and out through the archway.

Maya's tyrian smoke dissipated. She became her usual self again. She looked back at her hands; she looked over at David. Maya had seen inside his head and knew what he had done. She broke his gaze.

"At least now we know which way to go," Maya said.

The rest of the group inspected at her, dishevelled and weary, their faces a mixture of tired and relieved.

"One problem," said Jonah. "The other side of that archway is pitch black, and I'm assuming that goes for the rest of this place." He was right; they had to go into darkness.

Bennett was looking at his hands. His eyes were two golden swirls.

"I have a solution to that."

Thursday, July 5, 2040

4:13 a.m., TST
The Hedges, Minasyan Labyrinth, Far Reaches
Olindias Territories, Lyra Superior

Bennett laid his hands on their weapons. They glowed a warm yellow, lighting the way for each of them. They followed the string. It turned this way and that, weaving in and out. They had come across a few spots where the thread went into the hedges. Through trial and error, they found nothing there; an optical illusion.

Kay was sure they were going in circles. They made right turns. They were losing track of their faculties. One wall of greenery blended into the next. They turned right again, and, after a few meters, the hedges fell away. The thread leading them into a large courtyard.

There was a large open pit, too dark to see inside, taking up the entire breadth of the courtyard in the middle. At the midpoint was a bridge that crossed to the other side of the pit. The thread was on the other side of the bridge, waiting, with nowhere to go.

On either side of the pit sat a statue of a Gryphon, facing inward. Ronnie looked at the scene, and something wasn't right; she was queasy. She examined a statue. Its wings pointed down. Like its eyes, which stared at the midpoint of the bridge.

They split up to search the area for clues and fanned out. They inspected every inch of the courtyard on this side of the bridge. No one could find anything but some dirt, a few pebbles, and, of course, the perimeter wall of hedges. The entrance was gone, now a seamless wall of greenery.

Aiko sat and crossed her legs, tired and not knowing what else to do. She watched the others, like ants in a farm. They kept retracing their steps.

"Unless you have some x-ray specs," said Aiko, "I'm sure nothing is going to change." And like that, fifteen adults realized that even a child could see what they could not or would not. There was nothing to see.

"*Nothing that they can see,*" said the voice in Ronnie's mind.

Quoi? She thought. Ronnie was standing near the edge of the pit, looking down into the abyss. She held her glowing javelin in the air.

"*Take a better look, Ronnie,*" the voice said.

Ronnie peered behind her, searching for the source of something she knew wasn't real. She shook her head, focusing on the pit. She looked for something different, something out of place. There had to be something unique, different, to give them a clue.

"Should we cross?" Jonah said to the others. He stared at the thread.

No one responded right away. In fact, no one knew how to react. Bennett, Ronnie, and David were looking at one another. He held the weight of getting everyone through.

There was nothing else to do but try. David looked at Aiko.

"I'll go first," David said. "Once we know that it's able to support the weight, the rest of you can follow. Stay together. And Bennett, you and Ronnie take up the rear. Aiko, you're with me."

Twenty hours ago, they would have argued about this. Hell, five or six hours ago, they might have had problems. But that was before Aiko had defeated the Minotaur and David had died. Before Bennett and Ronnie had saved them many times with their lightning-fast reflexes.

David turned toward the bridge, a continuous extention of the stone beneath their feet. The naturally formed stone walkway arching up and across the emptiness to the other side. Aiko stood, and he grabbed her hand when he strolled by. Aiko and David walked up to the bridge, taking a closer look. The walkway spanned the chasm with an entrance that spanned over five feet and a bridge that David guessed to be three feet at the midspan.

They split up. David went left, holding a sword out. He inspected the side of the stone bridge. Everything was in order.

He peered across the bridge at Aiko, who peered back at him. *Nothing left to do but take a walk,* David thought, taking a deep breath. He went a few steps forward until he was on the bridge and past the curve of the pit. Nothing happened.

"That was underwhelming." He looked around, inspecting the arching path that sprawled out in front of him. The pit was about 250 feet across, and he figured it was about the same in depth. "Should I go across?" David asked, staring down the centre of the bridge.

"I don't know," Bennett glanced at Ronnie. "Can it hurt?"

"It can hurt," David said. "The question is," he continued, glancing back at them, "what happens if I fall?" He peered down into the abyss but had to look up after a few seconds.

"Is there another option?" Hayden said, looking around. No one piped up.

David turned and faced the midspan of the bridge, squaring his shoulders.

"Into the breach," he stepped forward.

"Wait," Kay said.

David stopped and turned back toward the group. They were all looking at Kay.

"For what?" David asked.

She didn't have an answer. Ronnie's stomach churned.

"Nothing," Kay stared down. "I don't know."

David looked at her.

"Don't worry," he said, "can't kill what is already dead." He flashed her a smile, and Kay lightened up. David turned back. He kept shuffling until he was three or four meters from the halfway point. The point where the two Gryphons' eyes stared, and he stopped.

Good, he thought. He looked back at the now-distant group.

"Don't say I didn't warn you," the voice in Ronnie's head said, and she looked at David. He crossed the halfway point. She was going to stop him, but nothing happened.

David turned around, smiling back at them, and Ronnie heard a buzzing sound that got louder. The Gryphons' eyes were lighting up when David turned to run back to them. The buzzing reached a high pitch, and David headed back. A wall of energy glinted into existence in front of him. He tried to stop but went through the barrier. His body disintegrated with a zap like a bug hitting a zapper. Momentum carried him through the barrier. A pile of ashes formed on the other side.

Kay screamed and passed out from shock. Slate swooped in and caught her before she fell. Hayden and Asher also yelled in surprise. Aiko ran toward where David had been, but four acolytes tried to stop her. Hudson managed to scoop her up.

"I'm sorry, little one," Hudson said, squeezing her tight. She wrestled to get away from him. "There is nothing you can do."

Tears streamed down Aiko's face. She sobbed into Hudson's arm. She stopped fighting, seeing the white smoke forming above David's ashes. Aiko pointed, and the rest of the group followed her finger to the small cyclone. It got larger. When the twister reached critical mass, it slowed, leaving David standing in its wake. Hudson stared at David, frozen in mid-step. He came back to life like someone had snapped their fingers.

He finished stepping forward, his front foot landing funny. David stepped wrong, and his knee gave out. He stumbled forward, and his whole body tilted. Bennett was running past them before anyone else could react; Hudson and Ronnie ran after him.

David crumpled, trying to stay on the bridge. His left leg slid sideways, dropping off the side. Bennett poured on the speed. David tried to hold on to something, scraping the deck with his swords. The bottom of David's body slid over the edge.

Ronnie wound up and launched a javelin forward. She yelled at Bennett.

"Catch!"

Bennett turned while running. He saw the javelin race past his body, and his hand shot out. It wasn't visible to the naked eye. He grabbed the javelin out of the air with both hands, one near each end of the javelin.

David's head dropped off the edge. Hudson gave it everything he had. Ronnie was ahead of him. Bennett reached striking distance. David's arms, hands, and swords slipped and scraped. They too disappeared over the edge. Bennett launched his hands forward. He slid along the dirt.

When Bennett's legs went up in the air, Ronnie reached forward, grabbing him by the ankles. She hit the ground. The top half of Bennett slid over the side. Hudson caught Ronnie around the knees with his right arm. He drove his trident into the ground at an angle toward the direction his body was skidding. The trident gained traction, stopping them in sequence. Hudson held on to Ronnie, who held fast to Bennett, hanging over the edge. Still holding either side of Ronnie's javelin, David's hook sword clinging to the bar. David grasped on by one hand, dangling into the dark abyss, the light of his second sword unable to pierce the black. David stared up.

"Thank gods. For a moment there, I worried."

Bennett stared back at him, wanting to be angry but unable to do anything but burst into laughter. David laughed and hooked his other sword onto the javelin.

"Try not to do that again," Bennett said. "Hudson pull us up, please."

Hudson heaved Ronnie. Pulling against his trident, he put his foot on the far side and anchored himself. Bennett's body slid over the edge, and David popped up. Once he was high enough, he put his leg up and stepped up, falling onto Bennett. Kay had come too, and the rest of the acolytes were grinning at each other like a smirk of Cheshire Cats.

Slate was examining the Gryphons. They sat still—guardians, standing watch over their gate, keeping an eternal vigil. She sensed they were mocking her, sitting there between them and the other side of the pit.

"*Why don't you do something about it?*" The voice in her head was talking.

Slate figured out that those Gryphons had to go, that if they stood, the gate stood. The frustration and anger at the situation had been building, and she let it go. Midnight blue filled her eyes. Slate raised one hand, pointing it toward the left Gryphon. She held her palm out, before closing her hand into a fist in one swift movement.

A booming crack cut the quiet of the courtyard. The Gryphon crumbled and split, falling forward into the darkness of the abyss. The left Gryphon slid into the pit.

Slate held up her right hand to the right Gryphon. After she closed her palm, another crack cut the quiet. The right Gryphons head tumbled to the side, and the rest of the statue crumbled. Slate came back to the group. The barrier that gated them in phased in and out, the energy dissipating. The invisible wall disappeared.

Hudson, Ronnie, Bennett, and David had straightened themselves out and up. They stared ahead, having seen the fall of the wall. David walked across the bridge, headed toward the far end.

Bennett grabbed him by the arm, stopping him.

"We have to make sure it's safe."

David turned and looked him straight in the eyes.

"One problem," David said, and Bennett's expression changed to confusion. "I'm the way we have of checking that."

David held his gaze, and Bennett realized that he was right. Bennett let go. David turned and walked forward in measured steps. He reached the midpoint of the bridge and stopped. Extending one arm forward across where the barrier had been. He waited, nothing happened. David crossed the line and stayed still, waiting for the zap. He peeked back at the rest of the group, smiling to the others in relief. He turned and walked forward another ten feet. Nothing happened.

"Looks like that worked," David yelled back at the others.

They were looking at one another; Hudson, Ronnie, and Bennett waited for someone to be the first one to move. Aiko sighed and walked along the bridge. And then, outdone by a thirteen-year-old, the remaining acolytes followed suit. Pierre and Maya brought up the rear.

David saw that they were all on the bridge. He turned forward and held a sword aloft, heading for the opposite side.

That was when the entire arch disappeared beneath them.

Friday, May 14, 1929
11:50 a.m., TST
233 Broadway, Manhattan, New York
New York, USA, Terra

Kushia's office was halfway up the Woolworth Building. Everywhere but his office window filled with volumes on all the available tradable markets.

He was pacing back and forth in front of his desk. The market had crashed that morning, along with his life.

He had one chance to fix it.

The phone rang, vibrating hard enough to dislodge from the cradle. Kushia grabbed the receiver and spoke before answering.

"Brandice and Stein, Kushia speaking." He listened for a moment. "I see," he bit his lip, "and that's all that you could do?" He listened again. His face fell. "Thank you for your time, have a good day." Kushia hung the phone up.

Kushia loosened his tie and took it off. He shuffled over to the window and opened it. He climbed up the frame and onto the sill.

Kushia took a step forward.

Friday, May 14, 2049
7:26 p.m., TST
Tunnel to Tartarus, Minasyan Labyrinth, Far Reaches
Olindias Territories, Lyra Superior

Sixteen people went into freefall in simultaneous surprise. They tumbled down into the darkness of the abyss. Sixteen lighted bodies fell for an endless amount of time. Kushia's eyes turned into pools of sparkling amethyst. He spread his arms and tilted his head back.

They dropped out of the bottom of the pit at the top of a massive underground cave. Kushia grabbed hold of them and they stopped. They hung three-quarters of the way from the ground to the ceiling. The rest of the group orbited Kushia, frozen in place, suspended in midair. The chamber was like a forgotten cavern one would go spelunking in. Cutting through the middle of it was a large, slow-moving river of dark, grayish-black water.

Kushia lifted them back up. They entered the pit and headed toward its mouth. They accelerated up the pitch black, until they shot out of the abyss, and stopped. Kushia lowered them back down and heading back; he dropped them all from a few feet above the side of the pit. Everyone hit the ground with a thud. Kushia floated downward until his feet touched down. He let go, and crumpled to the floor, drained.

Ronnie sat cross-legged, staring into the pit, her brain working a mile minute. She tried to figure out a way across.

"*You need to take a better look.*" The voice was back.

But this time, she challenged it. *How? How could I take a better look?*

"*Why don't you try on your glasses?*" the voice said. A weight dropped into her hand, and she glanced down. She was holding a pair of spectacles complete with wire metal frame and extended ear curves. They looked like the original pair of glasses, the lenses wide, flat circles. "*C'mon, put them on. What is the worst that could happen?*" the voice said. Ronnie hesitated, examined them, and put them on. Her eyes filled with an atomic tangerine. Now she could see it.

There was, indeed, a bridge covering the span of the abyss, invisible to the naked eye. It glowed orange with the power of the spectacles. Ronnie pulled the glasses down; her tangerine eye sockets saw nothing on their own. She put the glasses back on and traced the route of the glowing orange path.

On their left, it ran along the hedges to where the Gryphon had been. The first invisible bridge stopped at the platform that jutted out from the side. The site now an empty space. There was a second bridge covering the entire span of the pit. It went straight across the middle of the abyss from one Gryphon's sill to the other. It ended on the right side. The orange ribbon connected the two empty platforms. It ran from the right-hand platform, along the hedges, and ended on the other side. She could see their way across. Now they had to get there. Ronnie jumped up and turned around.

"Girls!" She yelled at them and stopped dead in her tracks. Ronnie was still wearing her spectacles, and when she turned, she looked at David.

His true form appeared before her. He was a decaying corpse, and the magik of the glasses allowed the thick waft of decay to reach her. She turned back and, throwing her head over the edge, vomited like there was no tomorrow. She pulled off the glasses, and the decay dissipated, calming her stomach down.

Ronnie wiped her mouth and peered back at the group. David looked normal again. Asher was by her side, attempting to help her up.

"I'm all right," she said. "I'm OK, a little sick. I stood too fast."

Asher raised an eyebrow, giving her a look like *that makes no sense*. Ronnie fired back a quick and side-eyed *I know but trust me—drop it*.

Asher took the hint.

"Let me know if you get sick again," he said. The rest of the group caught up to them and huddled around Ronnie.

"Will do," Ronnie said.

"What were you yelling about?" Harry asked.

Ronnie perked up.

"Right," she said. "There is a way across. I can see it."

The wave of relief washing over the rest of the group was tangible.

"It's right there, in the middle of the pit." Ronnie pointed.

The group's heart sank. They looked at the empty space and assumed Ronnie was losing it.

She clocked the looks on their faces and realized that she was talking about an invisible path. Ronnie held up the glasses.

"Look," she said, handing them to Jonah. "Look through these and tell me I'm crazy."

"No one zaid you wear crayzy," Pierre said.

"No one had to," Ronnie stared back at him with knowing eyes.

"Shit," Jonah said, holding up the glasses to his eyes. He dropped them down, looking over them, and held them up again. "There is a path down the middle like she said."

Hudson, standing next to him, motioned for the glasses.

"Do you mind?" he asked, and Jonah handed him the glasses.

"What do we do?" Jonah asked the group, and everyone went silent.

Hudson looked and handed the glasses back to Ronnie. Everyone talked over one another. Hudson turned toward the pit. His eyes filling with cerulean, he held his hand out, focusing on the river a mile below. The voices behind him fell away. Hudson closed his eyes, concentrating on drawing the water toward him.

Slate stopped talking. She could hear rushing water, and she looked down. The ground rumbled. Everyone went silent, staring down at the sand. The rumbling got louder. Slate looked at Hudson and past him at the pit. A column of the grayish-black water erupted from the mouth of the hole. It slowed until the top was about three feet off the ground.

"Jesus," Slate said, her eyes wide. The flowing water remained stationary. The rest of the group stared at the water, speechless.

Hudson looked back at them.

"I have an idea," he said.

"You think?" Hudson glared at him, staring him down until Kushia was uncomfortable.

"How about you girls take a look at the right edge," Hudson said, and Ronnie could see it. The water had not risen where the actual path lay. Hudson had found a way for them to be able to cross, but who knew how long the spell would last?

"The pathway," Ronnie said. "We can follow it." She looked at Bennett, Aiko, who was smiling, and David, who was staring at Hudson.

"How are you going to get across?" David asked Hudson, looking at him with genuine concern.

Hudson peered at the waters, and back at David.

"Simple. I'll walk across." He waved his hand with a flourish, and next to him the edge of the column lowered in increments, creating a few steps up to the top of the water.

The modification kept going. It built a bridge over the middle path that continued to the opposing side. It formed a few steps down to the ground.

"I'm sorry," Hayden said. "Did I miss something? Why can't he walk the same path?"

David glanced at Hudson, sending him a "do you want to take this?" look. Hudson OK with David explaining, but before he could open his mouth he noticed Zavannah's was already open.

"The pathway is an enchantment. As is the Acolyte of Water's current spell. A person can't be a part of two enchantments; one dispels at random in the process. If he were to enter the pathway, he might destroy it." The voice finished speaking through Zavannah. She came to, bouncing back faster each time.

"Yes," David said, "what she...he...*it* said."

Jonah gave an exasperated sigh.

"Shouldn't we already be on the pathway?" he said.

"Probably," Hudson's cerulean gaze hollow. He turned and strolled up the steps, walking on water. He headed for the far side.

"C'mon," Bennett said. He reached the left-side hedges, and the rest of the group followed suit.

By the time Hudson reached the other side of the pit, the others were waiting for him. He stepped down from the column of water and onto the ground. Hudson's eyes drained of cerulean, and the water dropped away. An audible splash echoed out of the hole a few seconds later.

"Thanks," Kay said to Hudson. He joined the group standing a few feet away from Ariadne's thread.

It had remained still since they had entered the courtyard, but now the thread lifted itself into the air. Hudson touched down. It was unravelling the main cord and piling it up beneath the shrinking rope ball.

When the ball unravelled, the end of the thread sat suspended in midair. It hung there for a moment before the strands that made up the main thread frayed at the end.

It twisted apart. Sixteen individual threads rolled themselves into balls again. The coil of rope pulled back up, unwrapping along the way.

The sixteen individual balls rolled up in unison until they pulled the thread taut. One of Ariadne's threads headed for each of them and swung around the middle of its acolyte. It met itself again and the ball wrapped around the thread. Tying one acolyte to one thread before all the balls dropped to the ground.

Each ball headed toward a different spot on the back wall of the hedge.

Weaving around one another. They ended up sitting equidistant from one another all along the back hedge. After a few seconds, the hedges parted in sixteen places.

A doorway forming in front of each ball. They rolled forward in unison. They vanished into their respective halls.

"To lead you to your own dark maze," Asher voice a loud whisper.

"What?" David said, not understanding.

"The last line," Asher said, "of the message on the floor." He pointed at the wall of hedge doorways. "To lead you to your own dark maze. That means we follow our threads."

David looked at the cord around his waist and traced it with his eyes. There was no mistaking it.

"We're going to have to split up," he said. His expression belied his distaste for the choice.

"Is that problem for you?" Avery asked.

"It should be a problem for you," David said. "It should be a problem for them." He swiped his hand around the group. "This is the part in the horror film where people start dying, like for real."

Asher gawked at him and laughed. Unable to reconcile the ridiculousness of that statement.

"What does it, matter to you, eh?" He managed to spit out through his laughter, doubling over. He waved one hand while clutching his abdomen with the other. "You have already died, twice." He gasped and stopped laughing. "I'm sorry. It's not funny. I'm punchy."

David arched his eyebrow. He looked at Asher.

"Are you going to be OK?" he said, wondering if Asher would pull it together.

"I'm OK," Asher said, straightening up. He wiped a solitary tear from his eye with a finger. "Though, do we have an alternative?"

Everyone was looking at someone else, trying to find a different choice.

"We have no other choice," Aiko said, and like that, the group knew she was right. There was no alternative and nothing else they could do.

Ronnie was peering behind them with her orange-coloured spectacles when she noticed.

"Umm, girls," Ronnie put her glasses back on, "the bridge is gone." She looked back at the group, no one able to process much at this point. They were losing the ability to focus. "We're coming up on twenty-three hours straight here. I'm wondering how most of us are standing." Ronnie stopped and thought about it for a moment. "How the fuck are we standing?"

"That is your question?" Jonah said, incredulous. "We've battled the Hydra; travelled through space and time, I can assume. David died and came back to life; we fought winged shapeshifters. A little girl got the Minotaur to kneel there and wait while she broke its neck. We are taking direction from a magikal piece of yarn. David combusted in front of our eyes before reassembling by magik. The part that you're having trouble with is that we've been awake for a day straight? A feat that is often accomplished by an ordinary six-year-old girl, on Christmas Eve?"

Everyone stared at him. Until now, none of them had had to look at the situation; they had not had an opportunity. But now they faced it.

By the time they realized Aiko had reached her doorway, it was too late. She wasn't running toward her path, though. She was running away from the others. They watched her entered the opening, and it closed behind her.

"Fuck me," Jonah said. "It was because of the Minotaur comment, wasn't it?" He looked at Bennett.

"It didn't help," Bennett said. "Guess we don't have a choice now, eh?" He looked over at David and gave him a quick salute before he headed toward his path. "See you on the other side," Bennett passed.

David sighed, leaning forward for a moment before straightening up.

"See you on the other side." David walked in the direction of his thread, everyone else followed suit. They entered the hedges, and the doorways disappeared behind them.

Sunday, May 7, 2056
2:56p.m., TST
Entry Halls, Minasyan Labyrinth, Far Reaches
Olindias Territories, Lyra Superior

Pierre entered the doorway and the hedges sealed behind him. It was him, his glowing trident, and endless halls. He kept following the thread. It turned right, left, or continued forward at each of the junctions he met. He was going in circles until he turned and came face to face with his dead wife.

When Hayden looked down and saw her son, she couldn't contain herself. Hayden grabbed him, crying, and held him tight. Keeping her promise that she would never let him go.

"Mommy," Joshua said, and she let go. She looked at him, holding on to him. "Come with me, Mommy. We can be together again." He smiled at her. He held out his arm.

"You don't have to worry," Sam said, holding Kushia's hands in hers and brushing the hair out of his face. "Not anymore."

Kushia stared at her, admiring her beauty again. Seeing the woman he loved but was never able to be with was more than he could bear. He was having trouble thinking.

Twenty-four hours ago, Maya would not have hesitated. She would have taken her mother's hand and followed her to the end of Terra. Twenty-four hours ago, she would not have thought about it. How her mother was talking about going in the opposite direction of the thread.

It was deliberate, she smiled too hard and too eager for Maya to go with her. Maya was talking to a copy of her mother.

Jonah had a pair of truth goggles, staring at his brother. It looked like Seth; it talked like Seth, it walked like Seth, but it wasn't Seth.

Whatever this was, it was doing a fantastic impression. Over the past day, Jonah had learned how to spot the difference.

Kay remained calm and looked into her sister's eyes, smiling,
    She raised her sword to Jess's chest.

"I would love to," Kay said before she drove her sword right through Jess's heart. Jess gargled and looked up, a serene expression on her face. "But you aren't real," Kay said. Jess put her hand on her face.

"Congratulations," Jess said.

Emerson's body disintegrated before Bennett's eyes, and the thread dropped to the floor. The hall the thread was leading him down lit up, becoming a bright tunnel of white. Bennett turned away from his lover's body, a single tear in his eye, and walked into the light.

He stepped out of the hedges onto a ledge, and the hedges sealed again behind him. He was the last one out. Everyone else was standing around the circular room. Well spaced around the ledge that ran its entirety.

"At last," Zavannah said in mock frustration.

"Don't listen to her," Harry said. "She was a moment ahead of you."

Zavannah shot daggers at Harry, who mock winced and laughed.

"You could at least let me try to have some fun," she said.

"Where is the fun in that?" Harry said.

"Anyway," David drew attention to the swirling multicolour vortex that the ledge surrounded. "Anybody think this is not the exit?" he asked. "I mean, it does have a sign. It doesn't say 'exit,' but it's better than nothing."

Bennett looked up. Above the centre of the vortex hung a sign: *Trust Falls*.

What? Bennett thought.

"Does that mean they want us to fall backward off this ledge into that thing?"

"Is there another meaning I'm missing? I would love another choice," David said.

Bennett looked around at the rest of them, realizing that some of them, like him, did not like the idea.

"OK then, I propose that we all go together, on the count of three. If we do this, we do it together; no one left behind, no one goes alone. Agreed?" He looked around.

David waited to respond, wanting to see their actual opinions.

"Agreed," said Hudson. Everyone else exchanged glances, realizing he had said it for everyone, except Pierre.

"OK, I guess everyone turns around and backs up," Bennett said. Pierre protested. Bennett saw Pierre backing up and looked over at Kushia, who caught his gaze. Kushia curled his fingers at Pierre. "Ready?" Bennett asked, and they sounded off one by one around the circle until they reached Pierre.

"OK," Bennett said. "One, two...three!" The other acolytes fell backward off the ledge. Kushia pulled Pierre by his ass forward and down. Pierre screamed in protest. They disappeared into the event horizon before it folded up and dissipated.

Chapter 5
The Gods Must Be Lazy

Friday, August 9, 2058
4:51 p.m., TST
The Clearing, the Gray Thicket
The Whitespace

Rafi and Mica were often the odd Prims out, but if anyone was the black sheep of the family it was Rafi. The average prim had reached an age above five thousand, had survived at least twenty assassination attempts, and had put four or five of their rivals in the ground.

Rafi was still in her early 4000s and kept countenance of who she crossed. She was also a product of the post-Jadiel age, having been fifteen when Jadiel, Gabriel's predecessor and the Empress' brother, was defeated and imprisoned in the Universe.

The Prim of Nature and Order had had to fight for her right to preside over the trials of Gadreel and Ezekiel, despite it being more than two millennia later.

Being the baby of the family was a double-edged—

"Oy," GadZeke said, now reformed into a singularity of half Gadreel and half Ezekiel. He motioned to the centre of the clearing. Black and white mana was swirling forward from the centre of the thicket, folding outward. It weaved into a larger circle.

Zed's mouth was agape. She tried to process the scene unfolding before her. GadZeke held his hand above his head. *Shit*, she thought.

"Excandescunt," GadZeke incanted, and a bright-yellow flare flew from his hand. It reached its apex and floated back to the ground.

The circle filled up. Her brain went a mile a minute.

"They are going to assume it's a prank," GadZeke said. "My signal."

Zed looked at him, still processing. She lifted her hand to the sky.

"Excandescunt," a bright-red flare shot out of her hand. She reached into her cloak and pulled out four injectors. She tossed two across the event horizon at GadZeke.

"Plan Omega," Zed said. "We are going to need time."

GadZeke looked at her. The portal finished forming, and Asher came flying out first. GadZeke vectored for him, being closest.

As Asher landed, managing to keep himself on his feet, GadZeke stuck the injector into the back of his neck. He counted to three under his breath and pulled the injector out. Asher wobbled for a moment and slumped to the ground.

GadZeke didn't have time to catch him or even pay attention to his fall. Hudson and Kay landed on either side of him. He spun right and hit Kay in the arm. GadZeke flipped the injector around in his hand and turned, heading toward Hudson.

Hudson saw him coming and grabbed GadZeke's arm with both hands, not seeing the second injector in the other. GadZeke stabbed the second injector into Hudson's arm, and, after a few seconds, Hudson let go and slid to the ground.

Zed had taken down Maya, Bennett, and Slate. She tried to strike Hayden in the neck, but Hayden blocked. Zed struck down with her other hand, hitting Hayden straight in the thigh. Hayden pulled her arm out, but it was too late.

As Hayden fell, Zed flipped the injector end over end and turned, heading toward Zavannah. Zavannah wasn't expecting anything, and Zed managed to hit her neck.

"What the—"

Zavannah dropped to the floor.

Avery and Ronnie had been easy enough to subdue, but Aiko was proving to be more difficult. She was small and fast and kept dodging GadZeke. He feinted, and she took the bait, allowing him a much-needed window. GadZeke contacted Aiko's neck. Three seconds after he plunged the injector in, it disappeared in a puff of purple smoke.

Out of charges, Samael's Sleeping Serum was gone. The slogan of the injector— "Now in a convenient quadrajector!"— popped up. It remained burned in the air for a second after the injector was gone, and disappeared itself.

GadZeke turned and focused on the last two he could get to, Harry and Pierre. He ran toward them, catching Pierre by surprise. Pierre came out of the portal dead last. He slid forward on the ground, hitting Pierre in the thigh on the way by.

GadZeke pulled the injector back and continued sliding toward Harry. Harry went to block his legs before realizing that GadZeke was going to bowl him over. They both tumbled end over end. GadZeke tried to get the injector into Harry's chest. The war machinist was war itself. They kept rolling until they hit a tree. The injector sandwiched between GadZeke and Harry. They collided, chest to chest. They tumbled down to the ground, Harry unconscious under GadZeke. He struggled up.

Zed was down to her last charge. Having managed to drug Kushia and Jonah, she needed to get David. David was backing up, panic in his eyes. He swung his swords at Zed, who grabbed it with her bare hand and pulled it forward. She was able to reach his forearm and jam the last injection into the fleshy underside.

Tuesday, January 30, 2063
2:04 p.m., TST
Med Bay, Headquarters
The Whitespace

Rafi leaned on her knuckles over the still body of Hudson. Mica checked his pulse and put his arm back on the bed. "How long are we going to keep them under?" Rafi asked Mica, who did not look up from the chart she was writing on.

"Don't know," Mica slipped the chart onto the end of the bed. She moved to the next patient, Slate, in the bed beside Hudson's. Rafi walked around the tables, looking at Mica.

"Are you condoning this?" Rafi asked.

Mica picked up the chart from the end of Slate's bed.

"Of course not. It's ridiculous," Mica said. "The reason they're here is to keep them under. This way Lucy can make a game plan, and Gabriel can make a backup plan." Mica grabbed Slate's wrist and checked her pulse. "I also don't blame them. What if the Empress finds out before the kids are strong enough to resist her? They do fall under her domain now." She put Slate's arm down.

"Right," said Rafi. Mica continued to make notes. "Gabriel and Lucy are scared, afraid that after all these years, after all this time, she will get her revenge."

Mica stopped writing, putting one hand on her hip. She looked at Rafi.

"Would that be bad?" Rafi said. "They deserve it. They killed their mother, used her to do it. In the process, they punished her for eternity by splitting her in two. They trapped the other half of her inside an Amethyst. Karma might bide her time, but she always catches up with you. They are going to take that hit. This is the first group of acolytes that has a real chance to work, to last. We need them if we're going to stop the Strangers, and our best chance of keeping them alive until ascension is to tell them the truth."

Mica stared at Rafi, who stared back. Mica knew she was right but doing this meant defying the family. She took a deep breath and closed her eyes.

"One condition," Mica said.

"Shoot," said Rafi.

"If we do this, we have to make sure they understand that they can never tell anyone, or else it won't work," said Mica.

"You think that if the others know, it will be a problem? Once it's done, it's done," Rafi said.

"Except Gabriel has not met a problem he can't fix by killing someone," Mica glared at Rafi.

"If we have to say that, we will."

"OK," said Mica. "I'll get the antidote. You figure out what we're going to say."

Saturday, May 17, 2064
9:37 p.m., TST
The Imperial Gardens, the Imperial Palace
Atlan, Atlantis Prime

The Empress was strolling with the prime minister of Poseidon, the largest of the Seven Sisters. The second-most-populous planet in the Atlantean System, next to Atlantis Prime itself. Diakitos of Pathos was unbothered by the presence of the Empress. She had known him since he was a boy, having worked with his mother years ago. They were staring up at the mothership, its skeleton completed with finished sections of it added daily

"There's been talk," the Empress said, "that the workers on Poseidon are going on strike on Monday. There would not be any credence to that rumour, would there be?"

"Unfortunately," Diakitos said, "Your Imperial Majesty, I won't indulge pleasantries. The workers are angry. They see these deadlines are arbitrary and hard to keep to. Not everyone can understand the intricacies of what you're trying to do. Your Imperial Majesty."

"One of the things I have always liked about you," the Empress said. "You get straight to the point. Then, I assume you have a plan?"

"As always," Diakitos said. "Your Imperial Majesty, I have set up talks with the union leaders. If they prove intransigent, plan beta is ready for when we are in talks. I'll make sure there is no hint of our signature."

"Excellent," the Empress said.

Friday, January 2, 2065
7:13 a.m., TST
The Gymnasium, Headquarters
The Whitespace

As the acolytes walked into the gymnasium, they saw the space for the first time. Four centre posts, set twenty-five meters apart, marked the central sparring space. Going up a few dozen stories, the posts supported a new platform every fourth story. The back wall housed a staircase that snaked around the wall. It went upward, attaching to the platforms. The stairs continued climbing up the walls.

Mica led them to the sparring space, where Lucy was waiting for them. She smiled at the acolytes. They walked in, still green.

Lucy said "ladies and gentlemen, can we go ahead?"

They around at each other, confused.

"Go ahead with what?" Kay asked, staring straight into Lucy's eyes.

"Your training," Lucy said, and she waited for their reaction. "For your destiny."

"What do you mean?" Harry asked, a small lump in the back of his throat. "Our destiny?"

"You're here because you were the best candidate for the position," Lucy said.

Harry became agitated.

"Are you saying that you picked us?" he asked. "Like I could be happy and dead?"

"Do you want the truth?" Lucy asked, looking at him to show that she was warning him.

"Yes."

"I'm saying," Lucy explained, "that if we had not chosen you—if Zed had not picked you, you would have...how should I put this...lived?"

Harry's eyes filled with rust, and he lost control, charging toward her.

"Arma," he grabbed the handle of his gladius, pulling it from thin air.

"Arma," Lucy said, plucking a Sai dagger from nowhere with each hand.

Harry jumped at the last second, swinging his sword downward. It connected with Lucy's crossed daggers. She was ready and leaned back when Harry hit, rolling them both backward. She kicked up her leg. Harry launched over her and Lucy popped up.

Harry pushed backward even after he managed to right himself. He scrambled forward, making it to his feet. Lucy spun in place to face him. Harry slid to a halt in front of Lucy and swung down on an angle. Lucy leaned back to avoid the blade; her cloak fluttered by. Her expression still had not changed. Harry spun around with the momentum of his swing.

Lucy turned to the other side. Harry's gladius came around, and she caught it in the bottom hooks of her Sai daggers. She flipped the gladius out of Harry's hand. He grabbed her close wrist. He pulled her arm to his left, bringing Lucy closer. He grabbed her other wrist, wound up, and headbutted her. Harry let go before they connected, and they both stumbled back. Lucy clutched her forehead.

She pulled her hand away, ichor running out of her nose. She smiled, turned, and spit the blood of the gods all over the marble. Lucy threw her Sai daggers to the side. Harry charged toward her. He bent down. He reached her, grabbing her by the waist. He dug in. She bent in the middle and slid her legs back to counter his momentum. She put her hands together in a double fist and slammed it into his back, causing him to drop in surprise.

Harry rolled to the side. Lucy's knee cracked the marble where his head had been. He lifted his leg and swung it around, hitting Lucy square in the back and knocking her forward onto the floor. Lucy pushed herself up and turned until she was sitting on the ground. She jumped to her feet. Harry came at her with a roundhouse kick. She grabbed his foot midair and turned it backward. Harry had to roll with her momentum, to avoid Lucy breaking off his foot, and spun in the air. He tumbled to the floor.

He went to get up, but Lucy put her foot on his back and stepped down, slamming him back into the marble. She stepped forward, one foot beside his head, the other under the arm on the opposite side.

Harry was struggling to breathe, the wind knocked out of him. He lifted his head. He panicked at Lucy's hands, one cupping his chin, the other cradling the back of his skull. She twisted his head, breaking his neck.

Lucy stood and stepped to the side, looking over at the acolytes. Their collective shock was palpable.

"What?" Lucy glanced at the group. "He needed to calm down."

"You killed him?" Kay said, incredulous.

Lucy looked at the acolytes with a wry smile.

Gabriel snapped his fingers and leaned back against the boulder he sat upon. After a moment, Harry's neck snapped back. He gasped. The entire sequence of events leading him there replayed in reverse. He picked his gladius back up, swinging it backward and pivoting. He ran back to his origin point, and the sword vanished into thin air.

Lucy looked at him, and for the first time, she saw it. Terror.

"Perfect," she said, "someone gets it." She looked at the other acolytes. "He's terrified, and he should be. You all should be." She surveyed their faces. "You all need to realize that this is the training grounds. A place where we can teach you the skill that you need to know: how not to die. But the moment—I mean the *moment*—you leave the whitespace; all bets are off. There are no more protections for you. If you die, you die. None of you are immortal—not even David."

There goes that theory, David thought, eying Kay. *What the hell?* He couldn't help wondering why they were important. *Could the Prims not handle this themselves?*

"No," GadZeke said. "To answer your question, no, the Prims can't interfere with the species that they protect. We are guardians, not warriors. Think Shaolin monks. That is where you come in." He looked at David. "We can choose two champions to fight for us, a pair of acolytes to act on our behalf. Terrans who can wield the power of the elements and don't have the same restrictions we do. You're our hope to make a large enough impact to change history."

"What do you mean?" Jonah asked.

"Some things happen," said GadZeke. "History wants these events to happen. It won't let you change things without a fight. The Omniverse is a living thing, and it will always try to balance itself by balancing the equation."

"If this is a formula," David asked, "what are we?"

GadZeke looked at him, staring at David's face and seeing that he already knew the answer.

"An attempt at changing the parameters of the formula, and thus its output." He kept looking at David, who held his gaze. He scanned the others, trying to see if they followed.

"You're hoping we change things enough that the previous outcome is no longer possible," Maya said.

"Actually," Gabriel said, "that is what we need you to do. Nothing more, nothing less." He looked at Maya, who sighed.

Aiko, still on the ground, stared at Lucy, "what do we do first?"

Lucy reset. "Who's next?"

Wednesday, September 19, 2068
7:13 a.m., TST
Women's Dormitory, Headquarters
The Whitespace

Ronnie stepped out of the hall and into the dormitory, as Mica called it. Exhausted after spending hours in the gymnasium, Ronnie wanted to go to bed. She saw the dorms. Eight stations, a post, a shelf, and bed. Each shelf was unique, creating a resting place for a specific weapon or set of arms. There was a place for each of them, the beds were on the left side of the room, pure white and leading to a door at the back, the women's baths.

Mica stood in the middle of the room.

She turned to face the acolytes. "Look, I'm sorry. I wish that things were different. Believe me," she said, looking off to the side, remembering something. "No one would like to interfere more." She turned back to them. "But us getting involved makes things worse. You all have the potential to make the Omniverse a better place. You must realize that no one ever affected change without sacrifice."

She walked toward them, heading for the exit. They parted for her, for the first time seeing some terranship by the Prims. Mica was at the door when Aiko spoke.

"Thank you," she said.

Mica turned around. "For what?" She asked.

"For telling us the truth," Aiko said, and Mica smiled.

"No problem, little one," Mica said. "Take care of yourself." She turned and left the room.

Saturday, July 27, 2069
8:14 p.m., TST
Dining Hall, Headquarters
The Whitespace

All sixteen of the acolytes were eating in silence. They had reached a strange place in their relationship. They knew too much about one another to act like strangers, but not enough to be friends. They needed to find a way to work together.

"Two truths and a lie?" Jonah asked the room.

He got a variety of reactions. Aiko's of confusion. David's furrowed brow spoke something akin to "What's wrong with you, eh?"

"The game," Jonah said. "Do you know it?"

David was still drilling into him with his eyes.

"Is that the one where you tell people two truths and a lie?" Avery grinned.

"Thanks for that, Boots," Jonah said.

"Anytime, JoJo," Avery made a pair of clicks like she was spurring on a horse.

Jonah got hot.

"Stop it!" He yelled at Avery, who smiled.

"Whoa, whoa. Calm down. Sorry, buddy. Pullin' your chain, eh?" Avery said, trying to look apologetic.

"What is the purpose of telling people these two truths and a lie?" Hudson interjected.

Jonah took a deep breath to calm down, turning to Hudson to explain.

"You tell people three things abou—"

The double doors bursting open deafened them. For a moment Jonah worried something was wrong. Gabriel, expression indifferent, burst through the doors. He was the loudest corpse Jonah had ever met.

Gabriel walked to the end of the table and stood to face the acolytes seated on either side of him. Holding a clipboard, he put it on his hip and his fist on the other, akimbo.

"OK," Gabriel said, "we've finished your assessments and divided you into four teams for training."

They exchanged confused expressions, and Gabriel raised an eyebrow and sighed.

"Right," he said. "OK, part of training is learning things, but part is practicing things. And while training with us will help you if your opponent is immortal, mortals tend to be wilier than their immortal counterparts. I must have the reflexes of a one-hundred-year-old man."

He took his fist off his hip and pointed around the table at them.

"You," Gabriel said, "ladies and gentlemen, are going to try much harder to win than we would. We divide you into teams and pit you against each other. To help you hone your skills in a semi-controlled environment. Does that make sense?"

"Doez it matter?" Pierre said, looking at Gabriel. Gabriel smiled.

"You either learn to adapt, or you die. There are thirteen days left in the whitespace. Make them count, because the freebies stop when you stop being here."

"Je-oot."

"OK," Gabriel said, looking at the clipboard, "I was saying. We finished your evaluations, and we've divided you into four teams." He reached into his cloak and pulled out four clips of bracelets. "Team Delta," Gabriel said, tossing the set of four white bracelets at Aiko. "Team Captain Aiko," Gabriel stopped. He had realized the dead silence was because fifteen pairs of eyes were staring at a little girl. She held the bracelets in her palms. She was staring at Gabriel, having found her moment of terror.

"Deep breaths, little one," Gabriel said, leaning toward Aiko. "Lucy would not have chosen you to captain her team if she did not believe in you."

Aiko wondered what scared her more: being a team captain or Lucy. She roused.

Maya remained shocked. "She's thirteen."

The look on Gabriel's face told her that a response wasn't necessary. She realized that they had not cared about that when choosing her to be an acolyte. Why would it matter when choosing a leader?

"I was saying," Gabriel continued. "The remaining members of Team Delta are Asher, Pierre, and Zavannah." Gabriel looked at Aiko, waiting for her to pass them bracelets. She eyed Gabriel.

"Yes," Gabriel said, "you should all be wearing the bracelets. Helps with the bonding."

Aiko blinked and unwrapped the bracelets.

"Team Gamma," Gabriel said. "Team Captain Bennett." He tossed the clear bracelets at Bennett, who caught them and untied them. "Other members are Avery, Jonah, and Slate."

"Team Sigma," Gabriel continued, tossing the gray bracelets at Ronnie. "Team Captain Ronnie. Other members are Harry, Kay, and Kushia."

"Team Omega," Gabriel said. "Team Captain David." He tossed the final set of bracelets, black in colour, at David, who caught them and sighed. "Members Hayden, Hudson, and Maya."

Gabriel looked around the table, staring at the ragtag group before him. They couldn't figure out how to put on the bracelets. Except for Aiko, their hands were too big. Gabriel reached toward Jonah's wrist.

"May I?" he asked, holding out his hand for Jonah's bracelet.

Jonah handed it to Gabriel, who put two fingers on each side, inside the circle, and pulled. The ring snapped apart between his fingers. The small trail of black smoke suspended between the two ends of the now-broken ring. Gabriel slipped it over Jonah's wrist and let go, it snapped back together. "Like that," he said.

Jonah stared at his wrist, and the rest of them were splitting their rings open.

"What happens when we want to take them off?" Jonah said. The last of them snapped their bracelets on. He'd discovered he was unable to break the ring.

"We'll worry about that when we get there," Gabriel said. "One last thing, Avery," he glanced at her. She stared back at him, nervous. "Your Pegasus is at the stable."

Avery bolted upright.

"My what?" She didn't trust her ears.

"Your winged horse," Gabriel said. "Called a Pegasus. It's at the stable. Your responsibility is to feed him, clean him, and care for him. I mean, it's your war-steed."

Avery looked like a kid. She got up and turned around to run out the door.

"Avery," Gabriel shouted, and she turned in place. Gabriel pointed in the direction opposite Avery's trajectory. "Through the kitchens and keep to the left until you hit the grounds. Hook it right, and if you hit the edge of the lawn, you've gone too far."

She looked at him for a moment and saw a hint of a smile on his face. Avery ran toward the kitchen, blowing past Gabriel, his cloak flapping in her breeze. She stopped in the doorway of the kitchens and looked back at the group.

"You girls coming?" She turned and disappeared down the hall. After exchanging glances, fourteen other acolytes got up and headed for the kitchens. Jonah looked at his plate.

"About yourself, and we all try to guess which one's a lie," Jonah finished.

Kay, the last one out, stopped and turned. "Are you coming, Jonah?" She asked, and he looked up at her.

"He said," Gabriel answered for him, "he will be there in a minute. He wants to finish eating, eh?" Gabriel was examining at Jonah, waiting for a response.

"Y-yeah," Jonah managed to stammer, before looking at Kay. "I want to finish up. I'll see you out there."

Kay raised an eyebrow, not buying it for a minute, and lowered it and smiled.

"Don't take too long. This is a fun moment, eh?" She turned and disappeared down the hall.

Jonah was staring at Gabriel. He took a seat across the table, collecting his robes up.

Gabriel put his hands together and set them down on the table. "I need to know what Mica and Rafi told you when they woke you up."

Jonah froze, remembering what Rafi had said to them.

"Trust no one, not even us, Lucy or Gabriel," she had warned. "They will do anything to get the outcome they want. Anything."

Gabriel met his gaze.

"Look," Gabriel said, "pretending that it did not happen won't work. I know they warned you about the reality of the situation." He leaned over the table, able to place his face a few inches from Jonah's, fogging up Jonah's glasses. Gabriel reached out his left index finger and wrote in the fog. On one lens he wrote the letters *u* and r, and on the other lens, he wrote: *safe*. After a few seconds, he waved his hand, and the fog cleared.

"But all I'm looking for here is some information—nothing more, nothing less," he said, leaning back in his chair.

"First," Jonah said, "answer a question. You want something; I want something. It's a logical trade." He leaned back in his chair, mimicking Gabriel.

Shrewd, Gabriel considered the proposition.

"All right," he said. "Shoot."

Jonah leaned forward.

"Why would your daughters tell us not to trust you as far as Aiko could throw you?"

Gabriel sighed.

"I guess I had that one coming." He looked at Jonah. "Do I have to tell the whole story?"

Avery was brushing the mane of the Pegasus. She admired the creature's yellow hide and spun-gold hair. It might have been the most magnificent creature she had ever seen. Jonah appeared from a distance in her vision, and she patted the Pegasus on the belly. She turned around.

When Jonah reached spitting distance, he said,

"Jesus. It's majestic."

"She," Avery said. "She's gorgeous."

"Where did everyone go?" Jonah asked, looking for the others.

"There are a bunch more Pegasus's in the stables," Avery said.

"Pegasi," Jonah said. She shot him a dirty look. "Sorry, bad habit."

"Anyways," Avery said, "the rest of them are checking out the Pegasi, though this is the only one whose pen we could get open." She turned back to her Pegasus, put her hand on its forehead, and pet it.

"Have you named her yet?" Jonah asked.

Avery looked at him, surprised.

"Why? Do you have a suggestion?" She asked.

"Actually," Jonah said, "she seems like a Pegi to me."

Avery smiled, patting Pegi on the head.

"How does that sound to you, Pegi?" She asked, and Pegi whinnied her approval.

"So," Jonah said, "Gabriel told me something that might interest you."

"Yeah?" Avery brushed Pegi more. "What is that?" She looked over at him.

"Gabriel says this can do more," Jonah said. "Try snapping your fingers."

She looked at him like he had three heads, then at Pegi.

"What?" Avery asked, patting Pegi on the neck.

"Try it," Jonah said.

Avery shrugged and snapped her fingers. Pegi's wings flapped. They folded up and disappeared into her shoulders.

"Uhh…" Avery was having trouble articulating, not processing.

"Gabriel said that sometimes you need to blend in," Jonah told her. "Try snapping both at once."

"What will that do?" Avery said. "Turn it into a Labrador?"

Jonah cracked a smile.

"Again, you'll never know if you don't try."

Sunday, December 3, 2073
1:12 p.m., TST
The Gauntlet, Oesterle, The Whitespace
The Whitespace

Harry, standing on the platform created by the capstone of a white marble column, looked over at Slate. She stood on an identical column beside him.

"Arma," Slate incanted, the handle of her two-bladed axe appearing before her. She pulled the weapon out of thin air.

"Arma," Harry said. He grabbed the handle of his gladius, pulling it out of the air and swinging it around a few times.

"You ready?" Harry asked Slate, smiling at her.

Her expression did not change. She took a ready stance. They both stood at the top of a giant staircase. Four-by-four-foot pillars descending to a pathway across an open gorge.

The pathway littered with obstacles, half and pony walls, boulders, and tunnels. Choke points for the several challenges they would face on their way to the other side.

"Get on with it," Slate glared at him.

Harry faced forward.

"OK! Three...two...one," he said, and they both jumped down to the first step. Harry edged out Slate at each level. He charged forward at breakneck speed. Slate was pacing herself. Harry reached his ledge and headed across.

"Armis," Harry said, celestial-bronze plates popped up around his body. The plates slid forward, covering his body in glistening bronze armour. Pillars rose on either side of him, offset, flames throwing out of machine parts strapped to the top of each post. They collided with the walls of the bridge.

"Armis," Slate running along her bridge. Void-steel plates covered her in shimmering armour. Fire pillars rose in front of her on either side.

Harry saw two walls of fire in his path. He ran, sliding under the flames, holding his arm up to shield. He rolled when he cleared the fire and kept running. He looked over his shoulder to see Slate charging headlong out of the flames.

Harry ran for the pony wall in front of him to vault over it. He rolled under the half wall and popped up on the other side. Harry grabbed the next wall by his fingers and pulled himself up. He swung his leg over and hauled the rest of his body with him over the other side, landing with a tumble on his ass.

Slate was catching up. He had pushed too hard. Harry picked himself up. Slate jumped off the wall at her side. He bolted forward and took an enormous hammer in mid-stride. Harry latched on, surprised but still able to grab the corner of the mallet and swing around. He launched himself back onto the bridge ahead of where he was. Harry rolled forward again, landing on his feet in stride.

He approached a pony wall, standing alone, and realized he should not try going over. Harry poured on the speed and vectored for the right side of the wall. He went over the right side of the bridge, grabbing the wall with his left hand.

A large saw blade appeared on the end of a pillar, slicing across the top of the wall where he would have been. He pulled with his left hand, swinging his body back onto the bridge and sliding to a stop. Harry looked over to where the blade on Slate's side was finishing its pass. Slate's head popped up from the behind the wall, and Harry turned. He headed for the stairs on the other side of the bridge, leading up to the ridge ahead of them. He vaulted up the first step, covering the three-and-a-half-foot vertical.

Slate was catching up. She pulled herself up the first step and managed to run up the rest. They were a half foot apart apiece.

"Slow and steady," she told herself. She reached the top a second behind Harry. He grabbed the handle of the zip line and jumped. Slate ran after him, grabbing the zip line and pointing her feet in front of her body. Harry was hanging there, and she whooshed past him. She picked up speed. Harry mimicked her, but it was too late; she was too far ahead of him.

Slate let go of the handle, bailing left and tumbling forward to slide onto her front. She got up and ran again, this time through a figurative minefield.

A thunderous crash to Slate's right informed her of a boulder barreling toward her on her right. Slate kept heading straight, the spherical block on a collision course with her. She dropped to the ground. The rock rolled by with a light clink against her armour. Slate stood and kept running, Harry trailing. She heard a whistling sound. An arrow blew through the space between her backplate and helm, brushing her hair.

"Clipeus," Harry said, and a circular bronze shield appeared on his left arm. He tossed the gladius into his right hand.

The arrows were coming from the left. Slate slowed to match his speed. Arrow after arrow bounced off his shield. She got overconfident and forgot to check her three. An arrow went straight through the middle of her right hand.

She cried out, slid to a halt, and dropped to the ground. Harry stopped running, staring at Slate. She broke the end of the arrow. She pulled the rest of it through her wound. She cried out. She was panting. Another arrow flew over from the right. Harry held up his shield, hearing the telltale clink of steel on bronze.

"Clipeus," Slate raised her right arm. A circular shield appeared and strapped itself to her forearm. She got up and held the guard up. She bolted forward.

"Fuck," Harry said, "you didn't wait for me."

"You have your own shield," Slate launched across the open pit and landed on a platform. Harry was behind her, jumping from platform to platform. He caught up over the empty space.

They both jumped from their final platforms and landed at the same time. Slate kept running, but Harry tucked and rolled, popping up ahead of her. He headed for the last obstacle.

The wall ahead of Harry had two sections cut straight out of the façade. He headed for the left space cut into the rock, a vertical ascension shaft with a ladder on one side. Harry grabbed the ladder, and the two side walls moved together. He rushed up the ladder and on top of the section, but the wall in front of him was blank.

He turned around and saw the ladder was on the other side. Harry headed for the other ladder, stepping over the space. The two sections met. The part Harry was in closed. He jumped on the ladder and scrambled up it before turning and vaulting to the other side and the next ladder.

Slate was three sections from the top, and the walls were getting closer each time she got to the top—too close. She stepped onto the third platform and headed for the next ladder. The walls closed again. She jumped to the midpoint of the ladder and scrambled up it, making it to the top in time to jump over the space. Slate gave everything she had to the five-kilometre course.

Harry rolled over the top edge and saw Slate climbing over her side. He scrambled to his feet and ran for the small pillar between them. Atop it sat a little gold bell. Slate reached for the signal, stretching to her limit. Harry edged her out, swiping the bell at the last second. He rang the bell, panting, and put it back on the pillar. Slate slid to the ground.

They heard someone clapping, and they turned to see Lucy walking toward them.

Harry's legs gave out, and he grabbed the pillar, propping himself up.

He shifted, he was holding on to the pillar behind his back. Slate sat up.

"Lucy," Harry said. His left hand gave out, and he dropped to the ground. He put his head in one hand and the other hand on his hip. "To what do we owe the pleasure?" He said it before he could stop himself. *To what do we owe the pleasure?* He thought. *Someone kill me now.*

It was bad enough that he kept thinking about her hands on his head. Every time he got within a few meters of Lucy, he turned goofy.

"I came by to see how things were coming along," Lucy said, without acknowledging Harry's act. "You two gave it everything you had. I don't know if I have ever seen such a matched set at the combat reflex test."

"That's me," Harry screwed up his face in an odd frown and made a finger gun with his hand. He pointed it at her, "A matched set," he cocked and fired the imaginary gun.

Harry thought it would be euthanasia if she snapped his neck again at this point. He stopped, *except that may be what I want.*

Thursday, August 24, 2079
5:33 p.m., TST
The Basement, Headquarters
The Whitespace

Hudson had gone into the basement to find a storage room where Rafi had said he could get some art supplies. Painting always calmed him and helped him find his centre. He had not expected anyone else to be there, though that should not have been a problem. He had stopped when he heard voices down the hall in front of him. His instincts were telling him to find out what they were saying without letting them know he was there. He got close to the corner and peered around it to clock the conspirators. It was GadZeke he was hearing, which wasn't surprising. But who he was talking to was.

Zavannah.

Why would GadZeke need to talk to his acolyte in the basement? Hudson thought.

"You have seen it? He fails?" GadZeke said.

"Yes," Zavannah said in a huff. "How many times do I have to tell you that he does not stop the invasion? I see this future. He will die at my hand. I guarantee it."

Hudson could hear her smiling.

"Perfect," GadZeke said. "That is two problems taken care of."

"What was the other problem?" Zavannah asked.

"Gad," Zeke replied. "He was a liability; plus, I need to be able to move about. I ditched the dead weight."

"Did you kill him?" Zavannah asked.

"Nah," Zeke said, "way too much work. I put him back in his cage—took like ten minutes." He brushed his hands together. "No muss, no fuss."

Hudson heard them moving and grabbed the handle of the door beside him. He slipped into the room without a sound.

Chapter 6

Aquarium for a Dream

Monday, June 10, 2080

11:27 a.m., TST
5, rue des Nations Unies, 92130
Issy-les-Moulineaux, France, Terra

Atelier Beaulieu was preparing to do her chores. She turned on her old OLED display. She connected to the satellite link on her roof. The signal quality was terrible today. The news poured in over the airwaves:

"Welcome back," said the news anchor, looking sombre for the camera, "to France 24 *News at Noon*. I am Collette Gagnon with breaking news out of Canada. A group of Americans entered Parliament on Capitol Hill in Ottawa today, armed. Officials say the men and women shot through security, wearing full body armour. They made their way through the Centre Block of Parliament to the House of Commons Chamber. The entire House was in session.

"The fallout of these events resulted in the closing of the Canadian border crossings, followed by a military barricade of the border itself. The Governor General of Canada made a statement at 10:13 a.m., declaring a national state of emergency. A report from the PM herself declared war against the United States. Canada cited 'an inability to allow acts of terror from any nation, big or small.' Evidence was presented that the automatic weapons matched US Army serial numbers. The US government claims the stock is in the federal armoury, but they have yet been unable to produce it.

"Witnesses say the first intruders shot for the prime minister. Four of them carried a large duffel bag into the room. The Honorable Jacques Gagnon, the leader of the official opposition, crossed the floor. He shielded Prime Minister Mallory Abignail with his body—"

Atelier had collected all the laundry and headed for the basement.

"—an unexpected level of resistance by members of Parliament. This included the Honorable Jessica Lansing of Nunavut. She was able to disarm seven of the assailants. She held her stapler to the back of the neck of an unsuspecting intruder. Reports state that the stapler model was Swingline—"

Atelier couldn't hear the television anymore. She descended the steps into the basement. After sorting her piles, she found that she didn't have enough of anything for a full load; she headed back upstairs. Once there, Atelier cleaned the living room.

"—prevented the blast from destroying the pillars supporting the bridge. Lieutenant Brigand's cruiser did not clear the bridge before it collapsed. Rescue crews were on the scene in minutes and were able to pull out Lieutenant Brigand. He is in critical. They also recovered the body of the unnamed CSIS agent. The man died from injuries sustained while shielding Lieutenant Brigand from the breaking windshield."

The newscaster put her hand to her ear. Someone spoke into her earpiece.

"I apologize. We've now received current information about the so-called unnamed CSIS agent. Canadian officials have confirmed that the man wasn't employed by the CSIS. His credentials were a prop from the television show *CSIS*, purchased at auction."

Atelier stopped working and looked at the television.

"Authorities believe that the man was a citizen visiting Capitol Hill that day." The reporter continued, "and that he impersonated an agent to speed up moving the bomb. They also estimate that he prevented over ten thousand deaths from the explosion. He also saved up to a million more deaths due to radiation and related causes."

Atelier put down her cloth and headed for the television.

"The death toll for the event is one thousand twenty-four."

Atelier switched off the television, walked over to the foyer, and opened the closet.

She reached up onto the high shelf, took out a large hat box, and walked it to the sideboard. She opened it up and removed a purse, a set of passports from various countries. She produced cash in seven different currencies, and a pair of Talaria, or winged shoes. She filled the bag and closed the hat box up.

Atelier slipped on the Talaria and returned the hatbox to its rightful place. She closed the closet doors behind her. She turned and opened the front door. She checked out the perimeter.

Atelier pulled a strap from her purse and looped it around her shoulder. She clasped it to the other side. She took a breath and ran towards the road; she needed thirty-three steps to get the Talaria charged.

Atelier bolted out the door before running into the invisible arm of Samael. Samael materialized and bent over the coughing sputtering body of Atelier.

"Hello, Merc," Samael said, using Atelier's real name, Merc, short for Mercury.

"Jesus Christ Sam," Merc managed to roll over and bolted for freedom. Samael's eyes spectred. He pulled out his wand.

A spark from the tip of his wand shot out and passed by Merc's head. It exploded a few feet ahead of her, knocking her back to the feet of Samael. He looked down at Merc, writhing in pain on the ground.

"Look, Merc," Samael said, "we both know you owe me some favours." Sam adjusted akimbo. He looked down, "we can do this the straightforward way."

Merc spat in his face.

Friday, March 3, 2084
4:27 p.m., TST
East Stairwell, Headquarters
The Whitespace

Hudson walked up the white marble of the east stairwell in measured steps. He talked to himself under his breath. He walked.

"David," he was saying, "I saw something in the basement, and I came to you first." Hudson figured the best way to handle this situation was by going to his team captain. David's job was to be on his side, right?

After four days sitting on this information, he needed to do something with it. David was smart, impartial, and invulnerable. None of the rest of them had transcended, as Gabriel called it.

Hudson walked down the halls of the administrative wing. He thought about how this was a place where they could learn how to survive. The gods they said they were—Hades, Zeus, Aphrodite, Athena, and the list goes on. The fact that they insisted on names like Rafi and Ezekiel worried him more. Were they the archangels or the gods, and if they were both, why not say so?

He remembered what Gabriel had said in class.

"Transcendence is the act of becoming a god. You become one with the spirit-god inside you. When you reach a state where you're strong enough to control your powers and let them control you."

Confused, Hudson had asked what happens, for example, to Aphrodite should Aiko transcend. She becomes the Acolyte of Love? Gabriel glanced at him, saying;

"Who said you were Greek?"

Hudson turned the handle on David's door—habit by now due to his open-door policy—and walked into the room. The sounds of David and the woman he was with hit Hudson, along with the scene. David, nude, leaning over the woman on his desk. They were in the middle of the act.

"What the fuck?" David said.

"Sorry, sorry, sorry." Hudson backed out the door. He closed the door. He realized who the woman on the desk was. Zavannah. Hudson ran down the hall and stairs and headed to the dorms.

Sunday, April 1, 2085
7:47 a.m., TST
The Capital Isles
Thoth, Atlantis Prime

The Empress wasn't impressed. She walked down the hallway to the Senate Chamber. Compared to the cost of building their fleet, the Atlan Shield Project was a drop in the bucket. The president of the Senate calling it a boondoggle was a step too far. She might not tell them why things were a certain way, but the Empress did not entertain boondoggling.

The royal guard opened the doors to the chamber, and the entire room stood for her entry. The president introduced her. The Empress's eyes filled with pure blue mana. She held her hand up toward him. The air around the president disappeared, sucking the wind out of his lungs with a gurgle.

She walked to her throne and sat. The president, his face turning purple, slid down the side of the podium. Everyone else in the room stayed quiet. The Empress leaned forward and put her hands together, eyes filled with blue.

The President, near unconsciousness, reached out for invisible help. "Are you ready to play, Mr. President?"

He nodded his head, and she leaned back in her chair.

"Wonderful," the Empress snapped her fingers. The air rushed back into both the space around him and his lungs. He took a deep breath, relieved for a moment until he tried to breathe out. His lungs filled, unable to do anything but suck air in. His eyes widened. The Empress pulled out a cigarette and lit it, sucking in hard. The ember burned red hot, before removing it from her lips and flicking it at the president. The other people in the room ducked and shielded themselves. The president was frozen in place.

The cigarette flew, getting to within a foot of the president's mouth. The air flowing into him burst into flames, engulfing his throat. He exploded in a fireball of limbs, tendrils, and blue blood. The walls spattered with blood, save the few inches that surrounded the throne.

"Unfortunate," the Empress said, "that I am not."

Tuesday, April 23, 2086
9:05 p.m., TST
Men's Bath, the Dormitory, Headquarters
The Whitespace

David found Hudson relaxing in hot tub, a favourite nighttime pastime of his. He took off his clothes and stepped into the container. Hudson came out of deep thought.

"Hey, Hudson," David said, "I'm sorry about that. That was inappropriate. I'm sorry you had to walk in on that." Hudson was relieved. "I forgot about my open-door policy, about everything, and it happened."

David smiled and put his hand on the back of his neck, rubbing it. He liked her. That was when Hudson realized that David was the target.

Hudson knew he needed to keep David in the dark. He could find a little help from someone he knew would always be on David's side. He might even be able to keep David in the dark until after he had fixed this. Hudson had a profound and sudden urge to kill Zavannah.

"Did you come to my office to talk?" David remained ignorant.

Hudson examined him and thought about how there was no right way to talk to David about this. He managed a smile.

"No. I was, ahh..." He also wasn't fast on his feet, but he powered through. "I was there on behalf of Gabriel," he said.

"Gabriel?" David asked. "What does he want?"

"You." Hudson kept going. "Yep, he wanted to talk to you, and I told him I would get you."

"Oh," David said, lifting his body out of the hot tub. "Did he say where he would be?" He went to the wall, grabbed a towel, and wrapped it around his waist.

"Yeah," Hudson said, lying again, racking his brain for somewhere to send David. "He said he would be at the Pantheon of Ruins, in the Celtic section." Hudson couldn't even imagine a reason why anyone, let alone Gabriel, would be there.

"The Celtic section?" David stopped and raised an eyebrow. "Are you sure that's where he wants to meet me?"

"I'm sure that that is what he said," Hudson forced a smile. His stomach churned. He hated lying. It was often hard for him to lie for a greater good or to spare someone.

David sighed and walked toward the exit. "What does he want now," he said.

Hudson was thinking, *who do I turn to now*, but found he had gained an instant ally.

"Hey," he called out to David, who stopped and turned. "Have you told Kay about this?"

"Why would I tell her?" David said, perplexed.

"No reason," Hudson said, realizing David was oblivious. "Wondering."

Saturday, July 26, 2087
3:57 a.m., TST
The Pantheon of Ruins, Oesterle
The Whitespace

David was walking through the pantheon, taking in the sights of the ruins. The Abyssinian ruins sprawled out the left of the entrance like a large terra-cotta hill. To his right was the Etruscan ruins, the gray stone ruins sprawling out to the side.

David kept on through the pre-classical section, headed toward the Asian civilizations. He turned toward the postclassical shortcut. He sauntered down the middle of the pre-classical and classical parts. He straddled their border. He reached the post-classical section, near barren compared to the other articles.

He found the Celtic section, a single stone henge inside of which were a half dozen relics. There wasn't anything else around for a hundred feet and no sign of Gabriel.

David heard the click of stilettos. He turned and saw Lucy approaching from the distance, head down. *Shit*, he thought. *The last person I want to see. What will she do if she finds me?* He didn't intend to find out, but because of the open space, he couldn't flee. He had to find someplace to hide, and he set out for the henge. David put his hand on what he thought was the wall of stone in front of him and realized it was cloth; it was a curtain. He pushed it aside and disappeared.

From inside the stone, he could see everything like some magikal form of two-way mirror. David watched Lucy walked up to the ruins and over to one on the far side. She sat on the edge, waiting. David heard footsteps again, this time offbeat. He glanced over to see Gabriel stumbling toward the henge. Lucy glanced up and stood, putting one hand on her hip.

"You're drunk," she said to Gabriel. He stumbled up the steps into the henge. An empty sixty-pounder of Crown Royal in his hand.

"And you're a bitch," Gabriel spat back at her. At least David assumed that was what he meant through the slurs and hiccups. Gabriel spread his arms. "But, we all have our vices." He took another swig from the bottle.

"No wonder you can't keep the acolytes in line. I'm assuming you did not know that someone sent a message to Poseidon."

Poseidon. David thought. The largest of the Seven Sisters and part of the Atlantean Systems. One of the first things they had learned was that they were hoping to stop the Atlantean invasion.

"That's obvious," Gabriel straightened up. "What is your point?"

"You aren't that stupid," Lucy said.

"High praise," Gabriel said. "What do you want me to do about it?"

"I don't know," Lucy said. "That is not my department. Fix it."

Gabriel put his fingers on his forehead and to be concentrating. He held that pose for a while and let go and glanced around.

"Hmm...that did not work."

"This is not a fucking joke, you simpleminded, Cro Magnon–looking motherfucker!" Lucy said, grabbing Gabriel by the collar, and pulled him down to her level. they were face to face.

He kept staring at her. He downed the rest of the bottle and threw it against a stone pillar. The bottle smashed into thousands of tiny pieces. The pieces flew back together, reforming into the container. It settled on the ground below.

"Listen here," Lucy said. "I need to be able to play my end game, not hers. Get your pieces in line, or I'll clear the board. Understand?"

"I never wanted this," Gabriel eyes sad. He stared at Lucy. "What choice did I have? You're the one who wanted to descend. I knew I couldn't live without you. Now I wish I could die, and I'm the person who can't. I am the definition of irony," he continued, "because I would do anything for you, and you know it. That is the sick part—that I know you use me for my loyalty to you, and I still let you do it. Yes, baby sister, I'll do what you ask."

Lucy let go of Gabriel cloak.

"Always the martyr," she said. "No one forced you to take that knife. No one made you kill Jehovah. You have made enough of your own messes that you don't need to blame me for your circumstances."

"You act like they are the same thing, but what I did, I did for the greater good. That is a price I'll pay one day, and not soon enough. Choosing you came at a price I never knew a person could pay, and I keep paying it every day of my so-called life."

"Make sure that no one else gets through," Lucy walked away from the henge. Her heels clicked in the distance long after she had disappeared.

"You can come out now," Gabriel hiccupped to the empty room. From behind a pillar appeared a hand. It moved back a curtain, invisible from this angle, and David stepped out. His head was swimming from the conversation he had heard.

Enthralled, he missed a boulder but moved at the last second. Gabriel stepped forward, caught David's outside arm, dropping onto a marble bench he made appear. Gabriel fell with the momentum of his whole body letting go at once. He slammed into the marble and shook it off.

Gabriel patted the bench beside him.

David slid over with a huff.

"What the fuck do you want?" he said.

"Whoa, whoa, whoa," Gabriel grabbed his robes and got close to David. "Hey, are you going to be OK?" he asked David, who was shell-shocked.

"Pawns," David stared up at him. His sunken eyes sharp enough to cut glass.

Shitfuck, Gabriel thought. *Why does he have to be so goddamn smart?* Gabriel sighed, choosing his next words. He realized honesty might save this.

"Pawns," he gave David the most empathetic look he could muster. "The pawns in the Omniverse that matter." He pointed up like they were gazing at a night sky. "It's the biggest game ever played," he continued, "though the chess analogy is not correct."

David stalled out. The raw truth was worse than he imagined. He wanted to scream, wanted to yell, "A game? Are you fucking kidding me?" He couldn't think straight and managed to say, "What game *are* we playing?"

Gabriel tried but was unable to prevent himself from guffawing. He suppressed much of his laughter.

"Uh, hmm...never thought about it," he stared off into the distance and cogitated on it for a minute. David was processing. "Battleship," Gabriel said, with an air of realization.

"Perfect. Intergalactic Civil War brought to you by Hasbro." David's tone was sardonic and ineffable.

Gabriel was already suppressing laughter when he continued.

"Don't tell me. Uniforms and furnishings by Mattel?" Gabriel lost it, laughing because he was too drunk to do anything else. He tried to stop but couldn't, and he went forward off the edge of the bench and landed on the ground.

"You're an asshole; you know that?" David eyed Gabriel, who kept laughing, unable to disagree. David got up in a huff, moving to walk away.

Gabriel stood and held up his arm, pointing at David with one eye closed. He swayed in a circle.

"Wait," he said, and David stopped and turned around. Gabriel hiccupped again. "There is something you should know."

Thursday, May 31, 2091
5:37 p.m., TST
Egypt House, the Estates, Northern Boundary
The Whitespace

When Gabriel said he had something to show him, Harry couldn't have imagined it was this. They were in the middle of the Estates, the retirement village for forgotten gods. Gabriel had said they were going to see how far gods can fall and how bad the fallout can get. They arrived at Egypt House, and Harry got sick to his stomach.

The Egyptians? He had thought they had a vast and successful empire for hundreds of years. He did not know what to expect when they entered the Egyptian mansion.

They descended a staircase for a half an hour. They turned every time they hit a corner platform. They continued down into the darkness. Gabriel and Harry reached a light and the basement, and Gabriel knocked on the door. Twice, a break; three times, a pause; once, and a final break before he finished with four raps on the door.

A panel slid open, the eyes behind it surprised.

They peered back at Harry for a moment. The woman behind the door raised an eyebrow, slid the panel shut, and opened the door.

Her dark skin and sharp features were set off by her gold-and-black dress. She had a shaved head adorned with a miniature gold throne sitting on top of her black headscarf.

She walked forward, her heels clicking and echoing in the large chamber. She spread her arms, and the two exchanged a hug. She stepped back, resting a hand on his chest.

"Hades," the woman said, "to what do I owe the pleasure?"

"Business," Gabriel said, "I am afraid."

The woman struck an eyebrow, again intrigued.

"What possible business can you have involving us?" She said. "Or are you trying to get this one hooked?" She motioned to Harry. Gabriel smiled.

"The opposite," he said and looked at Harry. "How rude of us. My sincerest of apologies, Harry. May I introduce Queen Isis of Egypt."

Harry's mouth fell open for a moment, shocked at the casual appearance of the Egyptian mother goddess.

Harry had always hoped Isis was real. She was sassy, and he liked them bossy and able to kill him, for some reason. He bowed.

"Your Majesty," was less awkward than letting the bow lie.

Isis burst into laughter, a dry, maniacal tone to her laugh. She smiled at Gabriel.

"Where did you find this one?" She asked him.

"He's smarter than he looks," Gabriel said. "He's shy. We came for the nickel tour. Do you have change for a dime?"

Isis smiled again.

"You forget it's per person," The two of them laughed.

Harry realized that at some point the two of them had fucked. On and off for years, based on the way they touched each other. *Great*, he thought. *I'm an excuse to see his side piece.*

"I am no man's 'side piece,'" the voice of Isis boomed in his head, and he almost shit his pants.

"If you want him to see us in all our glory, get on with it. None of us is getting any younger."

She led them down a short hallway and pulled back a curtain to reveal an enormous, lit chamber, surrounded with second- and third-floor mezzanines. Harry examined the gods and goddesses of ancient Egypt. They were either lying on lounges and couches or serving those who did lie around. They were all smoking from pipes and hookahs, or else straight up snorting and freebasing. Gabriel had taken them to some drug den for washed-up gods and goddesses, and this was the Egyptians.

"Are they all like this?" Harry asked.

Isis looked at him and at Gabriel.

"He's smarter than he looks," she said, and Harry wasn't sure if that was an insult. "This is somewhere in the middle."

"This brings you to the edge?" Harry at Gabriel. "Breaking you in the process?"

"This," Gabriel rested his fingers on Harry's chest, staring into his eyes. "It can destroy you faster than it can help you." He tapped his fingers on Harry's chest. Gabriel looked concerned to Harry. He said, "The best way to fight the demons inside of you, Harry, my son, is to realize that you aren't a group of strangers. You're now your own family. Like a house of cards, make one wrong move, and the entire house falls. This was a chain reaction that consumed all but a few of them."

"This was the result of hubris," Isis said, "and it has consumed even the those who don't waste away."

Harry realized she was talking about herself.

"I get it," he said, sick to his stomach. "Anything else I need to know? Or is this a lesson in being a happy sunshine family?"

Gabriel stared at him for a moment.

"if you get the gist, there is no reason for you to stay." Harry was relieved. "You can go on ahead. I want to catch Isis up on a few things."

Harry thought. *Need a quickie, eh?*

"Yeah," he said, "I know my way back to HQ."

As he turned to leave, Gabriel stopped him with a hand on his shoulder.

"One last thing," he said, and Harry turned around. In an ominous tone, Gabriel said, "There will be a moment when you can stop Aiko from going down this road." He investigated the room and off into the distance at the same time. "You, the others," Gabriel continued, "you can come back from this. You have a chance of beating this curse, but Aiko...for her, this is in her blood. Once she goes to this place, she won't ever come back."

Harry stared at him. Had this all been to warn him about Aiko?

Gabriel let go, and Harry kept going, heading up the unending staircase. He walked and walked until he reached the top floor and stepped off the stairs, headed back toward the dorms.

In the basement, Isis and Gabriel deliberated while they strolled to the back, to Gabriel's private room. Isis kept one place in the back empty and ready. She recognized he would be back; he always was. He entered the room and looked at the table.

All the usual suspects were waiting for him, along with a clean needle.

"This is where I leave you," Isis said, heading for the door.

Gabriel sat and examined the inside of his right elbow. He tied off the tourniquet around his upper arm.

Thursday, December 9, 2094
10:41 a.m., TST
Sparring Grounds, Vaestport
The Whitespace

Harry walked down the stairs toward the sparring area below. He watched Aiko and David battling each other in the sand. David was advancing on Aiko. She pulled arrow after crimson arrow from her quiver. David deflected them with his swords. David spun, hooking Aiko's bow out of her hand. He planted and swung forward. Aiko rolled sideways. David turned and kept swinging.

Aiko evaded his attack. She went back toward her bow. She reached her bow, putting it in front of her body to deflect a double downswing by David.

Aiko managed to hook both of David's swords on her bow and pulled, lifting her leg. They collided. Aiko's foot slammed into David's crotch, and he and the other men winced. David dropped to his knees.

"No fair," he managed to sputter. Aiko pulled out an arrow and cocked her bow.

"All is fair in love," she let the arrow fly, sending it straight through David's left pupil. His head flew back from the force, taking the rest of David with it, "and war."

As he watched the arrow disappear and the white mana stitching David up. Harry went to sit down next to Kay and Hudson, sequestered on the side.

"Harry," Lucy said from her observation post at the head of the sparring area, "good of you to join us." Harry could tell that she was wondering what he thought was more important than his training. *Did they ever talk to each other?* Harry thought.

"I would have thought Gabriel would have told you," he said, keeping a serious tone. "We took a tour of Egypt House."

The moment he said 'Egypt House,' Lucy stood; Ariel headed for the nearest exit.

"Gabriel gave you a tour of Egypt House?" Lucy was calm. "You and him?"

"The queen and I," Harry said.

Ariel looked back at Lucy. He paced up the steps. She returned his gaze. Lucy nodded, and Ariel turned his head and kept walking.

"Unfortunate," Lucy said. "I had hoped to send Ariel with you two." Lucy sat back down and changed the subject. "He has such a unique perspective on the issue, plus, you should be giving the others a challenge. Will you step into the ring?"

Harry walked to the edge where David was standing, hand out to help him down.

"Which of you am I up against?"

"Both of us," David said, looking at Aiko, who smiled. "To make it fair."

Harry sighed.

"Arma," he incanted. He spun to deflect an arrow with his new conjured gladius before parrying David's sword.

Thursday, April 19, 2096
2:22 a.m., TST
The Estates, Northern Boundary
The Whitespace

Ariel ran the moment he was out of sight of the acolytes, and he cursed his father. *Son of a bitch*, he thought. *Had to see her again.* Isis was like a bad penny: no matter how hard you tried to get rid of her, she kept coming back.

Ariel vaulted off Assyria House. He launched straight into Egypt House and slid on his side along the floor. He dropped off the edge of the staircase. He hit the wall of the stairs running and bounded off the walls all the way to the basement. He launched off the last wall and hit the basement door with both feet. The door splintered into hundreds of thousands of pieces, shattering all over. Ariel landed on his feet. Isis stood four feet to his left, and he reached her before she had time to process the bursting door. Ariel grabbed her by the throat and lifted her into the air, crushing her windpipe. He spectered, his orange eyes piercing through her.

"Where is he?" he demanded. Isis struggled against his hand, grabbing his arm. He let go enough for her to talk.

"Room six," Isis squeaked out. "In the back."

Ariel dropped her with a thud; he went to the back rooms.

"I told you," Isis managed to say, nursing her throat, "he always comes back."

"And I told you," Ariel said, his eyes still orange, "what would happen if you served him again. Ignis," he incanted.

As he walked away, Queen Isis screamed in pain. The flames sparked and engulfed her in less than three seconds. She collapsed to the ground, a Terran fireball.

Ariel opened door after door until he found Gabriel, eyes glassy. They moved unnaturally. It was like watching REM sleep. Ariel picked his father up, holding him in front of his body. Gabriel draped like a corpse in his arms.

"Regressus," he incanted. The two of them became engulfed in a tornado of orange smoke, disappearing when it dissipated.

Thursday, April 19, 2096

2:22 a.m., TST
Subbasement Iota, Headquarters
The Whitespace

Ariel appeared in the emptiness of the basement with a swirl of orange smoke. There was a trough of water on the other side of the room, against the wall. Ariel walked toward it with Gabriel still in his arms.

Gabriel was in a high dimension, a result of the combination of psychotropics flowing through his veins. When he opened his eyes, he found himself in the middle of his old stomping grounds, the Clearspace. It was like walking on a glass surface while suspended amid empty space, a star-studded void.

Lilith was waiting for him, her red hair growing through the bonsai tree atop her head. Her extended, elegant features hidden by her light-bending dress. It was clear but projected the image of what was behind it in place of a solid colour. She looked like a head and two arms suspended in midair.

"Gabriel," Lilith saw him, "it has been too long."

"Lilith," Gabriel walked toward her, "you don't know how I need you."

"I know," Lilith said. "I wish I could be there."

"No," Gabriel said, "it's my fault. I trapped you here."

"The alternative was to kill me. This was a better choice." She smiled at him. He got close to her. "Besides, you couldn't let Lucy become Lord."

"When can I bring you back?" Gabriel pleaded, his fingers brushing her cheek. Her smile faded.

"Time to go." Tendrils of water wrapped themselves around his body and pulled him back into a wall of water.

Ariel was pulling his head out of the trough by his hair.

Gabriel gasped, coughed, and sputtered. He fought against Ariel's grip. "Let go of me." Ariel let go and stood.

"Nothing will wash the blood off your hands," he screamed at his father. "Mother is gone, and your guilt will do nothing to bring her back." He headed for the door.

"My son," Gabriel said, but Ariel was already out the door, and it slammed shut behind him.

Friday, April 5, 2097
7:41 p.m., TST
Branching Diversions, Vaestport
The Whitespace

Kay and Hudson walked in a line down the bright-blue cobblestones set into the marble. They marked the path to the sparring area. Harry noticed how twitchy they were. They had not intended for him to hear their conversation when he got to the makeshift arena. They had stopped talking the moment they noticed he was sitting down, but not before he heard them. In fact, Harry had heard enough of their conversation to be able to fill in the blanks and figure out what was going on. He went to pass the two of them, commenting on the way by.

"You're worrying about your chickens before they hatch, but that is my opinion."

"I am sorry?" Kay asked, confused.

"Zavannah," Harry said, "and the fact that she's running a Russian honeypot on David. It will be much easier to figure out what her plan is after arrival." He looked at the two of them.

"If she plans to kill him," he continued, "she can't do it here, she must wait until after arrival, right?" He waited for a response, but they were both staring at him. "Plus, she's getting close to him with this weird relationship. It's possible she's looking to convince David that he should take a certain role. Or, more likely," Harry went on, "she saw that he would be the linchpin in the battle. Either way, she would be looking to take him out closer to the invasion. That way we have the least time to react. And we are already dependent upon the role David plays if she and Zeke are working with the Atlanteans."

Hudson couldn't believe it.

"How did you—"

"You girls gave me more than enough info," Harry said.

Kay examined at Harry.

"We will need him to infiltrate their ships," she said.

Harry's eyes went wide. *Of course*, he thought.

"Because," Harry said, "we can send him into anywhere, and they can't stop him; he'll keep coming back. I've got to hand it to her; she's five steps ahead."

"How do we beat her?" Hudson asked. "Because it will suck if she kills David."

Harry laughed.

"Hudson, my friend," Harry said, "promise me you'll never change." Hudson blushed and put his hand on the back of his neck. "For your question, we have to be ten steps ahead."

Monday, June 23, 2098
4:21 a.m., TST
Samael Laboratories, Headquarters
The Whitespace

Gabriel was unable to stand. He crashed into the stainless-steel worktables after he made it down the steps. He righted himself and stumbled toward the drawers.

Asher walked into the lab, attracted by the noise, and rushed down the steps toward him. Gabriel was digging through drawers. He opened them with fervour but was less diligent at closing them. Asher grabbed his arm, but Gabriel ripped it away.

"What," Asher asked Gabriel, "are you looking for? I can get you anything you need." He slammed the drawer Gabriel was opening. "I know where everything is."

Gabriel raised an eyebrow, staring him down, but Asher held his gaze.

"Nolambraxone," Gabriel said. "Two phials." Asher examined him and realized he was high as a kite, eyes glassy. He was having trouble functioning. Talking was a tremendous effort. This wasn't his first stampede.

"Here," Asher said. He grabbed an office chair and slid it under Gabriel, "you sit. I'll grab you some Ambrax."

Gabriel sat, and Asher went to the glass cabinet at the end of the row.

"Thank you," he said. Asher pulled out a set of keys and unlocked the door.

"You would have needed help anyway." Asher brandished two unblemished glass phials with purple writing. "Ambrax," the labels said. "Say no to drugs!"

"Samael gave you a set of keys?" Gabriel asked. "You're ahead of the curve."

Asher walked over to the drawers beside the cabinet and grabbed an injector gun. He leaned on the counter, phials in one hand, gun in the other, and stared at Gabriel.

"Further ahead of the curve than I thought," Gabriel said, surprised by the power move by Asher. "It's going to be like this?"

"I'm trying to figure this out," Asher said. "You don't have any reason to be an addict, let alone one that takes"—Asher tilted his head, sizing up Gabriel's condition. "Seven grams of black amber and three and quarter ounces of chrissy."

There was no way that Asher could know his recipe, which meant he was good at his job. *They'll need a good doctor,* Gabriel thought.

"Had experience with BA and C?" Gabriel raised an eyebrow, always the left.

"Lucy and I went to Valhalla," Asher said, his eyes becoming sullen, "out in the Northern Boundary. A couple of days back we responded to a call about Idunn overdosing. By the time we got there, they were all overdosing—some reaction to the possible loss of Idunn. The worst part was that we managed to save Idunn but were unable to get to everyone there in time."

"Loki didn't make it," he continued, choking on the words. "Why the hell should I waste this on you? You're not on an expedition here. What's going to stop you from doing it again?"

Gabriel thought about his response.

"Nothing," he said. "Nothing is stopping me from doing it again."

"At least," he stood, "tell me why you do it, so I can understand. You're supposed to be our mentors. Help me understand you."

Gabriel sighed.

"114,753,262,800 and change."

Asher furrowed his brow.

"I'm sorry?" he wondered what that meant.

"The cumulative total number of deceased Terrans," Gabriel said. "The number of individual souls"—he used a pair of air quotes when he said *souls*— "you call them, that I have reaped thus far."

"What do you mean," Asher asked, "we call them?"

Gabriel was struggling to stay focused.

"It's more like an imprint," he said. "A record of your life. One hundred and fourteen billion data files in my bank. Every happy moment, every sad one, I see everything from the origin. Would you not want a break at least?"

Asher now felt sorry for Gabriel and went to load the phials into the injector.

"Except," the two of them turned to see Ronnie standing at the top of the steps, arms crossed, "that is not the reason you use." She continued down the steps. "Hey, Asher, sorry to interrupt. I came to get you for hand-to-hand training with Zed, but that was what you wanted to know, right? Why he does it."

Fuck, Gabriel thought. *The fucking lie detector.* Asher glanced at him and at Ronnie.

"She's right," Asher said, "is she not?"

"OK," Gabriel said. "First, yes, she's right. Second..." The last of the chrissy left his system. It was him and black amber now. Unsure how long he could hold out, he grabbed the table beside him for support. "I give you my word that if you give me the Ambrax, I'll tell you the whole story of why I do this."

"Now that," Ronnie said, "is true."

Asher clicked the magazine into place and sauntered over to Gabriel. He stuck the nose of the injector against Gabriel's neck. He pulled the trigger. The first phial shoved down into the gun, and the clear liquid drained out of it.

Gabriel was relieved. The first phial popped back and ejected sideways. The second phial loaded into the chamber. The glass of the first phial dissipated into purple smoke after leaving the injector. The lettering left behind for a second. Asher pulled the trigger again, and the second phial drained into Gabriel's neck. It ejected and dissipated like the first. Asher put the gun down. Gabriel massaged his neck.

"You want the abridged version or the whole thing?"

Asher glanced at Ronnie.

"We don't have time, eh?" He thought about class.

Ronnie examined the room, "I'm supposed to come find you, and since I don't see you anywhere, I guess I'm still looking."

Asher smiled.

3

The Worst Day of the Rest of Your Life

Chapter 7

Reigning Day

Thursday, July 14, 2101
11:03 p.m., TST
Point Eastern, South Sea Shores
The Whitespace

Aiko was the last to arrive, along with Lucy. They were late because of Aiko's dress and hair. When the Prims had told them that they were going to have a party before their last day of training, Aiko had examined her blackened shirt and pants. She realized that she had been hiding behind her tomboy outfit. Mica had once told her that she would have to believe in her abilities to be able to use them. She would have to believe in herself. If she was going to be the Acolyte of Love, she should look like it. Mica told her that Lucy was who she wanted to see, and she had been right.

The crimson dress's sweetheart neckline and princess sleeves framed her face. The form-fitting top flowed into a breezy skirt that stopped after her knees. Lucy had finished it off with candy-red lipstick and put up Aiko's hair.

Aiko had never seen anything like it. Lucy had twisted and pinned up her hair into a huge bouquet of roses, by hand. Lucy had even put napoleon rose petals in each of the roses she made from Aiko's black hair. She placed a full napoleon in at specific intervals.

The outfit finished off with a pair of sparkling ruby pumps given to her by Samael. She had told him that the best book she had ever had read to her was *The Wonderful Wizard of Oz*. She'd talked about how she wished she had a pair of slippers like Dorothy's. Samael asked if she wanted the ones from the book or the ones from the movie. Her blank stare gave him the answer.

Aiko had never been pretty. She was uncomfortable. The other acolytes and the remaining Prims froze like a tableau, everyone staring at her. Pierre's mouth was hanging open, and Bennett elbowed him in the solar plexus without turning away. Pierre groaned, snapping the group out of their collective pause.

Maya stepped over to her, holding out her hand.

"If you aren't the prettiest girl at the ball, I don't know who is." She led Aiko back toward her seat. "Come, sit by me."

Aiko sat next to Maya and surveyed the group. They had all gotten new outfits for the bonfire. Hudson had a cerulean-blue three-piece suit. Maya sported an off-the-shoulder, sleeveless, floor-length tyrian number.

Each of them wore his or her own unique style, all decked out in their primal colours. They sat in a large circle on the pure-white sand of the beach. Their seats were large pieces of white driftwood and a few white rocks. In the centre of the ring was a large pile of wood set up like a bonfire.

"Hayden," Gabriel asked, "would you like to have the honour?"

Hayden smiled, her eyes filling with persimmon mana.

"Ignis," she incanted; the wood inside the circle of small white rocks burst into flames.

"Now," Gabriel continued, "the reason we've brought you all together is twofold." He glanced over at Lucy.

"First," Lucy addressed them, "tonight is to get ready for tomorrow when you will complete your final. Getting here is an accomplishment, but you shouldn't underestimate tomorrow. The reason we have a bonfire is to give you a sense of camaraderie, help you work together. To give you a chance to bond before you face this final challenge."

"Second," Gabriel said, "we like to celebrate your making it to this point with a bit of a party. Little feast, some nectar and ambrosia, and a chance to learn a bit more about your peers." He snapped his fingers. "Let them eat."

Aiko saw the sub-Prim gods strolling toward the group. All their councillors were carrying white marble trays with an array of food and drinks. She noticed that each dish had a plate, a glass, and cutlery, a personalized meal for each of them.

Eros, the god of love, sauntered up to Aiko and held the tray in front of her. He pushed against the back wall of the dish. She heard a click and whirring. Legs extended from the underside of the plate until the four legs tapped against the floor. A set of fifteen identical sound patterns happened within a minute of Eros's delivery.

"Lucy," Eros said, "she always did have a way with hair. Careful, though. People might want to stop and sniff the roses." Eros winked at her and headed back toward HQ with the rest of the gods, Alethia taking up the rear.

Aiko glanced at the plate. Teriyaki shabu-shabu with a side of miso and yakisoba.

She turned to where Lucy had been, but they were all gone.

Aiko caught Hudson's staring at his meal.

Every meal had a pewter goblet full of gold-tinted liquid.

"But," Pierre said examining his plate, "'ow did zey get zis recipe? It iz a familie secret."

The rest of them stared at him.

I worry about that one, David thought.

"They stole it," Bennett shot back. "I guess this is to remind us that we're each other's family now?"

"Gods," Hayden said. "They're about as subtle as a jackhammer."

"Will we toast to successful tomorrows, to family?" Jonah glanced around the circle and raised his glass.

"Hear, hear," David said, and one by one they raised their glasses.

"From sea," Kay raised her glass, "to sea."

The others repeated it in unison, and they all took a sip of the nectar.

Slate couldn't believe how delicious it tasted, even though she had never had the flavour before. She tried to put her tongue on it. The closest description she could produce was sunshine on a cloudy day, with a chaser of pure happiness. She couldn't stop drinking the intoxicating liquid, tilting her head back all the way. She lifted the goblet in the air. When the flow stopped, she scraped the rest into her mouth with her finger at first. After cleaning off her finger, she licked the inside rim of the goblet clean. Slate put the cup down, horrified that she had licked dinnerware.

She realized they had all chugged the strange liquid, and no one knew why they did it.

"What the hell was that?" Ronnie said. She was holding her goblet in front of her.

Zavannah spread her arms. Her head tilted back, and the oracle spoke. "Nectar, the juice derived from the four celestial fruits. Hera's golden apples, Tartarus cherries, Tri Goddess Pears, and Persephagranites. Drunk by immortals for its euphoric and uplifting effects. Produced from the nectar of celestial fruits. Also produces an effect like Terran spirits."

The Oracle retired, and Zavannah came back to them.

"I hate that," Kushia said. "I mean, is it me, or is it disconcerting?"

Avery smiled. "That's because you're afraid of what it would say about you."

Kushia looked at her sideways.

"You mean," he said, "because they gave it to a thirteen-year-old, and it sounds an awful lot like booze mixed with drugs." A warm, tingling sensation flowed through his entire body. He couldn't remain angry, no matter how hard he tried. "Though," he said with a giggle, "I now see their point."

They all had become inebriated, but David experienced nothing. He looked at the inside of his goblet. It had refilled itself with nectar, and David downed it. He noticed the glass filled itself every time he put it back down. He perused the rest of them: laughing, swaying, talking, and thought, *what is wrong with me?*

"*Nothing,*" repeated that voice in his head, the one that had persuaded him to fall off his pillar. "*It's the price of being dead,*" the voice said. "*Nothing animate means nothing to animate.*"

David realized he needed a beating heart, to have metabolic or neurological responses. He was a car without an engine—nothing to rev, nothing to turn over, *except.*

"Then how do I get animated when I am with Zavannah?" David's question met with laughter in his head. The voice stifled itself.

"*That perv Gabriel,*" the voice continued, "*it's a spell that death wardens use, necromancers and reapers, a rune drawn on your forehead in cadaver form.*" David put his fingers on his forehead. "*In animus sexualis, you should thank him some time.*"

Hudson noticed the cups refilled. *Shit,* David thought.

"Cheers," Hudson roared. He picked up his goblet, raising it into the air before he downed the contents.

Shitfuck, David thought.

Sunday, July 11, 2106
1:31 a.m., TST
Okhla Industrial Estate, Phase 3, 110020-0048
New Delhi, India, Terra

"It's official," Aishwarya Rainier said, staring into the screen. "Today is Sunday, the eleventh of July two thousand one hundred and six, common era. At fourteen minutes after midnight, the fifth world war commenced.

"Canada and the United States entered a state of cold war in 2080, after an attack on Capitol Hill that linked to the US Army. Now, documents from Mickileaks show that the US knew about the missing weaponry. Further, they hid their culpability.

"Documents sourced by Everyone, now public via Mickileaks and several mirrors. It's been twenty-six years of wondering what motivated the Capitol Hill attack. E-mails found about 'slowing the growing Canadian threat' hold the key. They came from China, the USA, Russia, Pakistan, and Saudi Arabia.

"According to Pentagon communications, a group of soldiers went rogue. They were under the guidance of a captain who had experienced a mental break. They speculate that a report that his wife's plane crashed due to friendly fire was the central cause. She was near a Canadian Armed Forces training exercise.

"The Captain convinced the group that the Canadians were the 'real' enemy. He led them across the Canada-US border and carry out the infamous attacks.

"Here is where it gets geopolitical. The United States released a report that implicated Canadian friendly fire, a coordinated political move aimed at destabilizing international relations between Canada and the Commonwealth, other countries in the EU.

"Plans were in the works for other countries to spread more political misinformation. The project ended after the unnamed corporal went rogue. The Pentagon tried to bury evidence of any US involvement. Pretending nothing was wrong for two weeks before the attack itself.

"The incident report showed that the plane suffered catastrophic mechanical failure. The incident was ruled accidental due to engine failure.

"The fifth world war has the smallest number of abstaining states in world history. This includes Sweden, Finland, Ireland, Switzerland, Albania, Mongolia, and Laos. These countries are less than one percent of the global populace.

"Let us hope that shortly, cooler heads will prevail."

Monday, February 25, 2109
4:17 p.m., TST
Point Eastern, South Sea Shores
The Whitespace

David sighed. He watched the other acolytes, drunk off their asses and thinking they were the gods' gift to comedy. Pierre and Kushia were performing some dance where they linked arms. They danced in a circle, turned around, hooked their elbows, and danced in the other direction.

It had been informative, the drinking exercise. He was sure that this was the point—drunks make the best interviewees. David learned that Hudson was Hudson Rivers. Heir to the Rivers Publishing House, he had crashed his plane into the western Rockies after a freak accident with an osprey caused him to lose his right engine. Hudson was sad to hear that they never found his plane in the dense forest on the side of the mountain. His family had set up a reward for any information about his fate after the authorities gave up. The case was still unsolved, at least to David's knowledge.

Avery died at the Calgary Stampede. David had remembered hearing about the sole Terran killed in the history of the stampede. Seven horses also died that year in the chuckwagon races, but no papers covered that story. Avery's boot had gotten hooked when she went flying off the bull, swept under its flailing legs. She hit the ground and took two to the chest; the force of a small truck hit her in the ribs, scrambling her like an egg. The listed cause of death was "internal hemorrhaging due to high-speed blunt-force trauma."

"That's a fancy way of saying kicked in the tits," Avery said. She giggled, and David realized they had lost their perspective and logic. Their lizard brains were becoming more dominant.

This revelation sparked memories in Slate, where a scaffolding fell on her during a Whitesnake concert; in Ronnie, who had jumped on top of an amatol shell that fell off the line at a WWI bomb factory; in Pierre, who swears a jealous competitor sabotaged his gear during a lumberjack competition; and Hayden, who had heard the paramedics discussing the aneurysm that she had while vacuuming.

David also found out that Zavannah was the chief coroner for the province of Nova Scotia. She had died when she went to work on a Friday night. Zavannah inhaled a cloud of hydrogen cyanide when she cracked a John Doe's chest. It would be hard to choose a worse way to die than spasming, gasping for air, immobilized. She lay there for what she estimated to be five hours before she died.

This led to the realization that they had two McCoys. Asher was a trauma surgeon working with Doctors Without Borders. He ended up in the stomach of an alligator on a three-day vacation safari near Lake Victoria. David wondered if anyone else realized the irony of Asher.

"Hey," Harry glanced down into his glass, "it turned dark red." He took a sip. "And this one tastes like home."

Fuck. Like this wasn't enough of a debacle, David thought. He was already worried that they would fall into the fire.

The rest of them were chugging this new nectar like it was water in the desert. David watched them finish their goblets, and drop like leaves. They all fell where they stood or sat, passing out and crumpling to the floor. David stood there looking at them lying on the floor in a peaceful slumber. He walked to his tray, picked up the goblet, and held it to his lips in hopes of joining them.

"Won't work," Samael said from behind him, and he lowered the goblet. He turned around. Samael and Ariel were standing there. Ariel gazed into the fire.

"Exite," Ariel incanted, and the flames went out.

David put the goblet down and faced the Prims. "What do I do, then?"

Samael sauntered over to Hudson, picked him up, and threw him over his shoulder in a fireman's carry. Samael continued toward the water, where David could see a large raft waiting.

"You," Samael said, "can grab your compatriots and load them on the raft."

David sighed, walked over to Hayden, picked her up in his arms, and carried her toward the raft.

They continued in this fashion. David reached Kay, the last of the fifteen unconscious acolytes, and picked her up. He turned and walked her past the fire pit and circle of stones and up to the beach. Samael and Ariel were on the raft, waiting for him. He stepped up and onto the white wooden structure. David laid Kay down. The raft moving away from the beach and south. He thought the South Point Sea was the end of the southern district.

"Where are we going?" he asked.

Samael smiled at him.

"To the bottom of the whitespace," Samael said. "Our version of the end of the world, the Island of Apple Trees."

"Great," David said. "They can make themselves more nectar and overdose."

Samael turned. The raft stopped.

"Don't joke," he said, his tone like death itself. "We lost a Norskin the other day. Terrans don't have a monopoly on suffering and pain."

"Jesus," David said. "Sorry. I didn't realize we could overdose." The raft moved again, "Or that nectar was dangerous."

"It is when you purify it down to the essence, combine all four types, and inject it into your thoracic artery." No hint of comedy to his voice, "besides, they aren't those apples."

"And there," David said, "was where I should have said 'Jesus.'" He looked over at Samael. "Is it because I don't have a pulse that I am awake, or is there another reason to keep me up?"

Samael commented to Ariel:

"Nothing gets past this one, eh? You see, someone must understand the rules. One of you should know what to expect."

David sighed harder, from the ever-present reality of his role. A pawn in whatever sick game they were playing.

"And what, pray tell, do I need to know?" he said, his tone dripping with disdain.

"OK," Samael said, "the sarcasm is one thing—it's both intelligent and witty. I would cut the sardonic attitude because it gets old before its young. Got it?"

David fought the urge to stand up straight, salute Samael, and bark:

"Yes, sir!" He figured he should not push his luck. "Got it," he said.

Samael continued, "tomorrow is the last day of training. The traditional final task is like a team-building exercise mixed with a logic puzzle."

"Sounds like a blast," David said. "What are the rules?"

"One rule," Ariel said. "You make it to shore all together, or not at all. Understood?"

"There's not much room for interpretation," David said.

"One last thing," Samael said. "A warning. Don't—I repeat, don't—touch the surface of the water under any circumstances. Things will get about a thousand times more difficult and a hundred times more dangerous."

David's confusion sank in.

"Are we not floating on the surface right now?" he asked.

Samael shook his head.

"If you noticed," Samael said, "when we left, the raft was hovering in the air not close to the surface."

David realized that was why they had had to step up to the raft—it was gliding through the air.

"Everyone must make it," David said, "but don't ever touch the water." He looked over at Samael, who nodded.

"That is the gist of it," Samael said. David saw the island appear in the distance and moved closer to see it better.

"Is that it?" David asked. He went to turn back around, but a sharp pain in the back of his head caused everything to fade to black.

Friday, December 9, 2112
3:48 p.m., TST
Avalon, South Sea Shores
The Whitespace

Kay's head was killing her. *Gods damn it*, she thought. It might have been fun last night, but she wasn't sure the hangover was worth it. She opened her eyes and sensed something was off. They were no longer on the east most point. In fact, they were on an island approx. 100 meters in diameter, inside a circle of multicoloured apple trees.

Kay sat up, fighting her queasy stomach. She looked up at the tree she was under. Various shades of gray apples hung from the branches. She had a sinking suspicion that the ripe apples were in that state always.

"What the hell?" Harry said, and Kay glanced over at him. He held his head. "Hey," he said to her, "were you hit by a Mack truck?"

"Mine was a Peterbilt," Kay said.

"Ow," Harry held his head. "Don't make me laugh."

"Sorry, couldn't help myself. Are you OK?"

"Other than the world's worst hangover ever, yeah, I'm getting there." He mustered a smile and stood. He examined the ground in the middle of the circle and read: "Avalon: sperare, qui ineo metus." Then, realizing what it said, he took a step back and looked at Kay in dismay.

It couldn't say that, Kay thought, and she scrambled to her feet, she could see the writing. "Sperare, qui ineo metus" written on the ground around the word "Avalon," the name of the island.

"Abandon hope, ye who enter fear? What the hell does that mean?" Kay hoping for Harry's guidance. But he opened his mouth and closed it. Kay glanced down again, but this time it said: "Insula grata pomorum," or "Welcome to the island of apple trees."

"Great," Kay exclaimed. Harry followed her gaze.

"Shit," Harry said. "I suppose none of the others will see that, eh?"

"It won't change back since it's a warning." She looked over at him. His head fell.

"What?" Hudson groaned. He sat up with an "ow." The rest of them were coming to, except for David, who was lying face down across the circle.

"The words on the ground changed," Harry heaved him up. "Give us a second, and we'll talk about it together."

Hudson stumbled and shook it off.

"Anyone else taste copper?" Zavannah scraped her tongue.

"How should we wake sleeping beauty?" Jonah asked, walking toward the others.

"Not sure," said Kay. "Do we wait for him to talk about the ground?"

"Do we 'ave to wake 'im?" Pierre stood. "Will 'e not wake up like us?" He looked at Kay, who was eyeing David.

"He wasn't drunk last night," Asher said, and he and Kay exchanged a look. "If we made it here after we passed out, he needed to get here unconscious too. My best guess is they knocked him out, and we have no way of knowing how."

"You think you can—" Kay said.

"Fix him?" Asher said. "Should do." Asher walked over to David's body and put his hand on top of David's head.

"Sano," Asher incanted. His hand flashed black against David's skull, and he came to with a jerk and a snort.

"Wha', where are they?" David, disoriented, scrambled to his feet. He stood and looked around, spinning in place. He staggered to a stop and slumped his shoulders. "Shitfuck. I guess this is the island of apple trees?"

"Avalon," said Harry, "according to this." He pointed at the ground. David followed with his eyes and read the writing.

"Of course, it's Avalon," he said with a sigh. "Where is Morgan?"

"Right in front of your eyes," the voice in Ronnie's head spoke, causing her to jump.

"I was kidding," David said. "I'm sure Morgan le Fey is not here, should she still exist." Something about what he said rang untrue, like a white lie. Ronnie put her hands on her tangerine-coloured glasses.

"Who were you looking for?" Maya asked; David saw the multicoloured apple trees.

He saw the primary-coloured apple trees—the reds, blues, and yellows. There were the secondary-coloured trees in their oranges, greens, and purples. The last four apple trees boasted two-toned fruit. One had white apples mixed with golden ones, and another had black apples mixed with silver ones. One had gray apples opposite bronze ones, but the last caught his eye. One set of apples on the last tree was clear, a trick of the light when you looked at the branches. The other apples changed between the distinct colours like a revolving door.

In the centre of the island was a small mound with a shrivelled-up sapling.

"Ariel and Samael," David said. "They brought us here. I helped them load you girls onto a raft, and we headed for this island. They gave me instructions and a warning, and I guess they knocked me out."

"Instructions?" Asher asked at the same time Aiko blurted out:

"A warning?" They looked at each other, and Aiko nodded to Asher, letting him know he could go first.

"I'm sorry," Asher said. "What instructions?"

"Everyone makes it to shore, or no one does. I guess it's more of a rule. Anyway, we make it out together, or we don't make it out at all."

"Neat," Asher quipped. "That is super helpful." He rolled his eyes before turning to Aiko and nodding.

Ronnie heard them talking. She had put on her truth-coloured glasses. She scanned the trees and the island for anything unusual.

Aiko stared David, "you said there is a warning?"

"Yeah," David said, right before he heard Ronnie scream. She was wearing her tangerine glasses, and her scream turned into a gurgle. Something lifted her in the air. She grasped at what appeared to be an invisible arm holding her neck.

"Morgan..." Ronnie's voice gurgled. David could tell she was staring down her attacker. He realized he should never have joked about Morgan in the first place. "Le Fey, nice to meet yo—" The end of her sentence cut off by Morgan increasing the pressure around her neck.

Her purple-and-black dress was a sleeveless over-the-shoulder number. Her red hair cascading down her back. Morgan looked at Ronnie. Ronnie pounded on her arm, trying to break free. Morgan lifted her higher, and her feet dangled in the air.

Morgan looked Ronnie up and down.

"What do you, treacherous Roman, know of me?"

Ronnie pulled on Morgan's fingers, and Morgan loosened her grip. Ronnie smiled.

"Arthur's sister," she said, "the queen of the witches—or should I say, bitches?" Morgan screamed at a low pitch, her eyes filling with gray. Her hair popped out of its clips and became a mass on her head. She flew forward, taking Ronnie with her until Ronnie dangled above the edge of the water.

"Don't let her touch the water," David said. Bennett rushed past.

Bennett was moving before he even knew it, vectoring toward Ronnie. She dangled in midair. He grunted when his body hit something substantial before he reached Ronnie. He dropped to the ground, winded from the impact, and curled up.

"Ah," Pierre said, grabbing an apple from the nearest tree, "zat will do." He pulled a forest-green arrow from his quiver and placed the apple on the tip. He pulled out his bow and cocking it. "Bennett, through ze legs." Pierre pulled back and let the arrow fly.

The apple smashed into Morgan's shoulder, and for a second, they could see the alabaster shoulder. The arrow split the apple in half and pierced her shoulder. Morgan's scream was audible, and she pulled her arm back. Ronnie came with it and tumbled forward onto the island. Morgan let go of her throat.

Ronnie passed over Bennett. He found Morgan's legs and pulled himself through them. The ground rumbled beneath his feet. He scrambled up, watching the two perfect halves of the apple. They fell to the ground. One flipped onto its flat side and stopped moving a foot and a half from the edge of the island. The other half landed on its edge and rolled along with a wobble. Bennett ran after it. The island was now shaking. Bennett dove for the apple, its uneven trajectory sending it straight off the edge. Bennett got his fingers around the apple and stopped it a few inches from the water.

He was relieved. He rolled onto his back, and the ground moved underneath him. The water broke open next to Bennett, an immense wall of dark-gray scales shooting out of the water. The wall tilted forward. Bennett realized it was the head of a gigantic beast when he heard its soul-piercing shriek.

Bennett scrambled to his feet and headed back to the centre of the island.

"The other half of the apple," the voice in his head warned him, and he whipped his head back. His neck cracked. The rumbling and shaking rattled the other half of the apple right off the edge. He turned around; his foot slid backward, and he landed hard on his ribs.

Ronnie had a javelin in her hands, one foot on the ground, and one foot on Morgan's stomach. Morgan held a bard sword in both hands, pressing the blade against the javelin. She turned her head, pressing the button on the side of her glasses to the ground.

Ronnie's glasses produced a new exterior set of lenses that sat in front of the frames. They engaged and disengaged. The set of exterior lenses that remained allowed her to see what she was fighting. Tangerine outlined the sword, and a line spread off to make a box that filled with the words "Weapon: Bard Sword." On a second line, "Name: Excalibur."

Ronnie looked at Morgan, and the lenses outlined her maniacal face. A line formed next to a box that said "Beast: Morgan le Fey," leading to Ronnie to think *Beast?* The box populated a second line, "Title: Mother of Monsters," and a third, "Species: Echidna."

Morgan pulled up with her sword and swung downward to cleave the javelin. Ronnie rocked up and met the descending sword mid slash. She fell back, bringing an unstable Morgan with her, rocking back. She used her foot to kick Morgan over her, sending her tumbling backward.

Ronnie rolled over and saw Bennett scrambling to his feet. One half of the apple shook to the edge of the island. Ronnie looked at the beast rising out of the water to face the island. Her glasses outlined the head of the creature, a line drawing to a box. The words "Beast: Jormungandr" appeared above a line. "Title: He without End," and a final line indicating, "Species: Ouroboros."

"Jesus," Ronnie said. Jormungandr looked at her and let out an angry shriek. Ronnie looked away and saw that Bennett had reached the apple. The scream sent it flying toward Bennett's hand. But it was like touching a bar of soap. Bennett did not expect to reach the apple and knocked it back. It flew off the edge and straight into the water.

"Shitfuck," Bennett said.

Suddenly gravity betrayed them. The world flipped upside down, and the sixteen acolytes fell upward. The water all around steamed until they floated in a column of air inside a circle of dense fog.

Kushia spectered, his amethyst eyes sparkling. He balanced out their gravity, and they stopped falling up. The fifteen of them bobbed up and down in place. Kushia flew down, the rest of them coming with him. He headed for the trees, bringing one or two of them to each tree; they could use the branches for a floor.

"We have a problem," Ronnie yelled to the group. "Morgan le Fey *is* on the island and is invisible to everyone but me."

"Where?" Pierre said

Ronnie continued through gritted teeth.

"Look," she said, "I am saying that we need a plan to deal with her Jormungandr there." She pointed over her shoulder with her thumb. Slate saw the head of the beast breaking through the fog behind Ronnie.

"Move!" Slate roared.

Ronnie, Jonah, Asher, and Hayden all jumped from their trees after looking behind them. Jormungandr slammed into the limestone and wailed from the force against his snout. The snake retreated into the fog.

"Let me try something," Maya said, and Morgan heard her. Ronnie could see Morgan standing on the one side of the island. She lifted Excalibur above her head, tip down, and drove the sword into the stone island up to the hilt. She let go and stepped back.

"Ostende te," Maya commanded Morgan to show herself. The witch became visible to everyone, Ronnie put her glasses away. Morgan was upside down to them, still grounded to the rock. Ronnie realized that she was distracting them.

She looked over at Pierre, Avery, Kushia, and Slate. The fog behind them darkened, and a large arrow shape was descending on them.

"Incoming!" Ronnie yelled. They looked over their shoulders and jumped to the neighbouring trees. Avery fell into Slate on the one side. Pierre cradled Kushia after Jormungandr's tail broke through the fog. It smashed into the limestone knocking Kushia straight into Pierre. They hit the branches.

"Bonjour," Pierre said in a sultry tone, smiling like the Cheshire cat, and Kushia pushed off with a huff.

"Very funny," Kushia said, offering his hand to Pierre. He looked over and saw the look in Avery's eyes. She gauged when the tail would free itself from the rock.

"Boots," Kushia yelled, and Avery jumped out.

"Arma," Avery incanted, and her two sickles appeared, one near each hand. After grabbing them out of the air, she grabbed the monster's tail. It flew backward and into the fog, taking her with it.

"No!" Kushia screamed into the haze. He turned back to the others, but there was nothing they could do.

"Morgan," Ronnie said, "I see your game, and I am not playing. David, can you take these jokers, Annie Oakley, and Buffalo Bill, and descend...ascend? Go up—it'll be easier to take on Jormungandr in the open."

"Sure," David said, looking for any dissension by the others, but none came. "What are you going to do?"

Ronnie batted another spell away with her javelin, looking at Morgan.

"I am going to kill Morgan le Fey," she said, provoking Morgan into flying at her, putting out both of her hands. Asher heard a flap, like a woman's dress and the rustling of feet. He couldn't place them.

"Arma," Morgan incanted, and a pair of sun and moon rings appeared, one in each hand. She came in, slashing her feet on the ceiling. Ronnie parried her swings and chops with her javelin. The branches broke under her feet. She deflected hits. She looked over at David.

"Go," Ronnie commanded, and every member of the Jormungandr team dropped off the trees. The eight acolytes ascended into the column of fog. Morgan deflected Zavannah's first two chakrams. The third embedded itself in her forearm, causing another scream.

Morgan turned toward Zavannah, pulling the chakrams out of her arm. Morgan whipped the chakrams at Zavannah. Morgan turned to the side, deflecting the shuriken as fast as Maya threw them.

Zavannah held up her hand at the last second, and her chakrams struck through her palm. It stuck out of the back of her hand and stopped short of her eye. She stumbled backward into Jonah, unable to keep herself from crying out in pain. Asher stuffed the sleeve of his shirt in her mouth, and Jonah held her down. Asher took the chakrams out of her hand.

The two enchanters locked in hand-to-hand combat. Maya's last two shuriken turned into improvised daggers. The clink of metal was audible in the background. Asher put his right hand around Zavannah's, holding the end of it. He put his left foot on her wrist and, grabbing the chakrams, pulled hard. Zavannah bit down on the sleeve and cried out, with Asher holding his hand over hers, his eyes filled with black.

"Curare," Asher incanted, the black magik stitching her hand back together. The pain stopped, and she spit out the sleeve.

"Thanks," Zavannah said. Jonah let go, and Zavannah stood.

Maya kicked Morgan in the head, sending her reeling and giving Zavannah a window. She threw her chakrams straight for Morgan's head. Morgan turned, exposing her back to Harry. She deflected the chakrams. Lucy burst through the fog and stood on the edge of the island.

"Wait!" Lucy yelled. Harry's sword, already buried to the hilt in Morgan le Fey's chest, cut straight through her heart.

Harry looked over at Lucy with a helpless look.

The light left Morgan's eyes, and now dead, she slumped forward and off Harry's sword. Harry sighed, slumping his shoulders. "I assume that you did not want me to kill her," he said, staring at Lucy.

The look in her eyes was a rare one: pure pity for the act of protection that would now define the rest of his existence. She sighed, not knowing what to do with him.

Kushia stopped them once they ascended a hundred meters, in a holding pattern around him. David had laid out a great multilayered plan for dealing with Jormungandr. After coordinating their movements, they were waiting.

Jormungandr's head appeared to Kushia's left. The darkening fog causing them all to jump into action. The snout pierced the haze. David was looking at Pierre, Aiko, and the others, checking that they were ready, when he heard it.

"Yee-haw," yelled Avery, spurring Pegi forward. They burst out of the haze near the trees and made a sharp upturn.

Thursday, January 15, 2122

11:51 p.m., TST
Basement, Ministry of Communications
Islamabad Capital Territories, Pakistan, Terra

Sunny Kasana turned the corner. He ran into the far wall. He stumbled and kept running. The wall behind him exploded. A hailstorm of bullets ripped into the concrete. Sunny put his hand on the door lock and dashed inside. He hit the emergency lockdown button beside the door. The assault team on his heels turned the corner. The door pushed shut with a hiss. He looked at the console in the room.

He walked over to the console, pulling his u-card from his pocket. That was when he saw his hand covered in blood, and he realized he took one in the abdomen. His fingers touched it. Sunny was at the console when he heard the oxyacetylene torch. He watched the molten spot forming around the door.

Sunny stuck his u-card into the terminal and typed. He threw everything he could think of at the government encryptions. He couldn't access the intercontinental emergency broadcast services. Sunny looked behind him. He saw the speed with which they were cutting through the door. Sunny realized he did not have enough runway.

Sunny was running several of the programs on his card. The windows populated the screen faster than he could execute the commands. The torch cut through the last of the electromagnetic connections. The assault team pulled the door open. The Captain shot Sunny in the shoulder; he clutched the console before sliding onto the floor.

The Captain walked over to the console. "Confirm Override Sequence? Yes, or No," flashed on the screen. The Captain clicked on "no," and the console spat back: "Override Sequence in Progress. Authorization Required to Cancel." Space to enter his authorization code followed. He typed in his clearance, and the console spat back. "Confirm Cancelation of Override Sequence? Yes or No."

The Captain hit yes and was relieved until he saw the console's status, "Override in Progress." The console was taken over by the command strings. The intercontinental emergency broadcast system took over. Broadcasting on every vidcom, caster, iScreen, television, and radio on and off Terra.

"How the—" the Captain said.

"No one," Sunny gurgled, "protects the text editor."

The Captain pointed his gun in Sunny's face but realized it was futile when he saw that the life had left his eyes. He turned and left the room, saying, "Burn the body."

A recording of Sunny came over the airwaves, explaining that two days ago the message had changed. He told how none of the governments and world leaders wanted the people to know.

Sunny finished with seven individuals who had delivered the new message two days ago. They acted possessed. They recited the new message several times over.

Sunday, August 22, 2123
9:14 a.m., TST
Avalon, South Sea Shores
The Whitespace

As Pegi turned toward their group, David huffed. "Change of plans, everyone," he said. "Kushia, collision course with Boots, on the double." He was looking at Kushia. Kushia rotated them along the horizontal axis and dove toward Avery and Pegi. The other seven were in tow. Jormungandr's jaws snapped around the space they had left.

"Wat ze fuck?" Pierre said. They vectored toward Pegi. She launched upward, a canary-yellow trail of smoke behind her. She climbed. Kushia pulled in front of the group, putting them into line behind him, Pierre at the back. Jormungandr's gaping maw chased after them. "Why me?"

Pierre pulled an arrow from his quiver, bulb ended, and fired straight into the mouth of the snake. It ascended on them faster than they were rising down. The arrow hit the roof of its mouth, exploding on impact, and causing Jormungandr to shriek and rear. It slowed him for a second before he climbed down fast.

"Shitfuck," Pierre said. He pulled out arrow after arrow, shooting the petards at the snake's weak spots, keeping him off their asses. He pulled to the side. Avery flew past him toward the maw of the beast. Pierre cocked one last arrow. The tail blew past him, the subsequent wind blowing him sideways while he focused on his target and let the arrow fly.

Avery snapped her fingers on both hands. A saddle of diamond and void steel materialized. Pegi's war armour spread out to cover her body, head, neck, and legs in checkered panels of diamond and void steel. Around the wings a pair of void-steel track wheels appeared, a mod she had requested from Harry.

"Oblatrantem," she incanted, spectered, her arm in front of her. Two canary-yellow rails appeared in front of her, and Pierre's arrow struck.

"Armis," Avery incanted. The arrow exploded in front of her, her void-steel plates coming up. She made Pegi perform a lateral and horizontal turn. The wheels hit the rails. A set of crescents shot them sideways out of the explosion.

The rails disappeared. The smoke cleared, and Jormungandr clamped down on his own tail. The paralytic in his teeth made the ouroboros return to its original state. The coil fell sideways into the fog.

Avery turned and headed for the others. Kushia was dropping them onto the treetops again.

Lucy had been standing there for a few seconds, trying to figure out if there were any options. She heard explosions and caught the end of the dinner show.

"Kushia," Lucy said. He brought the others to rest on the branches, "you need to pull back that half of an apple. Otherwise, you girls have to go through the fog."

Kushia nodded, looking over at Ronnie, who put her glasses back on, searching for the apple. Lucy stepped over to where Morgan had stashed Excalibur.

"Harry, over here when you're on the ground again," Lucy said and kept walking until she reached the sword.

Ronnie spotted the apple, sinking upward in the fog, and, tossing her glasses to Kushia, pointed at it. Kushia found the apple with his glasses. Focusing on it, he incanted:

"Accio," while Lucy said:

"Manufesto," revealing the sword stuck into the stone of the island. The apple half burst through the fog, straight into Kushia's hand.

"Boots," David yelled, realizing they were about to turn upside down again, "flip pancakes."

Avery knew he was referring to watching her make pancakes. She was right-handed, and flipped her hand inside out, or backward. She barrel-rolled Pegi at the same time gravity brought the others crashing down.

Harry rolled forward, sliding over beside Lucy. The fog came crashing down, and the lake surrounded them once more.

Harry had no idea what she expected. He looked at her, blinking, confused.

"That is Excalibur," Ronnie snatched her glasses back. "She's saying, he who kills its owner owns it."

"Go ahead." Lucy motioned for Harry to take the sword, and he pulled it out of the limestone with ease. Harry held it in his hands. It morphed from Morgan's bard sword style into a gladius, something more in tune with Harry. It's new owner. He couldn't stop looking at it, turning it over in his hand. He admired its glory, the power pulsing through him.

"Moventur in insula," Lucy broke the island free from the limestone beneath. It floated toward shore. The acolytes and Lucy remained locked in awkward silence.

Chapter 8
The Choking Gun

Tuesday, December 11, 2125
3:42 p.m., TST
Dis Pater Superdreadnought
Orcus Orbital Station, Atlantis Prime

Ten thousand Atlan soldiers lined the scaffolding and walls of the docking bay. They awaited their Empress. The silence of the bay was more apparent than the void itself. Soldiers straightened at the hollow tin sound of her heels against the metal floor. The clicking got louder until the two royal guards at the door stood to attention, and announced;

"Her Imperial Majesty the Empress of the Nine Systems." The Empress and the president of the Senate walked into the bay. They talked to each other like the ten thousand soldiers who snapped to attention did not exist.

"Yes," Synesis informed the Empress. They walked to the end of the catwalk. "We've completed fifty percent of the fleet. All the remaining vessels are at least twenty percent complete."

"Good," the Empress said. "I love to hear that someone understands the importance of a schedule. How are we doing on the advanced fleet?"

"Not what I would hope," Synesis said. "We are on schedule, but I had to adjust the work hours and increase over time. The budget can't absorb the fleet into the original estimates. I am going to have to propose an addendum to the bill for extra funding."

"Don't bother," the Empress said. She was always impressed when someone understood what to focus on. "I'll go before Parliament again. They take forever to make any decisions without me."

They were standing at the end of the catwalk, examining the polished ship. The name PAM *Dis Pater* painted on the side along with its call sign, "atlantikós midén." Its class, "paroplisméno thoriktó," listed next to its identifiers.

Synesis looked over at an officer, higher ranking than the others.

"Commander," Synesis said, saluting the officer, "please bring Her Imperial Highness the bottle."

The commander clicked his heels. He walked over to a table covered with gray-and-bronze cloth. On it was a single bottle of carbonated wine from the pomfolygódis region of Scylla, one of the Seven Sisters. Some people called it pomfoly, and others called it gódis, depending on what planet they came from. Scyllans called it pomfolygódis like the pretentious assholes most of them were. The commander picked up the bottle and marched over to the Empress, kneeling before her. He held out the bottle.

"Ah," the Empress said, "Phorcys, the best pomfoly in all Atlantis."

"Pomfolygódis," Synesis corrected her, and then, realizing what he had done, he froze in place. His eyes went wide.

The Empress kept moving, picking up the bottle up from the commander's now-shaking hands. She turned to the president, perusing the label. She stepped up to Synesis.

"Such a shame," the Empress said, "an authentic Phorcys pomfolygódis." She stared into Synesis, his pupils touching the white in all three places. "Am I saying that right?" She asked. The look on her face was sweet, and she smiled.

Synesis went to respond but when he opened his mouth, the Empress flipped the bottle and shoved its neck down his throat. She hit the bottom with her hand, and there was a loud crack. The light left Synesis' eyes, and he slumped back. The Empress spectered, her eyes turning gray. She held out her hand, and his corpse lifted into the air. Synesis' body turned in the air, his mouth toward the side of the ship, the bottle forward. The Empress flicked her wrist, and the bottle went flying at the vessel, taking Synesis with it. The bottle and his head exploded on impact.

"It was such a good bottle of pomfoly," she turned around. The rest of Synesis slid down the ship with a squeak until it dropped to the floor with a squishy thud. "Would you agree, Commander?"

Saturday, October 25, 2127
3:42 p.m., TST
Point Eastern, South Sea Shores
The Whitespace

Avalon, separated from its anchoring base, floated into the shore. It's base connected with the beach a few meters from the edge of the water.

"Hudson," Lucy eyed him, "would you mind?"

Hudson nodded and stepped up to the edge of the island. He spectered and held his hand out in front of him, pointing toward the shore.

"Distractus," he incanted. The waters in front of him parted, showing the sand underneath. Space for the acolytes to cross between the walls of water onto the beach. Hudson turned back to the others, his hand still in front of him. "Mind the gap."

David jumped down first, falling about a meter and a half before hitting the ground. He turned back and held out his hand, helping Kay down. Slate jumped down and followed suit, helping Aiko jump down next. The other acolytes trudged across the sand and up until they were on the upper beach, greeted by a full set of Prims.

Hudson turned to Lucy.

"Ladies first," he said to her. She walked up beside him, putting her hand on his shoulder.

"Thanks," Lucy said and took a step forward. "I can cross on my own." She took another step, launched herself into the air, and landed on the other side. The waters rushed back, Hudson having let go of the spell. He stepped forward, walking along the surface of the water until he stepped onto the sandy beach.

Lucy had already strolled over to Gabriel, who was leaning on his staff, and the two of them exchanged a look.

"He was too fast for you, eh?" Gabriel said.

"This is not funny," Lucy said. "Or do you think that taking over a curse that destroyed an entire civilization is a joke?" Lucy looked daggers at Gabriel, who smiled.

"The boy," Gabriel said, "will be fine." He looked over at Harry and added, "if he resists the urge to use it. Which I am sure he will."

Gabriel's eyes burned through him.

"Like, ever?" Harry gulped.

Gabriel turned and walked over to him.

Gabriel was calm, "you have two choices. Use Excalibur and succumb to its curse, like every other person to ever wield it has." His tone turned sharp. "Or you can heed my warning, and if you never use it, it can never use you."

Harry gazed at the sword, not excited about the prospect of owning Excalibur.

Gabriel walked up to him and held his hand out for the sword, which Harry handed over.

Gabriel grabbed the handle of the gladius and twisted the hilt around. The sword shrank. A chain emerged from the end of the grip until Gabriel held a necklace with a sword pendant. He handed the jewelry to Harry, who looked at it for a moment before putting it around his neck.

"How come you can hold it?" Harry asked. "I thought Lucy got me to grab it because only it's owner can wield it."

Gabriel smiled.

"You may be its owner, but everything knows its creator."

Harry looked down at the pendant in his hand and stuffed it into his shirt.

"Right," he said. "No use bad sword. Even I can get that one right."

Gabriel turned and walked back to headquarters.

"We should head back. Our intel suggests the Atlans are sending an advance fleet to establish a beachhead on Terra." He looked back at the acolytes. "We are going to have to send you soon."

Monday, August 1, 2129
8:24 p.m., TST
Tactical Chamber Upsilon, Headquarters
The Whitespace

The tactics quarters, a new addition that was waiting for them at headquarters. At three times its former size, the building now resembled a fortress on steroids. They each had their own quarters in the building with rooms for them to train and practice.

Although that was useless now that they had lost the last sixteen days of useable time. They had less than seventy-two hours before they were to leave. Harry, Pierre, Slate, Kay, and David were with Zed and Samael in the new engineering bays. The rest of the acolytes were with the remaining Prims here, going over tactics.

Rafi addressed the group, "they must have someone, or a few people, on the ground in Terra. The Empress is using our own resonance frequency against us. They will be exiting Higgs boson space on April 13, 2164."

Ronnie stood.

"Excuse me," she said, incredulous. "If they land in 2164, what the fuck year is it now?"

Rafi turned to Ronnie, holding up her wrist until a watch of some sort appeared. Rafi looked at it and put her arm down, it disappeared.

"It's 2130," she said. Ronnie sat, confused. She held up her hand, about to speak, but couldn't think of anything to say.

"Jesus," Avery said. "You think you might have mentioned the huge time gap earlier? That way, we could prepare?"

Rafi looked over at Gabriel and Lucy.

"You didn't tell them?" She asked, realized she did not need an answer. She walked over to the two of them, talking low. "You do realize that when you play with living dolls, sometimes the dolls play back, right? No wonder the ship has a leak."

Rafi walked back to the table.

"I apologize for my father and aunt," she said. The two of them remained stoic. "They oversee these things, we picked each of you up—after you died, of course. We held on to everyone until we got to David, and we released you. That was in 1995, after the trial and here in the whitespace, you have been on a different plane of existence. It happens to run on its own schedule and tends to be much faster moving than places like Terra. You have covered hundreds of years in days."

Aiko turned to Avery, "that is where you should have said 'Jesus.'"

"And," Asher snarled, "you did not think we would want to know that. That we would be coming out one hundred sixty-nine years ahead of the last time, we were on Terra? Two hundred fifty-nine years from Zavannah's exodus?"

"Two hundred fifty-nine years?" Zavannah sounded both surprised and distraught. Hudson thought she was laying it on a bit thick. "David's world was foreign enough, but one hundred seventy years further into the future? I'm not sure how much use I'll be."

"Nonsense," Rafi said. "If you were useless, I would not be wasting my time." She turned back to the table. "I was saying, they chose the dry day in the message cycle we set up. They're going to pretend that they are us."

"Using the 'we come in peace' angle we set up to lower their defences," Lucy said. "They won't need to worry about anything. At that point, resistance will be futile."

Mica put her hand on her hip. "I'm guessing at this point that she's a bunch of steps ahead of us. That if we try to work out a solution, then she prepared for it."

"I sense a suggestion coming on," Ariel leaned against a back wall.

Mica shot him a look, and Ariel smiled.

"I don't think she'll be expecting us to get the acolytes to make a plan and not tell us." Mica said, "I'm sure she thinks us foolish for trusting anyone at all. Am I wrong, Father?"

"No," Gabriel said. "Trust was never your mother's strong suit."

"Thus," Mica said, "I suggest that we have Bennett, David, Aiko, and Ronnie make a plan. They can roll it out at launch prep. No interval for error."

"Sealed that up tight there, didn't you?" Rafi said.

"I try," Mica said.

"Do it," Lucy said. "I can't see a better way. Let us do it, Gabriel?"

"Yup," Gabriel said. "Works for me." He nodded to them. "Excuse me, then. I'm going to go take a walk." And he left the room.

Mica said, "there is the business of assignments. For example, who are we sending to Patagonia?"

"Harry," Lucy said. "Least opportunity for collateral damage. Slate at least takes that into consideration."

Thursday, November 1, 2131
7:21 a.m., TST
Engineering Bay Gamma, Headquarters
The Whitespace

"And," Zed picked up the Xi One Fragmentary. The gun extending two feet above her head when she rested it on her hip. "This beautiful bastard is the Xi One Fragmentary or XOne-F. It can disintegrate an elephant in under a second. Not that you would want to, but it will do some damage to a ship's hull. Great for space battles."

Harry was in heaven. Surrounded by gadgets and equipment he had dreamt of—some he would have never been able to conceive of. Some he couldn't even recognize. Harry wanted to spend the rest of his life in this room. Gabriel walked in.

"David," he said, "we need you in the tactical meeting." David looked at him.

"Do you mind if I—"

"This is not a request."

David got up from his office chair and turned to the others before he left.

"Gentlemen," he said, tipping an invisible hat, "lady, I bid you adieu."

Gabriel waited until David fell in line beside him. They exited the room into the adjoining hallway. He waited until after they got to the junction and walked up the stairs. He even waited until they were halfway between the basement and the eighth floor. He turned, grabbed David by the throat, and threw him up against the wall.

"Are you insane?" Gabriel asked. David made gurgling noises. "Scratch that. You wouldn't know you were. How about this. You do realize that the five of you being together in the engineering bays wasn't some random thing, right?"

David pulled on Gabriel's hand, trying to speak. Gabriel let go, and David slid to the floor, coughing, and gasping. He rubbed his throat.

"What the fuck?" he said, looking up at Gabriel. "Get to the point already. Jesus."

"Point is," Gabriel said, "that we kept the suspects out of the meeting."

David's eyes widened. He finished his realization.

"You think I'm the one feeding the Empress information?"

"No. If you were the leak, we would not know about it, and you would not get caught. If it were you, we would have gone into your trap without blinking."

"Thanks, for the vote of confidence." David said, half offended, and half complimented, "what is your damage, Heather?"

"Don't act flip with me. The other Prims aren't easy to convince."

David got to his feet.

"What?" he asked, watching Gabriel's expression; *was it fear?*

"Like the fact that the acolyte who knew the date of our introitus was you."

David had no hint of deception on his face, "I would never betray them. You," he added, looking away, "but not them."

"I agree." He turned away from David. "Having said that"—David looked back at him, knowing what he was going to say— "there is one more possibility."

"You said," David said, "that the other four were with me because they are suspects, right?" Gabriel nodded. "Yet none of them are being interrogated like this, I am sure."

Gabriel sighed.

"They are persons of interest. You're a suspect." David's eyes threw daggers at him. "A position you're in because you're fucking the prime suspect."

"Wait," David said, confused. "If Zavannah is your prime suspect, why would you put her in the tactical meeting?"

"Victorious warriors win first and then go to war, while defeated warriors go to war first and then seek to win." David stared at Gabriel.

"Sun Tzu, *The Art of War*. Until you know, it's her. Until you know her plan and what she has told the Empress, you want to keep her around, and in a false sense of security."

The last line fell flat, and Gabriel looked at David, worry breaking his veneer again.

"I have to ask, Davie. There is no chance you told her about introitus, right?"

David's now-emotionless face stared up at Gabriel for a minute before looking away.

"Zavannah made a point of instituting a 'no shop talk' policy early on in our relationship." Gabriel looked wary. "In fact, she instituted that policy right away." David looked back at Gabriel. "And I can't, for the death of me, think of a reason to have the 'no shop talk' conversation before it comes up."

Gabriel frowned at David.

"You can't look at everything she does under a microscope," Gabriel said. David turned away; Gabriel sighed. "Has anyone ever told you that curiosity killed the clam?"

David back. "What? I thought curiosity killed the cat."

"Yes," Gabriel said, "what I am talking about is when scientists were examining Ming the clam. This was back in 2006, mind you. They opened it to examine it, see if they could see how old it was, causing Ming to go into shock and die. The oldest living creature on earth, five hundred seven years old. They killed it because they wanted to know more but did not consider the animal itself."

David turned away again.

"Your point?" David asked.

"Right now, we are that clam, and if you bust us open, most likely we all die."

"What is death anymore anyway?" David responded.

"I know it's hard to differentiate when you're in our position. You do realize that the lives of an entire civilization hang in the balance, not to put too fine a point on it."

"Do you think the Empress would annihilate the Terran race?"

"No," Gabriel said and sighed. "But the Strangers will if we can't find a way to make peace with the rest of the Omniverse and unify the civilizations."

"I presume I walked into that conversation in the middle. You want to back up a step there, chief?"

"OK." Gabriel straightened.

Tuesday, December 7, 2134
9:55 p.m., TST
Tactical Chamber Upsilon, Headquarters
The Whitespace

Gabriel left David behind at Tactical Chamber Upsilon. David entered and walked over to the table, where the three other people in the chamber were hovering. The door closed behind him. He looked around at the others.

"You may be wondering," David said, "why I brought you here today."

"You're a stitch," Ronnie said, "Do you want to know what we figured out, or do you want to make jokes?"

David raised an eyebrow, "I don't think you'll be happy with me if I answer, but I want to hear what you three have planned." David gave her a grin and could swear he could see the steam coming off her; she had no sense of humour.

Ronnie went first. "The main issue is our intel suggests they are sending 32 ships, across the entire planet. Aiko produced the idea of mapping the distance between each ship's estimated exodus location. Pair up the closest two ships and keep doing that until we have the closest pairs we can get."

Friday, June 17, 2135
10:23 a.m., TST
David's Quarters, Headquarters
The Whitespace

When David opened his door, he wanted to sleep. It had been a long day. What he found was Zavannah leaning against the island in his kitchen. She wore a see-through citrine teddy.

I don't care, David thought. *I am going to open the clam and kill us all. I don't care. Don't make me do this.* He shook it off and smiled.

He mustered everything he had, "are you not a sight for sore eyes." He walked into the room, closing the door. Zavannah walked over to him, hanging off him. He thought *if intelligence is not what you're after, what is your end game?*

"Hey, baby," Zavannah said, running her hands over David's chest. She put one arm around his neck and ran her finger along his lips. "Do you think you have enough energy left to make me a happy girl?"

David fought the urge to run and let himself sigh mentally. He was going to have to lean into the curve on this one. *I guess there could be worse problems to have,* he thought. He needed a Silkwood shower.

He picked her up by the thighs in the way he knew she liked, "we can work something out."

Zavannah kissed him. He walked into the bedroom and shut the door with his foot.

Thursday, February 23, 2136
10:23 a.m., TST
Engineering Bay Gamma, Headquarters
The Whitespace

David walked into the engineering bay and found Harry where he always was, in the middle of a pile of parts, covered in grease, and grinning ear to ear. He walked down the steps, and Harry looked up.

"Hey, David," Harry said, cleaning some valve. "What can I do you for?" David had liked Harry from the moment they met. It was odd for an architect and an engineer to get along, but he had a kinship with Harry. They seemed to get each other and had been confiding in each other.

"Can you change my situation?" David said.

"Would if I could, good buddy. Would if I could." Harry said, "Woman issues?"

"Yes, but not the kind you would think. I mean, there is no problem with our relationship, per se."

"I sense a but—phrasing, boom! —coming on," Harry said. "Do you want to skip to the important bit, or will we dance a little longer?"

"OK," David said. Harry reassembled a traversa injector. He often took things apart to see how they worked. "I'm caught between a rock and a hard place, and I don't know which way is up anymore."

"Go on," Harry said, assembling the injector without looking, eyes focused on David.

"I mean two days ago, I was thinking about asking Zavannah to marry me."

Harry jumped, pulling the trigger on the injector. The problem was that Harry was holding the dart guard in his other hand. With nothing to stop it, the dart in the chamber flew out and into David's neck.

The dart hit him square in the throat and collapsed his trachea, lodging in his spine. David tried to talk but couldn't, and the dart wasn't coming out of his throat. He fell to his knees. Screwing up was second nature to Harry. Instead of wasting time in surprise, he took the twenty-two seconds left and ran to the table with David's gear on it. Harry shoved everything on the table into David's backpack and two side packs. He scrambled together all the different pieces of equipment. Harry went over to the table with the XOne-Fs, disassembled one, and shoved it into a side bag.

Eleven seconds, Harry thought. He rushed over to David, who had slid to the floor.

"Sorry, bud," Harry said, slipping David's arms through the handles of the various bags. "I'm forgetting something." Harry was thinking aloud, but David managed to cross his arms with his fists closed. Swords, Harry realized.

"Mortis telum," Harry managed to incant in time to grab the two hook swords and stick them to David's chest. *Three*...he crossed David's arms. *One*. David folded into the pure purple mana before it shrank into nothingness, taking him with it.

"I guess I could change your situation," Harry reviewed the empty room.

Friday, August 2, 2137
1:46 p.m., TST
Samael's Quarters, Headquarters
The Whitespace

Samael awoke. A loud banging coming from his door. He sat up in bed, the banging getting louder and more frantic. Samael threw the covers off and went to open his bedroom door. He remembered he wasn't wearing anything. He slipped into a pair of purple boxer briefs, grabbed his robe, and slid into his fuzzy slippers.

"Who the hell is that?" Hayden said, sitting up in bed and rubbing her eyes. Samael didn't think she had woken up. He had thought you could slap her with a dead fish, and she would remain sleeping.

"That is the point of getting dressed," Samael, "and answering the door—to see who is on the other side."

"Samael!" Samael heard through the door. It was Harry, and he sounded distraught. *What has he done now?* Samael thought.

"Can I do anything?" Hayden asked.

"Yeah," he said, giving her a quick kiss. "Put some clothes on."

Hayden pulled up the duvet, remembering her exposure.

Samael walked into the apartment and over to the door. The banging resumed, and he opened the door. Harry fell to the ground when the door opened, panting and frantic.

"I shot...David," he was still panting.

"What?" Samael said. "I don't understand."

Harry shook his head and grabbed his side, a stitch hitting him.

"With the...serum...he...is gone," he managed to finish.

Samael's blood boiled; he lost his temper. He wound up to backhand Harry.

"Are you serious?" Samael heard Hayden say. Harry bent his head to the side.

"Hayden?" Harry asked.

"No," Hayden said, "it's someone else."

Samael lowered his hand and picked Harry up from the floor.

"Why don't I make us a pot of coffee," Samael walked Harry to the kitchen table. Harry sat while Samael rifled through the cupboards. "What happened?"

"I was tinkering around," Harry said, "in Gamma, looking at the equipment."

Samael spoke without turning around or stopping what he was doing.

"And by that, you mean disassembling stuff to see how it works and putting it back together. Even though I asked you not to."

"Yeah," Harry said.

"Continue," Samael said, loading the filter with coffee from the can.

"David comes in and talks with me. We often chat in the mornings."

Hayden walked out of the bedroom in her clothes from last night. Samael pushed some buttons and turned around to rest his hands on the island.

"Yeah," Hayden said, "old news. Get to the good part."

"OK," Harry said. "Yeesh, is she always like this in the morning?"

Hayden looked back at Samael, who did not change his expression.

"Answer the question." Samael's eyes on Harry.

"He was talking about something important. How his opinion of Zavannah had changed. I was listening to him and cleaning an injector—the dual-action dart gun/injector combo."

Samael put his elbows on the purple marble and bowed his head. He ran his fingers through his hair before looking up.

"Then," Harry said, "he said a couple of days ago he was thinking about asking Zavannah to marry him." Samael did a spit take, and Harry closed his mouth.

"I told Zed more times than can I can count that that was a dangerous combo. How do I have to say handguns are dangerous, no matter the ammo?" Samael let go and looked up. "Let me guess." "The gun went off in your hand?"

"Yes," Harry said. "I don't even remember pulling the trigger."

"That is because..." Samael turned around and grabbed the now-ready coffee pot. He spun back and filled the three coffee mugs in front of him. "Room for cream?" He held the pot above the last mug, waiting.

"Yes..." Harry said, and Samael finished pouring.

"Sugar?" Samael asked.

"Double, double," Harry replied. "Sorry...that is because of what?"

Samael poured in cream and flicked his wrist; the three spoons all stirred themselves.

"Right," he lifted the mugs with a movement of his hand and walking to the table. He grabbed his mug and sat. The other two mugs drifted into Hayden and Harry's hands. "That is because you did not pull the trigger." Samael took a sip of coffee. "At least not with your fingers."

Samael put the coffee down and pointed to his head.

"You willed it. Using that pesky fourth type of magik, *Sorcery*." Sam looked at Harry. "The ability to manifest your destiny or that of others through thoughts alone. Hayden, thanks for stopping me earlier. I should not have hit the greatest sorcerer I've ever met."

"I assume," Hayden said, "there is a reason other than the obvious."

"Yes," Samael said. "Because I would have done the same fucking thing. I have a deal for you, Harry." He looked across the table at Harry, who looked like a drowning man who had received a lifeline.

"I can fix this," Samael interlocked his fingers together. He put them on the table, "but I need something in return. I'll even sweeten the pot."

"What do you need?" Harry stammered.

"Tell you what," Samael said, leaning back. "You tell me that secret you've been holding for Hudson all this time. I fix this, but I'll also tell you the secret that Gabriel has been hiding from you about that trinket around your neck. Deal?"

Monday, May 2, 2140

6:41 a.m., TST
The Tower, Headquarters
The Whitespace

GadZeke strolled into the room and closed the door on the floor with a clangour. Gabriel glanced at Lucy, "we are all here. Will we commence?"

"Let us," Lucy scanned the table. Three chairs were empty. GadZeke grabbed the last chair, and thus four of them sat on one side of the table and four on the other. That left the heads of the table open—one for the Empress, and one reserved for Jehovah.

"What did I miss?" GadZeke

"The boat, dear," Mica chided. "Harry shot David with a traversa dart. He's headed to Terra ahead of schedule."

"Awesome," GadZeke said. "Do we have a contingency plan?"

Samael spoke up from across the table. "I already have something in the works. I have established a network on Terra." Samael opened a folder. "I have the action plan, and parts of this are already either in place or in motion."

GadZeke said, "what do you need from us?"

"Less talking," Zed said, "would be good." GadZeke leaned back, feigning offence. "The real problem that we face is getting David to 2164. He could become the property of some government agency. There is no telling what can happen to him. Do we know if any of the plants on Terra are acolytes?"

Zed was looking at him now.

"You told me not to talk," GadZeke said, causing Zed to give him a look. "It looks like the Voidkin is somewhere in western Europe, from the intel I have."

"And where is David set to drop out?" Zed asked Samael, who frowned.

"St Petersburg," Samael said in a deflated tone.

"That is closer than I would like," Zed said. "Anyone else worried that Russia is less readable than the Voynich Manuscript?"

Samael stared at the page in front of him, realizing that there was no way around it.

"Plan Rho then," Samael said, still looking at the paper. He shook it off and closed the folder before looking at Lucy. "I can't see a way around it."

Gabriel raised an eyebrow, turning to Samael but saying nothing.

"What," Lucy said, "is our chance of success if we go Rho?"

"Low nineties," Samael said, looking up. "Closest alternative is seventy percent."

"OK," Lucy glanced around, "Plan Rho it is then." She picked up her gavel.

"Wait," GadZeke leaned in and examined the table. "Am I the voice of reason?"

"It's a nice thought," Rafi said, "this idea that we always have options." She looked at him. "But unless there is something we've missed, it's an idea until you have options."

"Then," GadZeke said, "I guess I am a dreamer."

"Agreed," Lucy said, and she banged the gavel against the table.

Friday, November 10, 2141
4:37 P TST
Engineering Bay Lambda, Headquarters
The Whitespace

Rafi and Ronnie were looking over modifications Zed and Harry had made to Ronnie's bastard sword. The sword had gone from sleek and archaic to turn-of-the-century high tech. Ronnie wondered if she would remember all the distinct functions, or if she even needed half of them.

"Now, here," Rafi was saying, "is a cool function. You can extend a cable from here." Ronnie got queasy again. "You can use it to scale a wall." Ronnie's stomach got worse, and she ran for the washroom. "You can even...Ronnie?"

Rafi saw her head into the washroom, holding her stomach and her mouth. Rafi followed her into the toilet. She recognized the distinctive sound of heaving coming from the closest stall. Rafi walked up to the stall, pushed the door open, and knelt beside Ronnie. She grabbed her hair and pulled it up and away from her face. A second round hit Ronnie, and her face disappeared below the porcelain.

"How long," Rafi reached into her cloak, "have you been getting sick?" She pulled a handkerchief out, offering it to Ronnie. She pulled her head out of the bowl.

Ronnie grabbed the cloth and spit into the bowl before wiping her face.

"Two days," Ronnie said. "I've been sick for at least two days. I'm sorry." She leaned back against the opposite divider of the stall. "I didn't want anyone to worry about me, because I'm fine. It's a little bug."

Rafi half smiled, pitying her.

"Except you've had some unusual cramps," Rafi said. "Your breasts are sore and tender, and you are always tired." Rafi watched for her reaction.

Ronnie's eyes widened. "You think..." Ronnie was unable to finish the thought.

Rafi bit her lip, "let me ask this. When was your last period?"

"I thought that we didn't get those anymore," Ronnie was still in shock.

"Until you ascend, you're still Terran."

Ronnie figured something out.

"But it's been over two hundred years." Her eyes filled with hope. "I would have been pregnant two hundred sixty-five times over by now."

Rafi looked away from her.

She stared into Ronnie's eyes, "to your body, it has been about a month since you died. Time moves depending on where you are and what you're doing."

Rafi could see Ronnie's heart sinking through her eyes. She had to deal with the harsh truth. Ronnie put her head between her knees.

"I assume, that means I am correct." Ronnie met Rafi's gaze.

"Yes. It looks like I am pregnant."

Friday, February 22, 2143
1:46 p.m., TST
Amaze Gardens, Headquarters
The Whitespace

Kay walked along the hedges. Different in type from the bushes in the Labyrinth, rows of endless hollow leaves. The half-pint hedges were short enough to see over; she found her way to Samael.

He turned when she approached, his hands behind his back.

"You wanted to see me, sir," Kay said.

Samael pretended to get stabbed, but for a moment.

"Don't call me sir," he pointed to the bench beside him, showing that she should sit down.

"Sorry," Kay said.

Samael shook his head.

"Don't apologize." Kay sat on the bench, and he sat beside her. Samael put his arm on the back of the bench, crossed his legs, and placed his hat between them. He looked around at the gardens. "A few hours left," he leaned over to Kay, "and it looks like I may have some unwelcome news."

"Get it out."

Samael picked up his hat and fiddled with it, looking out into the gardens.

"I have to bring you out in Russia," he said. "Not Iqaluit, like we've discussed."

Kay straightened up.

"Is everything OK?" She asked, her tone serious.

"Yes, yes," Samael said. "In fact, I'm having David extricated by CSIS, he will be in Canada." He looked back at her, dropping the hat back on the bench. "And it's easier to get him to Iqaluit than Murmansk, you understand."

Kay stared at him for a moment. She wrapped him up in a tight hug.

"Woah," Samael said, laughing. "Whoa, whoa...you OK there, kiddo?"

Kay let go and sat back, wiping her eyes. "I am now," she said. "Sorry, I know it's silly. I worried that he would get lost in transmutation."

Samael smiled and put his hand on hers. "I promise he will be all right," he said, looking off into the distance.

"How can you know that?" Kay asked.

Samael peered deeper into the distance, putting his hands together. Before looking back at her. "The same way I know he told you the truth about his tattoo...and his father."

Kay held his gaze, surprised.

"David said that he had never told anyone about why he got the tattoo, and he didn't tell anyone else here about his father."

"For me," Samael leaned in, "the walls talk here if you're willing to listen." He undid the one hooked button of his jacket and took it off. "You know that he got the tattoo because it was the same one his father had."

"Why are you undressing?"

Samael sighed. He shimmied out of the arms of his jacket.

"Yes, or no," He unbuttoned his shirt.

"Yes," Kay said, an eyebrow raised.

"He also showed it to you, yes?" Samael asked, stopping after unbuttoning his shirt halfway.

"Yes," Kay said. "What's with the striptease?"

"Our tattoos," Samael said, exposing his right chest, "aren't in the same place."

Kay saw it, over his heart. The same strange and unique symbol that she had ever seen on the back of David's calf.

She looked down, "the reason that David's father never came back—"

"Was because I had broken the rules and was being punished for it. It was not because I did not want to." Samael was looking off in the distance again.

Kay bit her lip.

"Samael," she said, and he raised an eyebrow. "There is something that you should know."

"Wait," Samael said, smiling, "let me guess." He put his finger on his head and closed his eyes. "Zavannah, in the basement, with GadZeke. Wait – it's Zeke because he locked Gad up somewhere, since killing him would be too much work. Was it in that ballpark?"

Kay opened her mouth and closed it, unable to process.

"How did you—"

Samael leaned back.

"Harry. He needed help with his whole 'I shot David with a transfer dart' problem." Samael smiled. "I needed information. If it helps, the reason that I needed to get it out of him was that you had them stitched up tight. That code was ingenious."

Kay couldn't help but blush before she went to explain.

"No need," Samael said, holding up a hand. "You had no idea whom to trust with this. You were protecting him. It's not a problem." Samael turned his head, greeting someone. "Aiko," Kay turned to see her standing there, waiting.

"Hey," Kay said.

Aiko looked uncomfortable. "Should I come back?" She asked. "I did not mean to interrupt."

Samael turned, sitting up on the bench. "Nonsense," he said, looking at Kay. "We were finishing up." He looked back at Aiko, reaching into his jacket to pull out a locket on a chain. "I finished it last night." Samael held it out for Aiko, who rushed over, took it, and stared at it in her hand.

"Thank you," Aiko said, looking at Samael and holding the locket. "I don't know how to repay you."

Samael smiled.

"I need no such repayment, but if you want, you can repay me by kicking ass and taking names."

Aiko was confused.

Kay looked at Aiko. "He means, that it would be repayment enough to see you succeed, no?" Kay glanced at Samael.

"You do much and ask for little, Aiko. Consider it a gift."

Aiko squeezed the locket tight. She rushed to Samael and grabbed him around the middle in a big hug. Samael laughed and looked at Kay, who couldn't help but smile.

"Did I miss the memo or something? Is it Hug-a-Samael Day?"

Aiko let go.

"Thanks, Sammie," she said before she turned and headed out of the maze, she stopped. "Are you coming?" She asked Kay.

"Right behind you, hon," Kay said, and Aiko disappeared.

"You should go," Samael said, turning to her, "but before you do, it's safe to say, I keep your secret, you keep mine?"

"How is mine a secret still? People know," Kay said, wondering what the other shoe was.

"Yes," Samael folded his hands, "but David does not know you let him keep sleeping with a traitor for weeks after you found out." The other shoe dropped. "No one, like the other Prims, can know. If you think it's hard to keep him alive now, it would become impossible if they knew."

"I don't like threats."

"If you were a parent," Samael stared off into the distance, "you would understand. You do whatever you have to, to protect your children. Besides, that bad taste in your mouth will fade."

Wednesday, July 27, 2146
1:46 p.m., TST
Cargo Bay, Headquarters
The Whitespace

Hudson was standing, legs spread and arms out. Mica clipped a utility belt to his waist. She added more belts across his midsection and chest. Hanging straps that ran like suspenders over his shoulders. He had small bags and pouches, and they were all strapped to his body.

Hudson was head to toe in aquatic equipment. A suit made of an impermeable membrane. He would need the maneuverability in the water.

"All done," Mica said. She patted him down, "and ready to go."

"Hey," Hudson said, "private property." He feigned disdain.

"Whatever," Mica said, heading over to Slate. She had a diverse set of needs. Hudson surveyed the array of equipment that she needed. "Here," Mica said, handing him a harness, "help me get this on her."

"Hello, Slate," Hudson said. "Do you mind?" He held up the harness, and Slate smirked.

"Always the gentleman," she said and held up an arm. "Please go ahead."

Hudson slipped the harness over her arm and helped her put her head through the hole.

On the other side of the room, Pierre gets into the harness Samael had made for him. Pierre was stuck, arm in the air, head halfway in the hole. Rafi pulled, and he grunted.

"Samael!" Rafi yelled, giving up. Samael looked over from helping Maya and laughed. "It's not funny, Hekate—fix it!"

Samael quieted down. She used his Greek name when she was angry.

"One sec," Samael informed Maya. He walked over to Rafi and Pierre and ran his finger over the side of the harness, his eyes purple. "Dissecarentur." The pieces separated, and Pierre popped free. Samael pulled Pierre's head through the hole and adjusted the harness until it was sitting the right way.

"Consuunt," Samael incanted again, this time moving his fingers down. The straps repaired, allowing Rafi to close the other side. Samael headed back to Maya to help her with her jacket.

"Everyone has their instructions?" Bennett yelled. His outfit was somewhere between the sleek lines of Hudson's and the utilitarian heft of Slate's. He held up a scroll in his hands. "This is the help we can give you. All we know is that thirty-two ships are set to come out of orbit within three minutes of introitus."

"That means," Aiko picked up. "We have three minutes or less to get our bearings, read the instructions, and get into position. We have outdated intel on the areas, you will have to improvise."

"We get one shot at this, girls," Ronnie took over. "Let's make it count, and if you achieve your goal, don't forget there are more ships, help out if you can. None of us can be in two places at once." Ronnie looked at Lucy, who shook her head. "Hold the line if that is all you can do. Help is on the way."

"Anything else?" Bennett asked Aiko and Ronnie. "OK, good fight, and good luck."

Samael walked over to Bennett with the transfer injector and shot the serum into his arm. The dart ejecting sideways and tumbling to the ground.

"Next stop," Samael said, moving to Aiko, whom he injected next, "morning." He smiled. Gabriel had the other gun and was injecting Asher when Samael reached Ronnie. Samael leaned into her, opened a pouch, and slipped a bottle of pills into it before closing the flap.

"All-in-one prenatal," he said in a hushed tone. "One in the morning, since you get sick at night."

She was going to respond, but he injected her, distracting her long enough to move on to the next.

Bennett left by the serum's spell.

"See you on the other—"

The spell enveloped him, and he was gone.

Samael injected everyone but Hayden, whom Samael had saved for last. When the others were gone, Samael turned to the Prims.

"Give us a moment," he said.

"Come," Lucy said, turning to walk out of the cargo bay.

The others followed. Samael turned back to Hayden. They kissed, savouring the moment, and Hayden held out her arm.

"Be careful out there," Samael said over the hiss of the injector and the clink of the dart on the floor.

Hayden smiled.

"Don't worry," she said while running her hands through his hair. "I'll listen to my voice. It hasn't steered me wrong yet."

Samael froze.

"Your voice?" Sam holding her by the arms, staring at her.

"The one that's been giving me instructions," Hayden said. "We all have one that helps us."

Turning frantic, his eyes wild;

"This is important. Did you hear it before you became an acolyte?"

The purple of the spell had overtaken her, but she managed a final word before she disappeared.

"No."

Chapter 9
Reindeer James

Monday, May 17, 2151
10:43 p.m., TST (1:28 a.m. + 1 Day, LAT [Local Area Time])
79km East North East of Granitnyy, Murmansk Oblast
Democratic Republic of Russia, Terra

The traversa serum was not for this purpose. David appeared in the air above outer Granitnyy, about 5,843 meters from the ground. The dart disintegrated, David's trachea snapped back, and he breathed. *Wow*, David thought. He had no idea how beautiful Terra was. The lush green everywhere was mesmerizing.

He remembered what had happened and where he was—or where he was not.

"Fuck you, Harry, this is not what I meant." David sighed, and he realized that a bag had gotten away from him. He vectored toward the bag. He reached out, he rolled over. The rest of the bags flew off that arm.

Great, David thought. *This is going to hurt.* He tried to turn himself around, but he had one free arm, the other clutching his hook swords and the remaining bags. He flailed his arm, to no avail, and gave up on keeping everything. He grabbed the hook swords in his free hand and let go of the bags.

He didn't calibrate for wind resistance. He flipped around. He tried to hold on to both swords. One slipped from his fingers. It dropped out of his hand, the blade slicing through the air faster than David.

The ground was coming up at him faster than he could imagine. The air buffeted him around. He hit terminal velocity. He tried to stay calm. The trees became distinguishable from the blur of green that was the forest.

David closed his eyes to calm his nerves, and he spread his arms, falling through the sky. His body was dropping for the trailing Caucus Mountains. The cold stone surface, smooth and angular, was open and empty. David heard the distinctive clink of metal on stone. One sound, no accompanying clatter of metal.

David opened his eyes to see his other sword stuck by the handle into the stone side of the mountain. The end of the sword stuck straight up. It pierced David's chest. It cut through his heart and killed him, before his entire body turned into muesli.

Pavel Volkova was driving his Wheeler with a grin, his friend Igor held on tight. "Did you have to drag me out here, comrade," Igor said to Pavel.

"Of course, comrade," Pavel said with a thick broken accent. Pavel spoke both English and Russian, but Igor understood English. "Everyone should enjoy the rubber on the ground." He lifted his arm when he said the last part.

"Did you go home with that girl from the bar?" Igor inquired.

"The blonde?" Pavel raised a brow. "No, she found a comrade with a thick skull and a long inseam." Igor shot Pavel a pitying look; Pavel shrugged. "Win some, lose some."

"You're too polite," Igor was saying when Pavel came to a halt, peering over his wheel.

"Iggy!" Pavel said. "That's a body." He put gear in his backpack.

Igor undid his harness and stood in the Jeep, looking over the windshield.

"I call dibs," Igor yelled, "on the sword sticking out of it."

"You can't call dibs," Pavel said, undoing his harness. He opened his door, threw his backpack over his shoulder, and slammed the door shut again. "We are scavengers. It is first come first served, good buddy."

Pavel headed up the embankment, toward David's necrotic corpse. Pavel covered his face with his bandana to mask the stench. Pavel obsessed over the sword sticking out of the ground around the remains of some poor comrade. He was holding a sword like it in what might have been his hand, which looked like a Terran stew left on a few too many hours.

"You are in luck, Igor," Pavel grabbed the clean part of the second sword. He lifted it in the air, shook off the remnants of whoever that had been. "There are two swords." He put the sword down and looked at Igor, who was standing a few feet from the Jeep. "If you are good to me, I may let you have the second one."

"You're too kind, comrade," Igor said, staring off into the distance before he looked back at Pavel. Pavel was pulling tools out of his bag, setting up his gear. "It looks like these are his things over here, I am going to check it out."

"What makes you think it is his gear?" Pavel set a metal plate under the triangle beam that he had placed against the sword and clamped under the hook.

"They are white," Igor said.

Pavel looked at what remained of the guy's clothes. They were all white, even the socks and underwear, the one piece of gear he had, and both swords.

"Makes sense," Pavel removed the old car jack he had for his car, of course, and put it on the metal plate. He put the handle on the jack and pumped. "If you want, go for it, good buddy." The jack hit the plate on the brace, and the resistance increased.

Pavel didn't try to force it. He had made that mistake before and knew how dangerous brute force and ignorance can be. He applied constant and increasing pressure against the handle, and it made progress.

The resistance stopped, and he heard a loud crack. The sword came free of the stone. He unlatched the triangle brace, and the sword was still standing on its own. He collected the rest of his gear and put his pack back on.

David's skeleton, at the skull, assembled and stitched up with white mana. Pavel was too busy looking at the sword.

David gasped. His skull reassembled, he pulled his head up, and Pavel shrieked. Igor looked over and shit his pants. David's neck, and shoulders lifted his putrefied skull.

"Bozhe Moy!" Igor dropped the bags and ran to the truck.

"What's wrong?" David said, happy to know the translator chips worked. "Never seen someone come back to life before?"

Pavel's eye went wide. He scrambled backward onto his feet and fled for the Jeep. Igor was already in the driver's seat, and Pavel tossed him the keys. He jumped in.

David's skeleton had finished forming, allowing him to pick up his swords, left behind in Pavel's haste. He walked toward the Jeep, his decay reversing itself in the process. Igor got the engine to turn over and turned the wheel to the right.

Igor popped it into reverse, let go of the clutch, and went to hit the gas, but stalled instead. He jammed the clutch, left it engaged, and hit the gas. The Jeep spun backward, creating a massive cloud of dust. Igor looked behind him, jamming the clutch and the brake, they stopped a few feet from the edge.

David was whole again. He walked into the cloud of dust, and Igor put it in first. He turned the wheel all the way left. Out of the haze, David appeared a few steps away from the Jeep and was closing the gap. Igor let the clutch go and hit the accelerator.

He didn't see David's sword appear between the windshield and Pavel's head in time. Igor accelerated. Igor cut off his best friend's head. David pulled his arm back, and his sword bounced off the rails.

Igor screamed, his face covered in his friend's blood, and his windshield. Pavel's body kept leaning on him, and he couldn't see through the cloud of dust. He hit a bump, and Pavel's head went from the back of the truck to Pavel's lap.

Igor screamed again, looking at the head. The path disappeared beneath him, invisible due to the dust cloud. The Jeep went shooting off the edge of the mountain and into the open sky. The Jeep landed upside down, crumpling from the force.

David fell to his knees and leaned back, breathing in the fresh air, and enjoying the moment. He glanced around, realizing that he was on the side of some mountain in the middle of nowhere. Something dropped into the pocket of his jeans.

He fished out the small scroll and rolled it open. *Blow Me* written in the middle of the parchment. David sighed and thought he should have held the paper to his face when he did that. He held the scroll up and blew on it, and the ink swirled out and rearranged on the surface. David's DNA was opening the lock on the message.

"Head down the tracks until you see a willow among conifers. Take the path to a cabin in the woods. Wait for James."

James? David thought, looking at the watch that Harry had made him before seeing the year, 2152. *Great*, he thought. *I can wait twelve years.* David walked over to the bags that Igor had dropped, fell to his knees, and rifled through the packs.

Half his gear was there—less since he had had the makings of an XOne F in a side pack. He heaved the backpack over his shoulder, grabbed the other bags.

He turned and headed down the tracks left by the Jeep.

❧⚬❧

He had been walking for twenty minutes when he stopped and put his bags down. He approached a flat ledge. He held his backpack. He walked up to the edge, testing the ground underneath his feet.

The ledge overlooked the far side of the mountain from where he had landed, and David needed a break. He put the backpack on the ground, dangled his legs over the edge. He rifled through the main compartment, looking for a snack.

He grabbed the canteen off the side of the bag, twisted off the lid, leaned his head back, and quenched his thirst. He put the flask down and examined the silver package. It was like the packaging for something without the something. A silver zip pack without any contents.

There was a dot in one corner and the words.

"Press here above and below." The purple label read, "Samael's Safety Squares! Taste like shit, but if you are desperate, you will eat them." David smiled. Samael had a way with words. David pressed on the black dot. The silver package filled with a four-pack of the nutrition bars cut into squares.

He kicked his feet back and forth. He ripped open the package and popped apart the resealable lock. He stared out at the wonder of nature he saw before him and took a bite of the bar. His face screwed up. He spat the bar out and turned over the package.

"Ingredients: Tempeh, Kale, Cabbage, Spirulina, Brussels Sprouts." He stopped reading and threw the bar, plus the package, over the edge.

"I'm not that desperate," David examined the wilderness around him, "yet." He took another drink from the canteen and put it back on the pack. He stood, threw his bag over his shoulder, and went to take a step. The ground gave way underneath him, the section of the edge crumbling beneath him. He thought, *Fuck.*

He was leaning too far back when his foot went out from underneath him. No amount of flailing his arms would stop him from coming down with the backpack.

Trying to hook his leg ended up flipping him end over end. He tumbled down the mountain, hit the rocks, broke his neck, plunged through the air, revived, hit a tree, wash, rinse repeat.

David went off the final edge, flying sideways over the treetops and through the brush. He broke through the wall and window of a small cabin. His body rolled onto the floor, wood and glass sticking out of every part of him.

His body reactivated, and he grabbed the glass shard sticking out of his left eye socket.

David grunted when he moved. Everything hurt. *Why does my neural network still have to work?* But he knew the answer. He grabbed the glass, which cut into his hand. He screamed. The shard popped out of his eye.

David's arm dropped, and his head hit the floor, rolling to the side. He could see the small table in the kitchen section of the room. On the table was a card, standing on its edges, the side facing him said *David.*

"Son of a bitch," David's face finished repairing.

Tuesday, August 30, 2157

3:51 p.m., TST
The Archives, Headquarters
The Whitespace

When Gabriel walked into the archives, he thought a bomb had gone off, and Samael was nowhere.

"Samael?" Gabriel yelled into the chamber, his voice echoing off the walls.

"Gabriel," Samael said from the back of the shelving units. Gabriel walked toward him. "I am at the back."

"What happened?" Gabriel walked through the shelves. He noticed many of the volumes were missing from their places.

"Hayden," Samael said.

"Hayden is on her way to Terra," Gabriel said. "You're not making sense, good buddy."

Gabriel reached the back of the archives. Samael was wild-eyed, his hair a mess, his clothes disheveled. "Hey." Gabriel grabbed his arm and looked him in the face. "Are you OK?"

"No," Samael said. "The Romans are coming."

Gabriel let go of his arm.

"OK," Gabriel said, "now I know you're talking crazy. The Romans disappeared 2,600 years ago, Terran standard."

"Yes," Samael said, going back to his stack of papers. "And we assumed that that would be the last we heard of them. Shake the world like a snow globe and disappear. But what if they didn't go anywhere?"

"Are you suggesting," Gabriel asked, "that the Romans are nonmaterial spectres that have stayed trapped between the whitespace and reality this whole time?"

"Yes," Samael responded.

"Where is this coming from?" Gabriel showed concern for his brother.

Samael looked at him and took a deep breath before sitting down.

"Hayden said that the acolytes were getting instructions from voices in their heads. That first happened after they came back."

Gabriel stared up behind his glassy eyes. His brain went into overdrive. He stopped and looked at Samael.

"You should have come to me," Gabriel said. "You're looking in the *Chronicles of Pythia* for the volume. The one on the transubstantiation of the original Acolytes of the Void, correct?"

Samael nodded, standing. Gabriel spectered, eyes white. He held out his hand.

"Ad crusta," Gabriel incanted. The three hundred thousand volumes of the *Chronicles of Pythia* rose from the floor. Gabriel named them after the first Oracle. Pythia initiated the practice of recording their visions. The tomes shifted in place and moved through the air until they had returned to their rightful spot.

"There," Gabriel said, walking a few shelves deep into the archives. "Cousin would have had a fit."

Samael laughed, calming down.

Gabriel walked into the aisle and, after a moment, re-emerged with a specific volume.

"Volume 143,728, *Transubstantiation*, Chase." Gabriel put the book on the table and opened it to the proper page.

"Problem is," Gabriel said, "it is not the answer you wanted."

Samael looked at the page. It described the state that the Romans were in: a weak, ethereal state. The entry turned to a premonition.

"You knew," Samael said, looking at Gabriel.

"That it was a possibility? Yes." Gabriel said, "that it was happening, hell no. I may be stupid, but not that stupid. This is the point you come clean *before* all hell breaks loose."

Samael looked down.

"Fuck," he said. "How long?"

Gabriel tilted his head back, thinking.

"I would say one tries it by the end of the Atlan attack." He glanced at Samael. "At the earliest."

Samael put his head in his hands.

Friday, March 23, 2159
5:19 p.m., TST (8:19 p.m., LAT)
Outer Granitnyy, Murmansk Oblast
Democratic Republic of Russia, Terra

Like the last man on earth, David sat alone in a room. There was a knock at the door. David froze for a second and moved to the door, picking up a sword on his way. He put his back to the door and grabbed the handle.

"Who is it?" His voice was hoarse from lack of use.

The silence from the other side of the door ended with what sounded like a snort. David lowered his guard and opened the door a crack, peering around the edge. He sighed and opened the door.

On the other side of the door stood a reindeer, strong and majestic. Saddled up, its side pack labelled *James*.

"Took you long enough," David said.

James turned his head and stared at David.

"Yeah," David said, "that's what I thought." James turned his head, no longer looking at David. "Oh, how can I stay mad at a face like that." David grabbed the fur around James's neck and rubbed. "Eh? Buddy."

David opened the side pack and found some equipment and a scroll. He pulled out the parchment. Seeing the telltale "Blow me," he breathed out onto the parchment. The ink rearranged, and the message formed before him. "Take me to Zlata Zdorovetskiy at the Port of Granitnyy. Murmansk Shipping Company, 05864. Follow instructions."

"Super helpful," David tossed the scroll back into the side pack before he closed it. "Hey, James?" James remained stoic. "Strong, silent type. I like that."

David went back into the cabin and collected his gear, having managed to find all his bags over the years. He had duly gone out and retrieved his duffels and even found the two on the far side of the mountain. But, inspecting James, he didn't know how to take all it with him.

James turned and walked down the steps of the porch, and David saw it—a small sled sitting on the ground. It had two arms out in front to attach to James at the back of the saddle. James walked past the side of the sled and stopped and backed up between the sled's attachments.

James kicked his foot, hitting an on-off pad. The electromagnetic locks on the harness engaged. They latched to the saddle and hooked up to the sled. At the same time, the sled lifted off the ground.

"Huh," David said. He sauntered the bags over to where James hooked up and dumped them in the sled before stepping over to James. David rubbed his neck again. "Ready to go, buddy?"

James snorted, and David figured that was a good sign.

David hopped on the saddle. Then, remembering his other sword, David sighed and retrieved it before they left.

It took them under three hours to get to the city limits. The streets were quiet, and the city looked foreign to him, even by conventional standards. Well-designed buildings were all around him, but none of them appeared to have a single window.

A streetlight flickered on in front of them, spurred by motion sensors. Blinded, David held his arm up to his face for a second. He looked at the light floating there in the air, nothing attached to it.

The patter of James's hooves was now a telltale clip-clop. They walked down street after street. The lights turned on ahead of them and off behind them. To David, the city was like a maze.

"You sure you know where you're going?" David joked. James stopped and snorted. "Sorry, checking, good buddy."

James walked again. He knew where he was going.

James brought them to the Port Authority, and David stepped down. David opened the pack and rifled through it, finding the keycard. He brought it to what he assumed was the door and stuck the key card in the console. *ID Scan Required* flashed on the screen in red, and David put his hand on the hand outline in front of him.

It was not a solid, though, but a gel, and he pushed through until his hand was inside the outline on the panel below. Green and red lasers scanned his hand until an affirmative set of beeps and a green light told him he was in.

"Welcome," a woman's voice said, "David Blackstone."

David waited for the door to open. He heard a hiss and a series of clanks. The wall beside him opened like a gate, and James walked in.

"Hey," David said, rushing back to James, "wait for me, eh?" David stopped, seeing a woman standing inside the gates. "Zlata Zdorovetskiy?"

"Da," Zlata said. "You come now." Zlata turned and led them to a ship. "We take reindeer to Nunavut for caribou cross-breeding program." Zlata pointed at a crate. James kicked the switch to release the sled before entering the container.

"You," Zlata said, "get in barrel." She was pointing to a large metal drum that said Reindeer Feed. "We send you with Chames, and no one cares if dead body in reindeer food, OK?"

David hesitated.

"OK?" he managed.

"OK," Zlata confirmed.

David had a familiar pain, and everything faded to black.

Saturday, November 7, 2161

0:37 a.m., TST (8:37 p.m. -1 Day, LAT)
15 km North of the End of the Road to Nowhere
Baffin Island, Nunavut, Canada, Terra

When James and David had landed in Iqaluit over two years ago, he had been in a sealed, airtight drum of reindeer feed for two months. To him, he had woken up from passing out, halfway across the world. David awoke to the muzzle of a C8 GenV and a small squadron of CSIS agents.

"What happened," David had asked the Captain, "to Canadian hospitality?"

The Captain lowered his rifle.

"Sorry, sir," the Captain said. "Captain Lance Gurja." The other agents lowered their rifles. "You can never be too careful." Captain Gurja put his hand out in a fist, and David stared at it. "Oh, right. You don't know handshaking stopped over one hundred years ago. Sir, we favour of the fist bump, to help stop the spread of disease."

"Fist bump?" David looked confused.

Captain Gurja motioned for the Corporal to come over to him. He used her to show him first a formal, standard fist bump. The Captain saw the look in David's eyes and nodded to the Corporal. She nodded back.

"Also," Captain Gurja said, "if you're friends with someone"—he rested his fist against the Corporal's— "you can blow it up." The two of them made explosions with their hands. They retracted them.

David held his fist out to the Captain in amazement.

The agents all turned when they heard a bang from outside the hangers, which made David sad. He heard clicking and saw James.

"It's OK," David said. "It's James. Hey, good buddy!" David tried to get out of the barrel, and, knocking it over, he fell to the floor.

David picked himself up, having taken a hornful of snow to the side of the face. David packed a snowball and rolled over to throw it at the advancing James.

He hit James in the face, washing it with snow. James charged him and scooped him up in his horns, throwing David through the air into a snowbank. He giggled.

James kids dug David out. The juvenile David had named Kenji was a year old now, his nose wet and cold. He found David's face in the snow. Abigail, named for his mother and six months old, she hopped around him. She landed on his side. He grunted.

Kenji hooked him with his antlers and pulled him out of the snowbank. David laughed and crawled forward to grab Kenji in a hug around the neck. Kenji nuzzled into David.

"How about a snack, little buddy?" David asked.

Abigail jumped into his lap.

"I will take that for a yes, little lady." David got up and looked around for James but didn't see him anywhere. James hit him from behind and tossed him in the air.

David landed in the snow. He could do nothing but laugh.

"OK, OK. You too, James."

After they came back to David's cabin—a modern Igloo—David went inside to get some food for James and the kids. He brought out a skillet full of his special reindeer chow.

He put the skillet in the snow. James tested the heat of the food with his tongue and nudged away Kenji and Abigail until it had cooled off. David stuck his finger in the skillet and licked the contents off.

"Ready," David said, and James let the little ones at the skillet, cleaning up what they didn't eat. Like any good single parent, James put his kids first. He had had a beautiful mate, a caribou female that had complimented him.

James had shown up six months before with Kenji and Samantha, the name David had given James's doe, in tow. David knew something was wrong with the way Samantha was breathing. Abigail was in distress, the cord wrapped around her neck.

David did everything he could. He managing to unwrap the cord from around Abigail's neck. He tied the cord into two knots before cutting it with his knife. By the time he got back to her, Samantha had hemorrhaged, and he had no way to stop the bleeding. David had to watch her bleed out in front of his eyes, helpless.

James lay beside her, putting his head next to her. Her breathing slowed, and her eyes closed. James lay with her awhile. David cleaned up Abigail. David must have lost track of time because Abigail stood and walked around in front of him.

That was what brought James back. Since Abigail was unsteady, James stood and helped her figure it out.

He had raised them alone ever since, watching his little family, thankful to have them.

Friday, April 13, 2164
11:47 a.m., TST (7:47 a.m., LAT)
Confederation Pier, South Seawall
Iqaluit, Nunavut, Canada, Terra

David walked down the pier toward the end, carrying his bags. He was ready for introitus, thinking about the others and wondering how they were doing.

David sensed the neck of an agent break, and he dropped his bags. He turned to run back toward the seawall. David keyed his handset. An amphibious assault vehicle popped up in the water beside the dock.

"We have a problem," David said into his handset. The Atlan soldier on the bow fired the rail gun on the front of the ship. "Abort," David said before the rail gun blew up the dock behind him.

David reached the wall and ran over it. The rail gun blew out a large chunk of concrete.

Friday, April 13, 2164
11:55 a.m., TST (9:25 p.m., LAT)
Buckland Park, Near Adelaide
Dominion of Australia, Terra

Jonah materialized in the middle of a field, full of yellow grass and sparse clusters of trees. He unhooked his bags, letting them drop to the ground. He opened a side pouch, fished out the binoculars, and zipped the sack back up.

Jonah put the scope around his neck and looked at the timer on his watch—two and a half minutes. He picked up the bags and headed for the nearest tree.

As he ran, Jonah surveyed the area. From the people picnicking, he to be in some park. From the looks on their faces, he must have seemed like a lunatic, causing him to crouch and move faster.

He reached the tree and dropped the bags, jumped up and grabbed the lower branches. Jonah climbed to the top of the tree. He pulled off his backpack, detached his quarterstaff, and laid it on the branches.

He opened the bag and pulled out a triangle and a small hammer, with which he secured the base to the treetop.

Jonah placed his staff in the triangle, and it stood like a lightning rod. He pulled two metal bars with hooks out of the bag, sticking them into his quarterstaff to step up.

Jonah grabbed the top of the staff and, after testing a step, climbed up. He held on with one hand and looked at his watch. *Eight seconds.*

Jonah lifted the dual scope and waited, scanning the skyline. He saw them materialize, the circle of energy cutting through the surrounding area. When it left, a ship sat in its wake.

The vessel was enormous, visible with the naked eye. But through the scope, Jonah could see it was clear and filled with what appeared to be water. He changed the focus of the range, looking for the power source.

He saw it, through the infrared—a pair of nuclear reactors. Jonah spectered. Using his order magiks, he searched for and found a stray electron inside the reactor.

"We can't have that," Jonah muttered under his breath. He pulled on the electron, putting it into alignment. It bounced another particle off it in the process. A stray particle collided with a proton in the fissionable materials.

The resulting chain reaction turned the nuclear reactors into a pair of atomic bombs. The flames incinerated the first ship. Jonah searched for the other ship, finding it on the opposite side.

He pulled a stray electron back into alignment, setting off the second ship after the first.

Jonah fell backward onto the branches. After a minute, he looked at his wrist, the digital readout flashed:

Singapore, Japan.

Friday, April 13, 2164
11:56 a.m., TST (8:56 a.m., LAT)
Midpoint of Quetrequile and El Cain, Patagonia,
Argentina, USCSA, Terra

The winds were fierce when Harry appeared. He blew sideways, tumbling end over end. "Jesus*fuck*," Harry brandished his gladius and drove it into the ground. He held on. He ground to a halt, gaining his footing. The wind changed direction, but Harry managed to recover.

Harry dug out what looked like an empty tube, two inches in length, and let the air rush through it until it beeped. Harry glanced inside the circle, and *98.4 km/h* flashed in the space. He was going to need his gravpads.

Harry looked at his watch—*One minute and twenty-one seconds*. He unhooked his left side bag and pulled it down until he could reach the gravpads inside. But he hyperextended when he pulled them out, and the bag went flying off into the distance.

Harry stuck the first gravpad on the sole of his right shoe and clicked the switch. He stepped on the pad. His foot anchored to the ground.

Harry stuck the other pad to his remaining foot and engaged it.

The wind changed direction again, and Harry's hand slipped off the handle of his sword. Harry fell forward. His second set of bags flew off in another direction. Harry sighed and looked up. One of the ships appeared in the sky above him.

"Of course," Harry said. "Looks like the hard way." He walked over to the sword and pulled it out of the ground. Harry turned and squared his shoulders to the ship and wound up his sword.

Harry spectered. He wound up, launching the gladius with the forces of his war machine. The gladius flew, accelerating at a rate of 255.96 m/s2.

The blade hit the glass-like surface of the ship, breaking through the material. It embedded up to the hilt.

Harry focused his magiks, channelling them through his sword. The blade erupted with rust smoke. The smoke ate through everything inside the glass sphere and left an empty husk.

The ground beside him exploded. Harry tumbled sideways, and he turned around to see that the other ship had opened fire on him. Ten feet to his left was a crater twice the width and eight feet deep.

Another plasma charge headed for much closer proximity. Harry couldn't escape in his gravpads. He disengaged them and jumped, the wind blowing him out of the blast zone.

Harry reached behind him. The winds knocked him back and to the side, and he called back his gladius. He rolled when he hit the ground. He reengaged his gravpads and grabbed the hilt of his sword.

Harry launched the sword at the second ship and disengaged his gravpads. The wind pulled him out of the way of another plasma blast. The sword flew forward, but this time the ship's lasers deflected it.

Shit, Harry thought. They had him in an awkward position. Harry put his hand on the Excalibur pendant. He closed his eyes, took a deep breath, and, opening his eyes, ripped the necklace off his neck.

The sword grew to full size. Harry latched on to the ground again and wound up.

"Deflect this," Harry yelled. He launched Excalibur at the second ship. The ship hit Excalibur with a plasma blast and every laser it could, to no avail. The sword hit the ship's orb structure with a ping and, after a second, the entire structure shattered.

The ship turned inside out before pieces of it fell from the sky.

"Arma," Harry said. He held out both hands. He sheathed his gladius and twisted the end of Excalibur; it returned to pendant form. He looked at it for a moment.

"Gods forgive me," Harry said, putting the pendant back around his neck. "Portal," he incanted and jumped backward, on to the next battle.

Friday, April 13, 2164
11:57 a.m., TST (2:57 p.m., LAT)
Outskirts of Malham
Kingdom of Saudi Arabia, Terra

Slate appeared in the middle of the desert, dropped her bags, and looked at her watch. *Three minutes.* She blew on the scroll and waited for the ink to rearrange. A schematic of a ship appeared on the parchment. The weak points highlighted and numbered in order of how crippling they were.

She knelt and pulled the three pieces of the XOne-F out of her side bag. Slate looked around, she was near a road, but it was too far away for her to be visible. She was a blurry shadow at best.

She attached the butt of the rifle, interlocking the pieces until they clicked. Slate looked around again, taking a second this time to admire the stark beauty of the landscape. She put the barrel on the XOne-F and clicked it together. She checked her time—more than halfway there.

She turned to the other bag, put the rifle down, pulled out a tripod for the XOne-F, and set it up in front of her. After checking the legs, she twisted a dial at the centre, and the gravity locks bolted it to the ground.

Slate picked up the rifle and clicked it into place. She looked around and saw the dust cloud in the distance. Someone was coming for her, the Saudi government or military, but they would have to wait.

Slate checked her watch and knelt, closing one eye. She looked through the scope and adjusted the focus. The ship dropped out of the Higgs-Boson.

Slate turned and focused the scope until she found what she was looking for, the structural beam end. She fired the rifle and the beam of energy burst forth, but she didn't wait to see her handiwork.

Slate got up, still crouching, and walked around the tripod. Pivoting the rifle, she found the second ship. She adjusted her scope and targeted the support beam, the gun pulsing when she stood.

Slate dropped the end of the rifle, standing tall. She held one hand up to each of the places where she had blown out a chunk of the ship.

"Perdere," Slate incanted. Her midnight mana swirled in each palm. She created a pair of half-torpedoes, half-jellyfish projectiles. They formed and burst forth. They swam like Chinese dragons through the air too fast to track their movements.

They sought out the weaknesses created by Slate's assault. They latched onto the destruction and amplified it. The ship disintegrated. They left nothing behind.

Slate had not seen the outcome of her incantation. Instead, she turned and unclipped the XOne-F in one swift motion. She turned back toward the oncoming fleet of Hummer H2O-G90s. She kicked the tripod out of her way. She dialled the rifle from pulse to laser.

The leading G90 turned sideways and drifted toward Slate. She pulled her cigarettes out of her midnight-blue jeans.

The G9s came to a halt. Slate grabbed a smoke with her mouth. She slid the cigarettes into her jeans and replaced them with her Zippo. The soldiers filed out of their vehicles. They used them for shields and aimed their guns at Slate. She ran the lighter along her leg.

The Zippo ignited. Slate lit the cigarette, inhaling. She squared herself to the soldiers with the rifle pointed at the sky. The Zippo snapped closed, and she pocketed it.

"Who are you?" One of the officers demanded. Slate would have understood Arabic without the translator.

Slate grabbed the cigarette out of her mouth and exhaled a cloud of smoke that seemed to frighten the soldiers. The closest ones pulled out masks with biohazard symbols on them.

"Gwendoline Slate Haverford of Canada," Slate took another puff of her smoke. "What is the problem?" She looked forward and hoped she came off nonchalant. She would hate to have to kill them all.

Friday, April 13, 2164
11:58 a.m., TST (7:58 a.m., LAT)
Lower City
Iqaluit, Nunavut, Canada, Terra

David patted the CSIS agent's body, looking for more clips. He had another pair in a side pouch. David moved on to the next, ejecting and replacing the magazines.

He had traded in his hook swords for the moment. This was more efficient. There had been a squadron of Atlans, 144 soldiers and sixteen officers. He and the few CSIS agents who had survived had taken out all but six.

He had lifted a pair of Colt Double-Nines off a young agent, one he had talked to the day they opened the barrel. Agent Johnston had helped David out of the barrel, and he had later learned that it was his first day on the job. He grabbed the agent's ID.

David had closed his remaining eye before he moved on. His anger was helping, and he ducked behind a column. The leader opened his reticulated automatic rifle.

The plasma bursts destroyed chunks of the column. He ducked to the ground, and a thick cloud of concrete dust obscured his sight. He closed his eyes and listened, tuning his hearing to the frequency of heartbeats.

David dialled in like a radio, and he heard two heartbeats besides his own. There was a second soldier with the Captain, to help him reload. Those things took some finagling. *Shit,* David thought. He would have liked more time.

The rifle clicked and stopped firing, and David took his moment. Turning and aiming at the sound of the heartbeats. He shot both guns twice through the two soldiers' chests and once each in their heads, he hoped.

The sounds of two dead bodies hitting the ground in quick succession told him it didn't matter. He grabbed the biohazard mask off the nearest agent and, holding it to his mouth, set off for the nearest exit. This was not a safe house.

David made it to the bottom floor of the apartment building. He shot one Atlan on the stairs and two more in the lobby. David went out the back.

He opened the door, holding his gun out. He peered into the streets of southern Iqaluit, now empty. David surveyed the road.

David breathed out and stepped into the street, lowering his weapon. He was about to take another step when he heard the distinct sound of a plasma round charging up. David slumped forward. He waited for the soldier to fire. David heard hoofbeats.

"No..." David whispered. He turned to see James charging the last Atlan officer. She turned and fired off a single shot. James headbutted her in the chest.

James hit her with enough momentum to rip her hand off at the wrist strap. It attached to her rifle, which had caught in James's antlers.

The Atlan officer slammed into a concrete column at a forty-degree angle, head first. Her brains scrambled, neck snapped. Blue Atlan blood pooled beneath her.

James collapsed, his own blood gushing from a chunk missing from his flank.

Friday, April 13, 2164
11:59 a.m., TST (1:59 p.m., LAT)
0 MR3, Lobamba, Hhohho Region
Swaziland, African Unionized States, Terra

When Kushia dropped out of the Higgs-Boson, he appeared in the middle of a traffic loop along the MR3. He was between the two sides of the highway. His front faced one interchange lane, behind him the other lane closed off the patch of grass he stood on.

He was across the street from two illuminated signs in front of a driveway that descended to a building. The Potter's Wheel Church, the left-hand sign read. In front of that was a set of highway signs, one for Mbabane and an arrow pointing right. The same direction that the blue circular sign below it pointed, showing the road was one way.

Since all he had was his backpack and his morning stars, he took them off and sat on the grass. He looked back at the church. He read the second illuminated sign, declaring them a Challenge Ministry. Underneath, it said Swaziland.

Africa, Kushia thought. *Always wanted to visit Africa.*

He blew on his scroll; he could read it. Kushia straightened up and crossed his legs, putting his arms on his knees. He counted to three in his head, to clear it.

He was still counting when he sensed the ships drop into Omnispace. The power of the central electromag gravity cores was like wearing orange in the Arctic. It stood out. He realized he did not even have to get up to beat them. He could use their own technology against them, or at least the concept of it.

Kushia opened his crystalline amethyst eyes. He faced away from the two ships.

Kushia moved with deliberate grace. He channelled his spirit magik and the shards inside him. A small model of a ship floated above each of his hands.

The models were of purple and ultraviolet spectrum lights. They had an inverted twinkle, dimming not brightening but with a similar lustre. Kushia turned his hands to the outside of the two models. They stood suspended between his curled fingers.

Kushia flattened his hands. The models vectored for each other. The ships followed.

The models of light collided, collapsing into a single ball. The two ships collided. One of the vessels was off centre; the other ship burst the Hydroxy fuel tanks for the stabilizers.

The ensuing fireball ignited another ball of flames. Each one bigger until the reactors went. The dark-gray spheres of destruction appeared.

The Atlan technology used gravlocks on all their ships. Kushia might not have caught the four landing parties in dropships headed for the ground. They had managed to launch before the explosion and outrun it.

Kushia put his hands down again. The light remodelled into four smaller tetrahedron shapes. Tiny paper airplanes hovering in his hands. He bashed the sides of his hands together, causing the planes to fishtail in the air.

One of the pilots hit the throttle, pushing ahead on the one side. The other dialled it back. They spaced out to stop him from sidewinding them together.

Kushia smiled and made a motion with his hands. Like running them up and around a crystal ball until they met at the top. A circle of light formed.

The ships all rose backwards, toward the gravity well that Kushia had created. He pushed with his hands, and the twirling spirals of light sped up. The magik increased.

The back ship flipped, caught in the vortex, and spun out of control. The pilot passed out from the g-forces. It flew through the cyclone and came back like a boomerang, tumbling into the gravity well.

The next ship fell into the spell. The pilot managed to wrest back control of the vehicle in time. Kushia's eyelids dropped, and his head tilted forward.

The last two ships were tumbling toward the first. One of the pilots managed to hit eject. His plate shield flew off the front of the vessel, and his seat flew out of the gaping hole. Kushia's elbows slumped. His body tilted to the right.

The two trailing ships collided with the first one. The explosion caused the flying pilot's trajectory to shift. The chair tumbled sideways. The altimeter kicked in. The parachute opened. The pilot left the gravity well.

Kushia slumped forward, his hands still together. They pressed forward, and the forces increased. The plate shield curved back toward the centre of the well. The pilot slammed into the gravity well and folded into nothingness.

Kushia shut down and slumped forward into the arms of Pastor Augustine of the Potter's Wheel Church. Augustine had gone for lunch. The driver had stopped to watch the stranger in the sparkling amethyst vest, pants, and hat.

When Pastor Augustine saw him channelling light, she didn't know what to think, but she knew she had to help him. Augustine Mngomezulu paced near the man, who did not notice her. He continued with his ritual.

The man was shutting down, and Augustine knelt in front of him, still afraid to touch him. He shut down. She could not hold back. She scooped him up in her arms.

She looked up at the sky and saw a chunk of a ship, volleyed by the second crash. Heading straight for the man and herself.

She picked him up by the armpits and dragged him toward the edge of the field. She ran. The fireball closed in, and Augustine reached the side of the area and pulled him onto the road.

A truck screeched to a halt but still bumped into Kushia. The driver opened the door and climbed up above the window.

"'Eye," the driver said, "what ta 'ell is ya doin' now? You could 'ave killed someone!"

Pastor Augustine looked at the driver. The meteor became a meteorite with an impact that created a hole in the earth the like the field they had left.

The driver ended up on the other side of the road. Augustine and Kushia slammed to the ground. The driver got up and ran to them.

"'Ere," the driver said. He pulled out his wallet and charged an exchange card. "I'm sorry for 'itting you." He pulled the card out of his com and threw it at the pastor. "But I 'ad nothing to do with dat!" He shouted. He scrambled back into his truck.

The truck backed up and drove around the two of them, accelerating away on the MR3.

Friday, April 13, 2164
12:00 p.m. TST (2:00 p.m., LAT)
Commerzbank Tower Roof, 60547
Frankfurt am Main, Germany, Terra

Avery was standing on the edge of the rooftop. She looked out over Frankfurt. She counted. She stepped off the building and turned to land on Pegi. Avery flew by, patting the side of Pegi.

She had dropped out at the bottom of this building. She had looked up and hoped that there was not a grappling hook in her bag. Avery had opened the bag to see the whole kit, launcher and all, calibrated for 259 meters plus ten. *Jesus*, she had thought, *it was a fucking joke, Samael.* Avery shot the grappling hook onto the roof. She would need somewhere inconspicuous to meet Pegi. Grappling to the roof of the tallest building nearby might have been a joke, but she was also sure it would work.

"Thanks, Pegs," Avery said. She grabbed the reins and pulled her toward the storm clouds she was brewing. Her eyes filled with citrine. The dark clouds moved like a smokescreen over the city. She spurred Pegi. Avery pulled back, and they ascended.

Pegi maintained a slow spiral. She charged into the blackening clouds, and Avery snapped her fingers. The two of them burst out of the top of the shadows, both now covered in armour. The Captain of the far ship halted the launch sequence, and the closest ship launched its vessels.

Avery and Pegi reoriented and vectored toward the two ships. They crossed between both vessels. They descended. Avery leaned back, closed her eyes, and stretched her arms. She pointed her sickles out. She called on the energy in the clouds.

The left ship exploded first, the force of the lightning hitting it with eight hundred gigawatts of power. It became a glorified Roman candle. The right vessel exploded. Pegi crossed its primary axis. Avery's riding helm shielded her face. Pegi exited the blast.

They turned and climbed toward the ships, but Pegi was reaching peak altitude. There were not enough molecules per cubic meter of air for her to float, let alone rise.

Avery put Pegi in a holding pattern, calming her down. They glided around.

Avery hooked one sickle back on her belt, "time for plan beta." Avery threw the other sickle into the air with a twist. It flipped end over end until she caught it in her hand, and let it spin for a few more rotations before she stopped it.

She wound up and threw the sickle at the speed of sound. She watched it sail into the closer ship. The ship exploded, and two bolts of lightning turned it into a fireball in under a second. The sickle flew out of the inferno. It bounced off the hull of the first ship before it blew and tumbled into the shell of the second ship.

The far ship blew up when the combined 1,500 gigawatts hit it. Engulfing the entire vessel in flames. At the same time, the sickle bounced off the hull and vectored back at Avery. Avery caught the sickle by the handle and looked at her watch, it flashed:

Sapporo, Japan.

Friday, April 13, 2164
12:01 p.m. TST (8:01 pm, LAT)
Double Helix Bridge
Singapore, Terra

Designed in the millennium to resemble the structure of DNA, Singapore's Helix Bridge was a marvel of architecture. It's successor, the Double Helix Bridge, was even more intricate and detailed. To the point where the crossbeams were close enough together to stand on.

Ronnie lurched out of the spell and into the dead air a half-foot above the bridge.

"Shit," she said. She fell onto the top of the bridge's structure, her gear making her unbalanced. She slid to one side on the dome, struggling to keep from going over the edge. She pulled out a javelin and stuck it into a crook in the design.

Ronnie stopped, hanging off the side of the dome. She lifted her wrist to see her counter: "14 secs." Ronnie laughed and deflated, waiting out the counter and trying to regroup. When she tried to grab her XOne F, her duffel fell into the water. er weight shifted. Her arm sliding into the hole of the dome.

Two ships dropped out of the Higgs-Boson.

Ronnie grabbed for her XOne F and pulled it out of the holster. Realizing she would need both hands, she glanced at the traffic whizzing by beneath her. Ronnie wondered how big the fine was for letting go. If the let go, she could fire the Fragmentary; she would fall through the dome or into the water.

She let go.

Ronnie didn't have time to think about what was going to happen to her bag. She grabbed the XOne F and pushed off the dome. She sailed through the air. She aimed at the first ship. Ronnie fired, and the kickback threw her towards the water. She splashed down. She pulled the trigger a second time, aiming for the second ship.

Ronnie became disoriented. The icy water hit her. She lost hold of her weapon. She thrashed around, trying to right herself.

A force grabbed her and pulled her out of the water.

Ronnie sputtered and coughed. She cleared her eyes to see Jonah standing on the top of the bridge. His eyes were full of malachite. He manipulated her body.

A crimson portal appeared next to Jonah, and Aiko stepped out and into Jonah. She knocked into him, and he lost his concentration, dropping Ronnie back into the water.

Ronnie floundered again but managed to pop up out of the water.

"Girls," she yelled at Jonah and Aiko. They managed to balance on the beams of the bridge. Jonah held his hand back out and lifted Ronnie out of the water.

"Fuck me," Jonah lifted her, his lack of balance making it difficult.

"No," Aiko retorted, and Jonah doubled over, Ronnie fluttered in the air.

"Thanks for that," Jonah composed himself. He dropped Ronnie beside Aiko.

Friday, April 13, 2164
12:02 p.m. TST
Nouadhibou Autonomous Port
Nouadhibou, Mauritania, Terra

Maya slipped out of the portal. She stepped onto the sidewalk of the Port District and examined her surroundings.

Three buildings over, Rafi closed the curtains and sat in front of her workstation. She turned on the camera and sensor array and flipped an hourglass. She had a little more than 5 minutes until the authorities were on her for the vast assortment of concentrated surveillance.

❧

Outside, Maya walked tall and confident through the empty streets of the Nouadhibou Port. Confidence dripped off her. Maya halted. She stared directly at the building holding Rafi's setup for a moment. Maya turned and walked forward. Two ships dropped out of *Interspace*.

Maya stopped again and held out her hand. A cloud of purple smoke rolled in. An amethyst ball dropped into her hand. The cloud dissipated.

Maya's eyes filled with purple light.

❧

Rafi had stalled out from the shock. She had never seen anyone, but Gabriel, use the fifth type of magic or *Worship*.

The only part of *Gabriel's Daemonology* she remembered was the warning label: Demon Worship causes hallucinations, drowsiness, muscle spasms, tremor, dry mouth, blurring of vision, nausea, headache, nervousness, dysphoria, loss of appetite, sleep problems, mood swings, Parallel Lock Syndrome, mana drain, mystical disarticulation, spontaneous maximum entropy, horizontal deplaning, and death.

Rafi watched the video feed. Maya's eyes shone like two small flashlights. She wondered how the Sorceress had even discovered magik like worship. Rafi thought about how Maya had switched from afraid to capable to fast, too many times. About her attitude at times.

Maya had been playing the long con. Rafi watched. Maya summoned a demon from the Omegaverse. Maya's magik drawing a tyrian pentagram in the sky filled with ancient runes.

The demon ripped through the fabric of space and time like a dog through a shoji door. It's black-skinned arm, and moon-sized hand reached out of the nothingness and grabbed the nearest ship. A second pentagram formed in the sky. Rafi noticed that Maya was summoning a third demon. She stood and turned away from the portal she was conjuring.

The Etherverse demon Maya summoned third was human-sized and wrapped its hand around Rafi's throat. The beast opened its mouth, and Rafi's eyes went wide. It poured itself into her mouth.

The last of the eerie blue light flowed into Rafi's body, and she closed her mouth, her eyes still lit in the blue glow.

Rafi blinked. Her eyes returned to normal. She sat and dismantled her setup, piece by piece.

Chapter 10
Trap in the Face

Monday, November 12th, 2164
3:27 a.m. TST
Denny Abbey, Cambridgeshire
Camelot, Kingdom of Eireann

Gadreel walked into the large chamber, glanced up at the vaulted ceiling, and the two rows of men before him. The rows leading up the central hooded figure in plain brown robes. The knights beside him in various forms from gilded armour to handsewn robes.

Gad stopped ten metres from the man in the hood and waited.

"To what," Hood said, "do I owe the pleasure?" Gad smiled.

"I thought I would offer my congratulations," Gad said, "on a job well done," Gad took a few steps back and forth. "Few men can say they orchestrated the fall of their entire pantheon at once. I hear you even managed to track down your Pandora and imprison her."

"What do you want, trickster?" Hood wasn't interested in the bait, "I have things to attend to."

"I came to warn you about a problem," Gad added a flourish, "you're about to have."

"Let me guess," Hood asked, "you came to offer a solution?"

Gad continued, "I could think up a few options if you insist."

"Not interested," Hood dismissed him, "thank you for your time."

Gad turned to walk away. Hood stood. "That's it? No fighting me?"

"If you don't want to know what happened to your sister," Gad took a step. "That's none of my business."

"Morgan? What has this got to do with her?" Hood inspected his men, but they were useless.

"About that problem you are going to have." Gad took a few steps toward the man.

Friday, April 13, 2164

12:03 P TST (8:03 a.m., LAT)
Lower City
Iqaluit, Nunavut, Canada, Terra

David stood in shock, his hands and forearms covered in James's blood. He sauntered like a zombie down the street. Topless, he had ripped off his shirt and applied pressure, but his efforts were futile.

He sensed it. He watched James bleed out, he closed James's eyes and rose, shaking. He stepped over the body.

Something inside David broke or instead clicked. The voice inside him protested.

"Sorry, Pluto," David said to the voice in his head, having learned her name at some point. "It's first come, first served."

❧

The 'hydro gene' a drunken Gabriel had called it during his tricky explanation. After making him stay behind, Gabriel had outlined how every acolyte had the Hydro Gene. A leftover from when the gods had borne half-Terran children. Demigods that had integrated into society after the fall of the Titans and the rise of the Prims.

Hydros, the Titan of origin waters, was the most prolific among them. Two out of every five carriers of the C9orf158 gene, or the Hydro Gene, is a descendant of Hydros.

The Hydro Gene shows an indelible link to the gods and marks candidates for acolytes.

The purpose of the acolytes, Gabriel explained, was to transcend and form a new set of gods to replace them. No one was successful yet at overthrowing these new *Primum Immortales*.

Gabriel handed him the communicator and asked David what he saw before him.

"A hunk of metal."

"You...going to keep joking?" Gabriel managed.

Sighing, David looked down until he realized the underlying truth.

"Progress?" David asked, and he assumed that whatever Gabriel had said meant yes. Gabriel stopped him and waited for someone else to contact the Universe. He had not needed David to break the treaty.

Terrans will break their own laws and turn on their own principles, given enough rope. Gabriel had chosen him; he was the best hope for the future. And until now, David had not given it much thought.

❧

The landing parties filed out of the assault vehicles. They were crashing into the ground all around David. He found transcendence came through love, and let it take him over.

Armed soldiers filed toward him from every angle. He spread his arms and rose.

"I am David." His voice boomed. White mana swirled around him. He glowed with the power of his shards. His hair turned white, beard and all. "God of Death."

His words echoed. His face became a skull. His mandible lowered. David sucked in and ripped the souls from the soldiers. David left one officer in the landing squadron.

David rose further and faced the two ships looming in the distance. He used the Automata spell on the Atlans still in the vessels. The officer made his way to behind David where he floated. David dropped down and landed on the street with a small thud. When he stood straight, the Atlan officer put him in a chokehold.

David was confused:

"I thought you were here to kill me," he gargled. The officer increased the pressure.

"Orders are to take you alive," the officer said.

"This is a sixteen-person kidnapping attempt?" David gurgled.

"No sir," the officer said. "One."

David raised an eyebrow, another piece of the puzzle falling into place.

"Guess," David said. He elbowed the Atlan in the stomach. He let go. "I have to do everything myself since you can't even kill me."

David grabbed his own chin in one hand and the opposite side of the back of his head with the other. Smiling at the officer, David broke his own neck. David's Automata spell mimicked the motion with the heads of every Atlan on either ship.

"This is Corporal Diaphones," the officer said into his wrist com. "We have a problem down below." He waited for a response, David's head turned back, and he stood.

"There is no one to answer," David said, standing up and looking at the officer. He held one arm out. "You are the last left." One of David's hook swords flew into his hand.

David used the momentum. He sliced through the officer sideways. His arms dropped to the ground.

"Asshole," David heard a radio key, coming from around the seawall. David knew he was too far away for that to be natural.

"Are you going to get that?" It was Pluto's distinctive voice, but it was coming from the soldier, the one he had met the day he had arrived in Nunavut.

"Found a carrier of the Hydro gene, eh?" David said. "You're hard to get rid of."

"Thanks," Pluto said. "But if you will stop playing murder, death, kill," David didn't like how much he liked how Pluto said that. "Who is on the other end of the walkie?"

"I don't know, find out." David walked toward the seawall. Pluto, arms crossed, leaned against the concrete wall, his shoulder and legs crossed. "You going to come with?"

"Nothing better to do." Pluto walked with effortless grace. David kept going. The soldier's body was much taller than David, and Pluto caught up with David fast. "I have to hand it to you," Pluto said. He matched strides with David and looked at him, "would not have pegged you for the first one to go."

"Thanks?" David said, unsure if Pluto offended him.

"Oh no," Pluto protested. "Don't get me wrong. It's not that I don't believe you should be a god. We need all we can get." They kept walking down the street, side by side. "But the elements of death, if you will—we stay somewhere in the back half of the pack."

"And I ran to the front in your thinking?" David asked.

"It's a bold move, and it does put a large target on your back." Pluto sped up. "This is taking forever," David hustled to keep in time.

"Does that body you're in have a name?" David asked, wanting to change the subject, "or should I call you Stretch?"

"You may call me Pluto," he said. "That will suffice." Pluto kept walking forward, and David couldn't leave it alone.

"Come on," David said. "What is this poor sucker's name?" He had stopped walking, and when Pluto stopped, David noticed that the name tag wasn't on the uniform of the soldier. "What could it be that I can't handle? Tell me the poor guy's name."

"Can I at least register my protestation of this?" Pluto asked. "Because I got my hands on his body after he was gone. There's nothing of him left in here, this is all I have." He stepped toward David and handed him the name tag.

"Noted," David said, taking the name tag from Pluto before he continued. He glanced at the label and found that Pluto had come to his realization. David would instead call him Pluto than refer to him by the last name of the deceased corporal: *James*.

David let the tag fall to the ground and caught up to Pluto. They walked in silence for a moment before David broke it with an inane comment. They deliberated. They headed for the constant clicking of the handset keying.

They reached the seawall. David rushed over to the remnants of a bag. He looked for the handset in the rubble. David realized that the mic and speaker were out of the housing. In fact, everything was; it was innards and no casing.

David found the button for the mic, or more its wires, and keyed the rubble twice.

"Hello, over," Mica's voice came from the speaker.

"Mica. Go for David. Over," David said.

"David." Mica's voice came out of the speakers. "I assume that you girls have destroyed the ships. Over."

"I killed the entire crew of my two ships, but the vessels are fine," David said. "But given how long it's been, I would assume most of them are gone, yes. Over."

"It was a setup," Mica said with a pause. "Over."

"What do you mean it was a setup? Over," David demanded of Pluto.

"You know how they're coming in eight months, and we thought this was their shot across our bow? I guess the Empress found a reason for them to go to war. We destroyed thirty-two of their hospital ships that she says were an act of goodwill, gods know why. Over."

"I'm sorry; *Hospital ships?* They tried to kill me and take me hostage." David's anger was bubbling inside him. "And they were in hospital ships. She wanted a good shot for her ad campaign?" David breathed for a moment. "Over."

"Umm," Mica's voice came through the speaker, and then silence.

"Yeah, that about sums it up. Over."

David smashed the remaining pieces of the walkie with his bare hands. He screamed and threw them against the seawall.

"Better?" Pluto asked.

"Little bit," David's breathing was slowing down. Pluto helped him up.

"Where to next?" Pluto asked, and David looked at his watch. It flashed:

Sapporo, Japan.

Friday, April 13, 2164
12:35 P TST (9:35 p.m., LAT)
5 Chome Kita 8 Jonishi, Kita-Ku, Sapporo-Shi, Hokkaidō 060-0808
Japan, Terra

Stepping out of the portal from Nunavut was like stepping out of the wilderness. Civilization was in utter chaos. David grabbed Pluto and headed for the blasted-out doors of the university hospital. Hayden stood alone in the middle of the street, outside the building. She fended off the advancing waves. A dance set to music you couldn't hear.

She wielded her fans like extensions of her hands, daggers flying out of the folds. She opened and closed them, batting back plasma fire and bullets alike.

David and Pluto ran inside the building. David followed Pluto up the motionless escalator. They saw Aiko, Pierre, and Ronnie kneeling behind a chesterfield. They delivered suppression fire to their flanks and forward position.

Hudson was trying to get information out of a catatonic Zavannah. She kept repeating the same answers over and over in a monotone and dry voice. Not hollow, like the oracle. This was despair at its finest, and she registered David's presence.

"Vannah," David knelt beside her and held her face. And for the first time since he had known her, she was fragile.

"I want to change their intention, stop them from attacking." Zavannah bore into him with empty eyes.

"What is she talking about?" David asked Harry, who had picked up a pump-action shotgun with a modified scope.

"She tried to use the Oracle," Harry said, firing and reloading, "to show them that if they fought they would die. She thought they would turn around or something. Instead, they went berserk. They even turned on each other."

"Here," David said to Pluto, "watch her." David stood and grabbed Harry by the arm, pulling Harry with him.

"Where are we going?" Harry asked.

"You're going to grab Hayden," David walked for the blown-out windows. He pushed Harry back the way they had entered. "I'm going to finish this." David ran through a busted-out window and landed on the street. He kept going toward the alley ahead.

David ran up the side of one building and pushed off. Using the walls, he scaled the taller building and landed on the roof. David spectered, searching for the souls of the Atlan soldiers. His face turned skeletal again. He lowered his mandible and inhaled, sucking the souls out of the remaining soldiers.

The sounds of gunfire stopped. David looked around the smoke and the rubble, and all he saw was calm. Sapporo's emergency services and citizens were to stay away. The military had converged on the city. A chopper hung in the air a few feet from his face, and someone yelled into the speakers.

"Freeze, you are under arrest," the soldier commanded. The Japanese filtered out by the translator chip.

David put his hands on the back of his head and got on his knees. Two officers jumped from the helicopter and grabbed David. They slammed him to the ground and cuffed him. The two of them threw him on the floor of the plane.

Back at the university hospital, Harry and Hayden were caught by surprise and had no time to warn the others. Pluto had been around the block once or twice before. She knew that the military would take control of the situation.

"Zavannah, is it?" Pluto asked.

"Yes," Zavannah said.

"Is everyone here? Is there anyone else?" Pluto asked, looking at her.

"Kushia has not arrived yet," Zavannah said, her eyes still empty.

"Anyone know where Kushia is?" Pluto yelled. The Japanese military came up the steps.

"Lobamba, Swaziland," Aiko said.

But Pluto had already grabbed Hudson and Zavannah. White smoke swirled out, and they disappeared. The remaining Acolytes put up their hands and surrendered to the Japanese forces.

The Japanese cuffed them and brought them into custody. They military hog-tied and dragged them to the nearest military establishment. The Japanese tossed them into a dark room, alone. Jonah was thankful they had at least undone the cuffs.

He got up and nursed his wrists. Looking around, he saw that something was off about this room. He was in some janitorial closet—a dirty one. He twiddled his fingers, his eyes filled with malachite; Jonah cleaned up the room to calm his nerves.

The objects moved in their places. They shook off the layers of dust, which collected themselves into piles on the floor. The last of the last of the toilet paper rolls bounced into place. The dirt and other assorted refuse walked itself into the swinging lid of the garbage bin near the door. Jonah was relieved.

A room like this at a military establishment meant that they were in various parts of the base. They had not prepared for this.

Jonah had to respect the way in which the military was responding—because of how they worked together. Because you couldn't help but appreciate someone who gets the drop on you. Jonah wished the soldiers thought they were friends, not enemies. *It would make this a whole lot easier;* Jonah snapped his fingers and the door unlocked.

Jonah opened the door and heard the clicks of several soldiers' rifles. He stepped out. He was holding his hands up. He strolled into the adjoining room. He was in a hangar bay, an inactive one.

"Get back in the room, now," the soldiers yelled at him. The soldier stepped forward and motioned with his gun for Jonah to get back in the room.

Jonah looked at the soldier.

"I am not your enemy," Jonah said. And then, with two left fingers, he made a scooping motion. All the soldiers' guns pulled forward out of their hands. "You have nothing to fear from me." The firearms disassembled themselves. The pieces rearranged themselves until they were in size order on the floor.

"Enough," the General arrived on the scene. "Seize him. I'll interrogate him myself."

Jonah put his hands behind his head and knelt. The soldiers patted him down before putting his arms behind his back and walking him out of the hangar. The General lead the way into the main building.

They strolled down endless halls until they reached a junction. Another General escorted David to the same interrogation room. David looked at his General, bowing his head. David walked over to Jonah's General and bent again, the General nodding back.

"What are you doing here?" David asked Jonah.

"I was going to put things back in order," Jonah asserted. "Everything is out of balance." David smirked at him.

"It's all good now," he said. "Being the god of death has few perks but knowing where the bodies are is one." David looked at his General and back at Jonah. "And I mean that this interaction is hush-hush." Jonah stared at David.

"Mum's the word?" Jonah said.

David punched him in the shoulder.

"Much obliged, good buddy."

"What next?" Jonah's General motioned to the guards holding him, and they let go.

"I know," David walked him down the hall, "of a machine that flies through the air." David put his arm out ahead of them.

"You know," Jonah said, "all this power has made you an asshole."

David smiled at him.

"Don't worry; you'll get there." David winked at Jonah. "I guarantee it."

Thursday, April 13, 2164
6:07 Þ TST (9:07 p.m., LAT)
0 MR3, Lobamba, Hhohho Region
Swaziland, African Unionized States, Terra

Hudson, Pluto, and Zavannah followed hordes of people headed to the Potter's Wheel Church. They called for the heads of the blasphemers. Hudson motioned to the back of the building, where there was no one. The other two followed him through the crowd.

Hudson jumped down from the top of the driveway to the back of the church. Zavannah and Pluto jumped down behind him. The back door of the church opened, and a congregant exited, lighting up a cigarette. The woman dialled her holocom, and a hologram of another woman lit up above her wrist.

"Hey, Mum, checking in like I promised. How are you and Dad?" The girl said.

The hologram flickered while the woman's image moved and responded like the real person.

"Your father is angry with the neighbour again, and he swears it has nothing to do with him being a Texan." The woman laughed. "But that's life here in Missouri. How's the mission?"

"Other than their love of electrocrusifiction, great." The girl's smile faded.

"Is that why you're outside smoking and holochatting with me? To avoid your duty to defend our values?" The mother went akimbo, staring her daughter down.

"Fine, Mother," the daughter said. "But don't say I never listen to you." She put her cigarette out. "OK? Love you," her mother blew her a kiss. She turned off the holocom and opened the door to re-enter the church. One of Zavannah's chakrams lodged itself between the door and the jamb.

Hudson looked at Pluto, who nodded and at Zavannah, who followed suit.

Hudson ran to the door and opened it wide. Pluto and Zavannah prepared should anyone exit the building. Hudson inspected the doorway and motioned for the other two to follow him inside. The three of them entered the back of the church, heading for the main altar.

He peeled back the curtains of the side entrance to the altar. It was like something out of a fantasy novel from the turn of his century. In the middle of the platform was a minister of some kind. The man wore white robes and had a microphone headset.

On either side of him was a cross, from each of which a crucified body hung. One of them was Kushia, and the other was a woman he had never seen before. Zavannah pushed past Hudson.

"And we 'ave being too patient with da so-called 'new tinkers.'" The minister was whipping the crowd up into a frenzy. "Dey say dat dese new tinkers are preaching caution and dat day does not know betta." He looked around the still room. Zavannah stopped, unable to continue concealed.

"You want to know what I tink?" The minister asked, and the crowd shouted affirmatives back at him. "They know what they do." The crowd screamed with him. He pointed to the woman, and she stood up by a strap around her neck. "Do you deny saying you saw a god come to life?"

"I saw," she gurgled, but the strap was too tight. Pastor Augustine couldn't talk. The minister motioned with his hands, and they loosened the strap. "I saw this man save us from two warships." Augustine lowered her head. "Two alien warships, and he did this using purple light. I won't lie."

"And yet you do," the minister said, and he gave the signal.

"You aren't even from this church."

A copper spike drove through the pastor's chest on the far side from them, piercing her heart and the copper foil, and sending one thousand amps straight through her heart.

Kushia was still unconscious. Zavannah lost her ability to deal, and she charged at the minister. Zavannah threw her arms out. The minister's head was between her hands, her eyes spectered.

"Posterus," Zavannah incanted, and the word hit the minister like a punch in the face. He saw the future, saw everything that Kushia would do, and knew that he was a god. The minister fell to his knees, the visions cleared, and he turned to Zavannah.

"Goddess," the minister pointed to Zavannah. "Goddess." He reached toward her, and she pulled her arms back.

The crowd screamed:

"Witch!" "Blasphemy!" "The devil!" Zavannah lifted her leg.

"I am no goddess," Zavannah put her foot on the minister's chest, "of yours." She kicked the minister into the bloodthirsty crowd he had created. She turned to the cross Kushia was on.

She ignored the screams of the minister. She untied Kushia.

"Are you two going to stare?"

Hudson rushed forward and untied the straps, and Pluto snapped to action.

"Here," Pluto said, holding out his hands they could each grab one, completing the circle with Kushia's hands. Pluto transmuted them out of there.

Friday, April 13, 2164
7:23 p.m. TST (2:23 a.m. + 1 Day, LAT)
De Havilland Bombardier Elite Wingless Dual, RR EI-R244
Cambodian Airspace, Terra

David bartered for their freedom. An alliance with the Japanese government to provide them with their Spirit Technology. A plane to take them where they needed to go, he underestimated Japanese hospitality.

He had refused the proper number of times when the Emperor offered extra aid. He accepted the members of the Imperial Guard to go with them in the end.

The dilemma was that he painted himself into a sharp corner. He hoped he could give the Emperor something he would find respectful. That was why he hesitated to touch him but explained that his gift was a vision. He hoped he wouldn't offend the Emperor.

The Emperor leaned forward. David touched his forehead. He inhaled when David did. The Emperor's eyes rolled into the back of his head for a second, and David let go. He had allowed the Emperor to see something he wanted—he had talked to his daughter again.

A single tear fell down the Emperor's cheek. He thanked David for the gift.

"Your gift humbles me," the Emperor said. He bowed to David, who returned the bow and bid him farewell.

Looking at the guards now, he wondered if he had made a mistake.

The other four acolytes appeared out of thin air. The guards moved with lightning precision to surround them.

"Hold on, it's okay," David said, "they are with us."

The guards lowered their weapons and returned to their posts. Asher jumped up to tend to the unconscious Kushia.

"What happened?" Asher was asking. He lay him down on the floor. He checked his vitals. "Pulse is thready. He's hanging on. Any idea how long he's been like this?"

"No clue," Hudson said. "By the time we got to him, he hung from a crucifix and next in line for an electrode spike through the heart." Hudson shivered at the thought. "It's possible anything happened to him between."

The story sounded ridiculous, but it was because it was Hudson speaking that it rang true.

"Integro," Asher put his hand on Kushia's neck to increase the effectiveness of the spell. Black swirls ran over his skin.

Kushia came back to them with a gasp. Asher pulled out a flashlight and pulled down Kushia's left eyelid. Asher did a dilation check on his pupils, all three points equal and responsive. He held up the now-off flashlight.

"Follow the centre, please." Asher tracked Kushia's eye movements. He moved the flashlight back and forth. He put the light away and held up two fingers.

"How many fingers?" Asher asked.

"Fuck off?" Kushia said.

"How many fingers?" Asher said again.

"Two," Kushia said. Asher changed his fingers. "Three," Kushia said, and Asher changed them again. "One."

"Good," Asher said. "I'm keeping my eye on the situation regardless, but you seem to be OK."

"No shit, Doc," Kushia said. "How big is the bill?"

"And back to your old spirits," Asher said, getting up. "That's also good news." Asher pulled Kushia up.

"Why don't you take a break?" Ronnie asked. "You should lie down. The seats become beds." She motioned Kushia over to the front by Aiko. She went past him and over to where David, Pluto, and Hudson now stood in a huddle. Zavannah walked past her, and Ronnie bumped into her.

"Sorry," Zavannah said.

"Excuse me," Ronnie said, and then, in the Canadian custom, the two women continued without a glance.

"Have you tried Mimir?" Pluto suggested, and David looked puzzled.

"Mimir," Ronnie walked into the empty space and glanced around. "Norse god of wisdom. The Rememberer. He's my patron."

David looked at her for a second.

"The guy that took Odin's eye?" David said. "How will he be able to help us?"

Pluto looked at David. *Naïve.*

"Something here is off," Pluto said. "Or am I the only one who sees it?" The looks coming back to him from David, Hudson, and Ronnie said he wasn't. "If you can barter with Mimir, he can answer any question for you."

"But doesn't he work off bartering items of equal value? Odin went to him and lost an eye. Anyone have a spare they can lose?"

David's joke did not land.

"Yet, Harry does have an object he may want." Pluto stared at Harry, down the way.

"Excalibur?" Hudson asked, and Pluto nodded.

"What would Mimir want," Ronnie gazed at Harry and back at Pluto, "in a sword he can't wield?"

"Ah," Pluto said. "The value of something does not always lie in what you can do with it. Sometimes it's what others can't." He turned to Ronnie. "Harry used Excalibur, right? Yet the curse has not taken hold.

"Something would have happened by now, but there is one explanation." He was staring through Harry now. "That boy is already cursed. Can't curse the cursed. The first rule of hexes."

David, Hudson, and Ronnie exchanged looks. It made sense. Harry had a way of finding himself in compromising situations. He was always behind the latest snafu.

"You're saying that Harry can wield Excalibur, and Mimir wants to keep him from doing so?" Ronnie said.

"Would you not?" Pluto said. "Being able to wield it makes it more dangerous for him."

"Wait," David said. "You want us to all pickup and head over to Mimir and hope we're back in time?"

"No, no," Pluto said. "There's far too much to do here. And, Harry is needed for the trade. I can take him."

David looked at Pluto, wondering if this was a trick. "What do you get out of this?" David asked, wary.

"There is this business of the rest of my team. And since we got me out in one piece"— Pluto batted his eyes at David. "I figured if I get Harry back safe and sound, you make sure that we get a chance to hop out before anyone else transcends."

"Of course, you do," David said. "Fine, but he has to make it back before the Atlans do."

"Deal," Pluto said.

"I'll inform the Captain," David said, "that we have a new destination."

Saturday, April 14, 2164
10:42 A TST (5:42 a.m., LAT)
1000 Airport Parkway Private
Ottawa, Ontario, Canada, Terra

The wingless touched down on the cold tarmac with a screech, and Aiko let go of her armrests. Air travel had been scary enough in the 1930s, and those planes had wings. Hudson was across from her, grinning from ear to ear, and had been for most of the flight.

Beyond the fence, people packed tighter than Aiko had ever seen them. *Are they here for us, or because of us?* Aiko thought. She undid her harness.

"Sport," Hudson said to Aiko. He jumped up, "ready to meet your fans?" Hudson held his hand out, but Aiko looked at him and down at her hands.

"What if they don't like me?" Aiko said to Hudson. "All those people out there?"

Hudson chortled and laughed. He took a moment to compose himself.

"Sorry to laugh," Hudson said, "but that's funny." He put his hand out again, smiling at her this time. "The idea of someone not liking you."

Aiko took his hand, and they headed for the front of the plane, queuing up. The crew opened the door.

The sound of the screaming crowds burst through the opening. Avery turned around and smiled, "I'm a Beatle."

"Why," Aiko said back to her, "are you smiling about being a bug?"

Saturday, April 14, 2164
11:16 A TST (6:16 a.m., LAT)
Rideau Hall, 1 Sussex Drive
Ottawa, Ontario, Canada, Terra

Clandestine meetings at the hall were in the Pauline Vanier Room or the other drawing rooms in the Monck Wing. The ballroom was a bit open and had too many points of entry for security's liking, and Jonah couldn't disagree.

Fifteen acolytes and eight imperial guards make for a large party in and of itself. The guest list for this meeting to include a who's who of foreign dignitaries. The presidents of the Americas to the crowned Queen Elizabeth IV.

Every security agency was on top of one another in any space they could find, including the broom closet. One could understand caution, but at this point, the security officers were in the most danger.

They sat behind a table, some water for them and microphones. The officials sat in rows opposite them, like an audience at a children's play.

Jonah spoke into the translucent plastic ring about an inch in diameter they said was a microphone. He cleared his throat and took a sip of water. "We would like to convey our gratitude to each of you for being able to accommodate us on such short notice. We also express our sincerest apologies on behalf of Harold Pennywhistle.

"He was, unfortunately, needed elsewhere," Jonah continued. "He will be unable to attend today. We are taking a moment of silence for the Canadian agents, technicians, and civilians lost. We regret we couldn't save them."

The entire room went silent. The most critical heads in the world bowed in respect of people they did not know. The silence held a minute before Jonah looked up.

"I understand," he said, "that the Emperor of Japan filled you all in on some things. As for what you need to know, it would be best if we started with questions."

The dignitaries looked at one another, whispering and talking. They performed the refined equal of standing up and shouting for attention. They jostled for space and held their arms out, waving their notebooks at him. Jonah rolled his eyes.

"Here," he said, quieting them down. "We will go by number of citizens under your purview, which means Her Majesty the Queen. Your Majesty."

Elizabeth IV stood, intending, one can assume, to curtsy to the acolytes and David. Jonah put up his hand to stop her and waved her down.

"There is no need, mum" Jonah said. "Besides my pale-skinned friend here"—he motioned at David sitting on the throne. "We are still Terran."

"What?" David said. "I should sit beside the throne?"

Jonah looked at him and realized that it was going to be a long day.

❧

David walked into the master bedroom and flopped on the bed beside Zavannah.

"Long day, dear?" Zavannah said.

David glanced over at her, "it has been a long twelve years." He put one hand behind his head and stared at the ceiling. Zavannah rolled onto her side.

"Twelve years?" She said, putting one hand on her hip and the other under her head. She leaned on her elbow. "What was it like?"

"Lonely," he said and looked back at the ceiling. "I spent most of my time alone in a room." He paused a moment. "The most exciting moment was scaring the two Russians who found me after I landed."

"Russians?" Zavannah said. "Like you were in Russia, or two Russians found you?"

"Russia," David said. "That's where I came out." He looked over at her again. "I went to Nunavut and stayed in a room by myself in the tundra. Did you know there is a road called the Road to Nowhere?"

"No," Zavannah thought for a moment before getting up. "You didn't go out and see the sights?"

"There wasn't much to see," David said. "Snow and trees, a wild animal or two, some birds." David looked back up at the ceiling.

Zavannah came around the bed and grabbed David's hand, pulling him off the bed.

"Then," she said, "will we remedy that?"

David held onto her. He stumbled forward, and Zavannah stepped back, smiling. David spun her around, holding on to her hand.

"What were you thinking?" David pulled her back toward him.

"How about we find a bar," Zavannah said, looking up at him, "and you can watch us get drunk. It makes you smile. Hearing Pierre unable to speak anything but French is your favourite thing."

"It's not fair to Aiko," David said.

"I'm sure," Zavannah said, "Aiko won't mind. She'll be more interested in sleep anyways." Zavannah peeled away from David. She went to the closet and moved the hanging clothes aside to rifle through them. "Now, let's find you something to wear."

Jonah was much better now that he had showered and changed, and he walked out of his room to see who else was about. When he got to the foyer, there were two Imperial Guards, and Jonah sensed it had happened again. He rushed down the steps to the entry, bowing to a guard.

"Where are the other guards?" Jonah asked of this guard, who understood English but answered in Japanese.

"They went to the Chateau Lafayette," the guard said, and Jonah sighed. He was invisible. *What did Maya ever contribute?* Jonah thought. But they never forget her.

"Take me to them," Jonah said to the guard, who exchanged another bow with him before walking him outside. The last guard remained.

Sunday, April 15, 2164
5:17 a.m. TST (12:17 a.m., LAT)
Chateau Lafayette (The Laff)
Ottawa, Ontario, Canada, Terra

The crowded bar was loud, but the ambience was unbeatable. Everyone was in high spirits. Zavannah excused herself and headed toward the restroom. She passed the bar, the bartender flagged her down. Zavannah walked over to the bar.

"Are you Zavannah?" The bartender asked a folded piece of paper between his index and middle fingers on his left hand.

"Yes," she said. "Can I help you?"

The bartender held out the note for her.

"No," he said, "but I can help you."

Zavannah took the note. The bartender opened the register, pulled out a key fob, and tossed it at Zavannah, who caught it. The register closed with a ding.

Zavannah opened the paper.

"It's time. Parking lot—Zeke," it read. She looked at the key fob and sighed.

"Thanks," Zavannah said and headed for the washrooms. She would have to sneak out the back.

Sunday, April 15, 2164
5:18 a.m. TST (12:18 a.m., LAT)
The Garage
Headquarters, the Whitespace

Zeke watched the Ford Shelby GT 5000 E-Series melt away in a wrap of yellow smoke. He took a step back and hoped that she would make it in time. Zeke turned around to see Gad standing behind him, covered head to toe in ichor. The golden ooze made him glisten all over.

Gad was holding his stiletto dagger in his hand.

"I suppose," Zeke said, pulling out his misericord dagger, "you aren't in a magnanimous mood."

"Not since," Gad said, "I let a glorified spell lock me in a cage." Gad lunged at Zeke, and the two of them grappled back and forth, swiping at each other. Gad kept on the advance, forcing Zeke's back up against the wall of the garage.

"You know," Zeke said to Gad. His hand on the cold marble behind him, "I have always hated this place." Gad smiled at him, enjoying the moment. "You're all terrible people. You do realize that, right? I mean, you girls are in a fucking ivory tower—"

Zeke's eyes widened. Gad's stiletto sliced through his neck. Zeke dropped his misericord, and his two hands clutched his throat. Gad stuck his stiletto into Zeke's chest and, twisting, pulled out the dagger. A fountain of golden ichor poured out of him.

Zeke decomposed via purple smoke. The spell undid itself. The smoke removing all trace of him until all that remained was a two-inch long amethyst crystal. Inside the Amethyst, yellow and bronze liquid swirled around each other. Gad bent down.

"Ezekiel 2.0" written on the side of the crystal in Samael's telltale script. Gad smashed the stone with the hilt of his stiletto, releasing the magiks trapped inside. The yellow magik swirled out and hit him in the chest, knocking him back a bit. He returned to his full strength.

The bronze magik came out to a ball and folded into itself. Gadreel was back to full form now that he had control of lightning wisdom, and he spectered.

"Trabea," the now complete Gadreel incanted. He transmuted in a swirl of yellow smoke.

Sunday, April 15, 2164
5:22 A TST (12:22 a.m., LAT)
St Andrews Street and Sussex Drive
Ottawa, Ontario, Canada, Terra

Jonah was unsure yet what had compelled him to tell the driver to turn here. The driver still turned and headed down Sussex Drive. The Imperial Guard was unnerving. He sat across from Jonah, silent and unmoving.

"Do you have a specific location for me to head toward?" The driver asked.

Jonah closed his eyes and concentrated on the out-of-place entity that was drawing it to him.

"Corner of St. Andrews and Dalhousie, across the street on this side," Jonah said.

The driver nodded.

"You got it, chief," the driver switched lanes.

"You can stay in the car when we get there. I'm not sure what I'm in for so go back to the cottage and guard Aiko," Jonah said to the guard.

He nodded; Jonah stared out the window at the passing cars.

The car pulled up to the building and turned in to the parking lot, pulling up to the side entrance.

"This good for you, boss?" The driver asked.

"This will do fine," Jonah said, pulling out the ID card that he had gotten from the Canadian authorities. He put it in the tablet the driver handed him. He paid and left a good tip—the service had been excellent—and authorized it with his thumbprint.

Jonah handed the tablet back to the driver.

"I authorized the same amount for the return trip," Jonah said. "You can do whatever you need to get the most out of that. He can take it." Jonah motioned to the guard and stepped out of the car. The driver reversed into space and pulled out onto the street, heading back to the cottage.

Jonah closed his eyes again and opened them and walked to the end of the building. He turned the corner and headed down the short alley, which ended at a wire fence. Jonah heard a gun cocking from the blackness of the space where the fence met the wall.

"Don't come any closer," a voice said from the darkness.

"Sorry," Jonah said. "I didn't mean to frighten you." He investigated the darkness. "You can at least look me in the eyes before you kill me."

"I don't want to hurt you," the voice said.

"I see that," Jonah said. "I also believe that you're out of place here. Am I correct?"

The woman stepped out of the darkness. Her above-average frame and long dark hair led to her robust features. One look at her, and he knew she was a Stranger.

He had never seen such eyes. The irises were round perfect circles of black. They held a square of neon-orange light. She was more than out of place; she was out of verse. Jonah realized she was from the universe.

"Hi," he said. "I am Jonah."

"Claire," the woman said. "My name's Claire." She unstiffened a bit.

"Claire," Jonah said, "I take it you're not from the Omniverse?"

Claire stiffened up and held the gun higher. Jonah put up his hands and took a step back.

"Whoa, whoa, whoa," Jonah said. "Look, I'm not going to hurt you, I promise."

Claire looked at him and lowered her gun.

"What do you want from me?" She asked.

Jonah relaxed and put his hands down.

"Me?" he said. "I want to help you return to the universe."

Claire eyed him for a second. He was telling the truth, and at this point, she either had to trust someone or risk further exposure.

"Honest, it's my job."

"How can you help me?" Claire asked. "What can you do?"

Jonah smiled, "I happen to know how to make a portal to the universe. All we need is the right location."

"Do you have something in mind, or are we going to have to find something?" Claire relaxed.

"No," Jonah rubbed his fingers together, "I know a place."

Claire pulled out a key fob and clicked it. The lights on the nearest car flickered.

"I'll drive," she said.

Monday, November 12, 2164
3:32 AM TST
Denny Abbey, Cambridgeshire
Camelot, Kingdom of Eireann

"About that problem you are going to have." Gad took a few steps toward Hood, who raised an eyebrow.

"Oh, you want something?" Hood sat back down and relaxed into his throne. "You need me more than I need you."

"You need me, I don't need you." Gadreel crossed his arms, "all I want is a little help. The target is an acolyte that can cause you problems, I have seen it."

"Your vision is now useless," Hood put his fingers together, "they are the new order of the Omniverse, you are over."

"I saw the Sorceress defeat you before they incarnated," Samael spoke too soon.

"The Sorceress?" Hood relaxed; "she is not an issue."

"Maya may be innocuous, but there is much more to her than you would comprehend. Besides, I could take it back, you know," Gad made a fist, "the magic I leant you." When Gad swung down, it sounded like he slammed his fist against a table. "Hell, I could tell the Faithfull you allow Gall to use it."

Hood leaned in; "I don't like threats."

"And I don't like the word no," Gadreel smiled, "we all have our vices."

Friday, April 11, 1947
12:01 a.m. TST
312 Bolton Crescent
Thunder Bay, Ontario, Canada, Terra

Maya opened her eyes. She sat upright in bed and examined the room. There was nothing there but darkness and furniture.

She floated down, seeking sleep.

"Now Maya," a voice said in the darkness, "did you summon me, or did you want to keep sleeping?"

Maya sat back up so fast her hair flew forwards.

"Unless I got your message wrong?" The voice permeated the room. "Do you still want to be my queen? To release me unto this world and rule it together with me for all eternity?"

Maya couldn't conjure words, so she shook her head affirmative.

"Then I have a job for you, I need you comprehend that if you do this job well, you will sacrifice your mortal body and leave this Terran form. Do you understand?"

Another nod from Maya.

"Perfect," the voice rumbled with satisfaction, "there is only one thing left." Maya's breath became cold enough to be visible. "Say my name."

Maya opened her mouth.

"Leviathan."

Epilogue

Sunday, April 15, 2164
5:24 A TST (12:24 a.m., LAT)
Royal Chambers, the Imperial Palace
Atlan, Atlantis Prime

The Empress was sleeping in her bed. A ball of bronze mana appeared above her, swirling into silent existence. It burst forth, and the bronze smoke snaked into the Empress's chest. She smiled. She put her arms out and grabbed the sheets.

She sat up, her heart racing. She looked at her hands, the power returning. She flexed her hand. She examined it. Thunder clapped in the sky outside the palace.

A celebration commenced for the return of the original Ezekiel.

"Electrifying move," Empress Ezekiel said aloud, a smile creeping toward her eyes. "Looks like someone came to *play*."

TEAM OMEGA

Guardian: Gabriel
Captain: David

David Blackstone
Acolyte of Death
Colour: White - Age: 36
Died: 1995 (Heart Attack)
Ancestral Relations:
Samael - Weapons:
Hook Swords
Ascends to God
of Death

Hayden Crawley
Acolyte of Fire
Colour: Persimmon
Age: 41 - Died: 1953
(Aneurysm) - Ancestral
Relations: Prometheus
Weapons: Korean Fighting
Fans - Relationship
with Samael

Hudson Rivers
Acolyte of Water
Colour: Cerulean - Age: 56
Died: 1911 (Plane Crash)
Ancestral Relations:
Queen Isis & Loki
Weapons: Trident
Allied with
Ronnie

Maya Dhaliwal
Acolyte of Magic
Colour: Violet - Age: 27
Died: 1947 (Strangulation)
Ancestral Relations:
Ganesha - Weapons:
Shuriken - Practices
Demonology

TEAM DELTA
Guardian: Lucyfer
Captain: Aiko

Zavannah Zhuang
Acolyte of Wisdom
Colour: Citrine - Age: 39
Died: 1905 (Cyanide)
Ancestral Relations:
Phoebus Apollo
Weapons: Chakram
Guardian of the
Oracle

Pierre Chrétien
Acolyte of Nature
Colour: Forrest
Age: 33 - Died: 1923
(Internal Hemorraging)
Ancestral Relations:
Silvanus - Weapons:
LongBow - Afraid
of heights

Aiko Tanaka
Acolyte of Love
Colour: Crimson - Age: 13
Died: 1935 (Overdose)
Ancestral Relations:
Uzume - Weapons:
ShortBow - Intuitive
Youngest modern
Acolyte

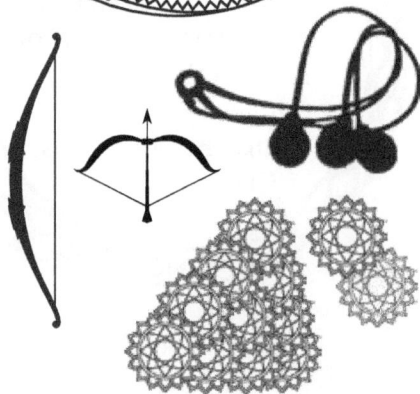

Asher Townsend
Acolyte of Life
Colour: Black - Age: 63
Died: 1965 (Friendly Fire)
Ancestral Relations:
Brahma - Weapons: Bolas
Veteran - Medical Doctor
Oldest Acolyte in
history

TEAM GAMMA

Guardian: Gadreel
Captain: Bennett

Slate George
Acolyte of Destruction
Colour: Midnight
Age: 38 - Died: 1983
(Crushed to Death)
Ancestral Relations: Etu
Weapons: Battle Axes
Can be a Blank Page
(Book of the
Dead)

Bennett Fairchild
Acolyte of Light
Colour: Gold - Age: 21
Died: 1941 (Shot Down)
Ancestral Relations:
Lucyfer - Weapons: Hands
Can move fast enough to
be invisible and use
all weapons

Avery Saunders
Acolyte of Weather
Colour: Canary - Age: 45
Died: 1989 (Trampled)
Ancestral Relations:
Hydros - Weapons: Sickles
Has 2 dominions
(Lighting & Thunder)
and sides

Jonah Caspary
Acolyte of Order
Colour: Malachite
Age: 32 - Died: 1977
(Hit-and-Run) - Ancestral
Relations: Ariel - Weapons:
Quarterstaff - Loner
Interacts with
a Stranger

TEAM SIGMA

Guardian: Ariel
Captain: Ronnie

Harold
Pennywhistle
Acolyte of War
Colour: Rust - Age: 26
Died: 1971 (Heart Attack)
Ancestral Relations:
none - Weapons:
Gladius & Excalibur
Subject of two
curses

Véronique
"Ronnie" Gagnon
Acolyte of Truth
Colour: Tangerine
Age: 31 - Died: 1917
(Explosion) - Ancestral
Relations: Rhea
Weapons: Javelins
Allied with Hudson
Pregnant

Kay(la) McIntosh
Acolyte of Time
Colour: Grey - Age: 35
Died: 1959 (Beaten to
Death) - Ancestral
Relations: Cronos
Weapons: Bard Sword
Believes it's a dream
or simulation

Kushia
Schlossberg
Acolyte of Gravity
Colour: Amethyst - Age: 40
Died: 1929 (Asphyxiation)
Ancestral Relations:
Hydros - Weapons:
Morningstars - Powers
have largest area
of effect

CPSIA information can be obtained
at www.ICGtesting.com
Printed in the USA
LVHW090509151218
600529LV00005B/15/P